Heart Of
STONE

A BAD THINGS NOVEL

New York Times and USA Today Bestselling Author

CYNTHIA
EDEN

PROLOGUE

"Do you think that I like coming to you?" Sabrina Lark asked as she stared into the bright gaze of Luke Thorne. A shiver slid over her body. Anytime she stared at Luke too long, Sabrina shivered. She didn't think she was the only one with that reaction. Smart people knew to fear the Lord of the Dark. "But I'm desperate, and I'm willing to do anything." *Well, almost anything.*

Luke put his fingers beneath his chin as he peered back at her. He cocked his head to the side. "Just what is it you think I can do for you?"

Sabrina gave a bitter laugh. "What *can't* you do? Every dark creature in this world jumps at your command." That was one of the perks of being the Lord of the Dark. Luke had ultimate control when it came to the so-called "bad" paranormals who roamed the world.

Luke's stare swept over her. "I don't see you jumping."

Okay, she was one of the bad ones. So sue her. "I didn't ask for this. I never asked for *any* of this."

Luke let out a long sigh. "Like I haven't heard that line before. Same song, same old dance. Paranormals are always whining for the world to change."

Sabrina sat a little straighter in her chair. Her hands fisted in her lap. "Are you going to help me or not?"

His expression never altered. "You still haven't said what you need."

"Protection," she gritted out. "Isn't that obvious? I've got a killer on my trail, and I need help."

He gave a bitter laugh. "Inspired someone too much did you?"

Inspiration. That was kind of her gig. Sabrina was a muse, one of the last of her kind. *The last*, actually. She'd been around for centuries. Sabrina had seen every good and bad piece of humanity out there. She'd watched her friends die. She'd seen lovers vanish. And she'd seen evil. So much evil. That was the thing, though, even after all these centuries, evil could still fool her. She hated that she could be so blind to its true nature. "Let's just say that I misjudged someone."

"Are we dealing with a human? You can usually handle those fairly well on your own."

"We're dealing with a monster." A monster who was stalking her. No matter where she went, he was there, following her every move. "I need a guard. Someone unstoppable. Someone to protect me 24/7."

"Are you sure that you don't just want a killer? Someone who will get rid of your monster problem?"

Sabrina swallowed and tried to keep her breathing nice and slow. "That may be necessary." Did that make her sound like a coldhearted bitch? Too bad. A desperate woman would do desperate things.

"And what will you give me in exchange?" Luke's eyes had narrowed. "Because that's generally the way this type of situation works. I give you what you want, and you offer me something in return. Something I want."

"What *do* you want?" Sabrina hated the fact that her voice trembled.

His mouth hitched into a half smile. It wasn't a very reassuring sight. "I want the same thing that every man wants from someone like you...I want inspiration."

At his words, the thick knot in her belly grew worse. "If you don't help me, I'm dead." Simple fact. "So I will give you any inspiration you want. I will inspire the fucking hell out of you...Just help me."

Luke rose slowly from his leather chair and stood at his full, commanding height. He stretched his arm across the table, his palm open. Sabrina rose, and she stared at his offered hand.

"When the deal is set, I like to shake on it," Luke said. His hand waited for her.

Sabrina eased out a slow breath as her fingers touched his. He squeezed her hand, and his eyes gleamed. "You just got yourself the best protection in the world."

She tried to pull her hand from his, but his grip just tightened.

"Though I should add," Luke murmured darkly, "that I never said the inspiration would be for me."

Her mouth got very, very dry as she gazed into his eyes.

"The best way to fight a monster," he continued in that low rumble that was his voice, "is *with* a monster. Don't worry, I have the perfect beast in mind for you."

Once again, Sabrina shivered.

CHAPTER ONE

The people in the ballroom smelled rich. The women wore glittering ball gowns as they spun around the dance floor, while the men were all clad in the same perfectly cut tuxedos. Fake laughter filled the air, and flutes of champagne were being passed out by the handfuls. Adam Cross knew how this scene worked. It was a charity ball. The drunker that the humans got, the more likely they were to donate that precious money to the cause of the night.

But to be honest, he didn't really give a shit what the humans did. He wasn't there for the humans. He was there for her.

The crowd parted before him, and suddenly Adam could see his prey. Sabrina Lark. An honest to God muse. This wasn't his first encounter with her, though she didn't know that fact. She didn't know about their shared past, and Adam intended to keep things that way.

She was wearing a body hugging blue gown. Probably topaz or some technical color shit like that. Her perfect breasts pressed against the top of the gown, while the material cinched in tight near her tiny waist. There was a slit along the left leg of her gown, one that revealed far too much skin. The gown had obviously been designed to tempt, and judging by the flock of admiring males near her, Sabrina's gown was certainly doing its job.

As he watched, she tilted back her head. Her long blonde hair trailed over her shoulders, and she gave a quick, light laugh. She seemed to not have a care in the world. Sabrina hardly looked like a woman on the run from a killer. Had she lied to Luke? If so, then the lady had made a fatal mistake.

It doesn't pay to jerk around the Lord of the Dark.

Just then, Sabrina's head turned and her eyes met his. Her eyes…For a moment, Adam actually stopped breathing. He'd never seen eyes like hers before. So big and blue and deep. The color of her eyes matched the dress perfectly. Adam was sure that was deliberate. She knew her appeal, and she was fully using it. The human males would be helpless against her.

But as she stared at him, something happened to that beautiful face of hers. *Fear.* Adam knew that emotion when he saw it. All too often, people looked at him with fear in their eyes. For some reason, he hadn't expected her to look at him that way. His mistake. One look, and she was staring at him the same way all of the others had. His body tensed, and Adam took a lunging step toward her.

As if right on cue, Sabrina turned and stumbled away from her admiring crowd of males. She rushed toward the open balcony doors, her high heels clicking against the gleaming floor. One of the men tried to stop her, but Sabrina just shrugged him way. The guy didn't follow after her.

Adam did. When people tried to get in his way, he just brushed the fools aside. After all, he was a man on a mission. She was his mission.

He swept through the open balcony doors and felt the brush of the wind against his face. He expected to see Sabrina standing on the balcony. It wasn't as if she had anywhere to go. Unlike him, she didn't have the luxury of possessing her own wings. But when he stepped outside, she wasn't in front of him. It took him two seconds too long to realize that he'd just walked into her trap. He spun around, but she'd already lunged at him. *She'd been hiding right next to the balcony door, pushing her body flat against the bricks there.* In a breath, she had a wickedly sharp knife pressed to his throat. Instantly, Adam stilled. After all, wasn't that the reaction a normal man would have to this situation?

"Who in the hell are you?" Sabrina demanded. She was tall in her heels, but she still tipped back her head to stare into his eyes. "What are you doing in a ballroom full of humans?"

Very slowly, he lifted his hands. Adam wanted to show he wasn't armed. He'd brought no weapons with him to the charity ball. It wasn't as if he needed weapons. "I think you're confused." Adam kept his voice soft and calm, or as soft and calm as he could manage. His gaze swept over her face.

What a fucking fabulous face it was. A perfect oval, with those wide, unforgettable eyes. Her nose was small and straight. Her cheekbones almost ridiculously high. And her mouth...Talk about the stuff of the darkest fantasies. Red. Full. Too tempting.

"I'm not confused." Anger tightened each word. "You think I don't know a predator when I see one?" Her left hand fisted around the front of his tux. Then she yanked him toward the nearby wall, making sure they were away from any prying eyes. Not that there was anyone out there to watch them. All of the rich humans were inside getting drunk. Only he and Sabrina were outside.

Adam offered her a weak smile. "Predator?" He lifted one brow. "I hardly think so. You took one look at me, and you went running. I just followed you to make certain you were okay."

The tip of the blade pressed to his throat. "Bullshit," she whispered the word like a caress.

"Your aura is the darkest one I've ever seen. Trust me on this, I've seen plenty of dark ones."

Adam blinked at her even as he kept his hands raised. "Aura?" he repeated. "You want to run that by me again?"

Her delicate jaw hardened. "Yes, aura. Yours hangs around you like a dark shadow of death."

Adam didn't know much about auras, but her description of his? Yeah, that seemed pretty spot on with his life. Not that he would tell her that particular truth. "You got me all wrong, lady."

"I have enough shit going on in my life right now. I cannot deal with you, too. Go look for inspiration somewhere else." She drew in a shuddering breath. "If you don't, you'll be sorry."

Adam had to admit, the muse was impressing him. And he wasn't one who was easily impressed. But she was doing it. Impressing him *and* turning him on. Sure, most men wouldn't like it if a woman put a knife to their throats. He wasn't most men. Technically, he was far beyond being just a man. So he offered her a small smile, then said, "You're the muse I was told about."

Sabrina cast a quick, nervous glance toward the open balcony doors. "Keep your voice down."

Adam laughed. "And maybe you should keep your knife out of sight."

It was interesting to note, Sabrina hadn't broken the surface of his skin. Not yet, anyway. She was being very careful with her knife.

"Who are you?" she demanded.

Instead of answering, he asked, "Can you really inspire a man to do anything you want?"

For an instant, she bit down on her plump, lower lip. Then Sabrina gave a quick, negative shake of her head. "That isn't the way it works. I don't know what you've been led to believe, but that's just wrong."

Adam wasn't so sure it was wrong. "Try it," he dared. "See if you can control me."

At his words, Sabrina gave a quick gasp. She yanked the knife away from his throat. "I want you to stay away from me. Do you understand? Far, far away. You carry a darkness…I can't handle you now. I *won't* handle you." As he watched, she tucked the knife back into a sheath that was strapped to her thigh. Hmmm. So that was why she had such a long slit in her dress. The slit gave her easy access to her weapon.

Clever muse.

Sabrina turned away from him. She'd obviously drawn him onto the balcony so that they could have a one-on-one chat. Only the chat hadn't worked out so well. And now she was trying to ditch him…again.

His hand flew out and curved around her shoulder. In a blink, he'd pinned her between his body and the brick wall. Adam leaned in close to Sabrina. If any humans walked onto the balcony, they would just assume he and Sabrina were two lovers making out in the dark. The humans would be wrong. But what else was new?

His right hand slid down to her thigh. Her skin felt like silk beneath his touch. His fingers moved lightly over that silk.

"What are you doing?" Sabrina asked, her voice little more than a whisper.

He pulled the knife from the sheath and held it easily in his hand. "I'm making sure you don't get the urge to slice my throat again."

Her incredible eyes narrowed to slits. "I didn't slice you the first time."

Laughter drifted out onto the balcony. The moon was full, and a million stars glittered overhead. But even without that light, he would've been able to see her perfectly. Paranormal bonus. Monsters always saw well in the dark.

"Let me go," she ordered.

Instead, he leaned in even closer to her. Barely an inch separated their mouths. He couldn't help but wonder...What would the muse taste like? Perhaps he would find out. But not right then. "You have me all wrong. I'm not the villain. Sweetheart, I'm your hero."

"Bullshit."

Time to seal the deal. So Adam said those few, soft words that were guaranteed to seal the deal for him, "Luke sent me."

He felt the tremble that shook her body. Adam prepared for gratitude. After all, he was there to save the day for the muse. He was the protection she'd ordered. He was—

"No."

Just that one word. A hard, flat denial.

In response, he nodded. "Yes."

"Luke's insane. I won't trade one psychopath for another."

Her sweet scent wrapped around him. It was a light, flowery scent. Just another part of her appeal. His body pressed closer to her. "That was just mean." And, really, did she know him well enough to decide he was a psychopath? *Not yet.*

She bared her teeth at him. "Get the hell away from me."

Adam took his time. His very sweet time. The fingers of his right hand trailed down her arm. He slowly stepped back.

"Give me my knife."

He tucked the knife inside his tux. "Not happening." Maybe they should get to the introduction part? "I'm Adam Cross. Bodyguard protection, at your service."

"Luke is a sonofabitch."

That might be true, but...

"I ask for help, and he sends someone like you? No, no, this can't happen." She lifted her hand and pointed at him. "You aren't the kind of man I want." Her hand fell back to her side. "What am I saying? You aren't even a man. I knew it the first moment I saw you."

He wouldn't let her piss him off. Okay, he would. Anger pulsed through him. "Hate to break it to you," Adam told her quietly, "but you aren't exactly an angel yourself."

Just then, a human couple walked onto the balcony. The woman staggered a bit, and the man's arms wrapped around her. The guy pulled her close, and their mouths met in a deep, hungry kiss.

Talk about shit for timing. "Get a room," Adam muttered.

Sabrina took the opportunity right in front of her, and she jerked out of his reach. She marched off the balcony, not bothering to glance back at Adam.

He didn't race after her. Didn't follow her like a lost puppy. That wasn't his style.

He'd made contact. He'd told her who he was and what he would be doing. Protecting her.

The human couple stumbled back inside. Maybe they were off to get that recommended room. Good for them. Adam stalked toward the balcony's wrought iron railing. His hands lifted and curled around that railing. He gazed out into the night. The night was his time. He lived for the darkness.

The muse hadn't been wrong when she said that he carried a shadow with him. He'd carried that shadow for centuries.

The air was crisp and cool. Adam took a few deep breaths. And he gazed down below. Some of the humans were leaving the ball. The valet attendants were bringing up their fancy cars. As he watched, Sabrina appeared below him. She handed her ticket to one of the valets. Moments later, she was climbing into a black convertible. The top was up, so he couldn't see her after she slid into the car. She drove away with a screech of her tires, moving way too fast.

As if she feared that something bad was chasing her.

Hunting her.

I'm not hunting you, sweetheart. I'm protecting you. Not usually his gig, but he owed Luke.

Sabrina's car turned right at the stop sign. Then she squealed away. But…Another car followed immediately behind her. A big, dark SUV that almost seemed as if it had been waiting for her.

Adam spared a quick glance around him. No one was watching. Typical. Humans were always fully involved in their own lives. He lunged up and over the balcony railing. He hurtled through the air, and seconds later, his feet touched the ground. Adam's knees didn't even buckle. He brushed off the shoulder of his tux, straightened his tie, then he handed his own ticket to the valet. Soon, his ride was ready. A dark beast of a bike, its engine growling like a wolf. The motorcycle was totally out of place in the middle of all those expensive rides.

Like he gave a damn. Adam climbed onto the bike. His fingers reached for the handle bars. He revved the engine a little more. Then he gave chase as the motorcycle shot forward into the night.

The muse needed protection. She was going to get it.

Whether she wanted him or not.

***

Luke was jerking her around. Sabrina should have expected it. Luke and his games…He never stopped. She'd been foolish to think he would actually help her.

Her hands tightened around the steering wheel. Her heart wouldn't stop racing.

Adam. The stranger had said his name was Adam. Adam Cross. She'd never heard the name before, and Sabrina didn't remember ever meeting the mysterious Adam in her very long life. He would be a hard man to forget.

Dangerous. Deadly.

Sexy?

Why did she always fall for the bad ones? Why did she take one look at a guy like Adam and think *yes, please*? He was definitely tall, dark, and handsome. His hair was thick and a little too long. His eyes…gazing into them had been like looking straight into darkness. His nose was a bit hawkish, and his lips oddly sensual. His jaw had been perfectly square and cut, and a faint cleft had been placed right in the middle of his chin. She'd wanted to lick that indention. Such a wrong response.

A much better response? Her urge to flee as soon as she saw his aura.

Auras. Most folks didn't believe in them. Sabrina wasn't most folks. She'd been seeing auras since she was a child. It was kind of a muse thing. She saw the auras that clung to people, and those auras told her things. Things like…

If a guy named Mike had insane artistic vision.

Or if a fellow going deaf could actually make the most incredible music imaginable.

Auras showed her passion. They showed her promise. They showed her what could be. But they also showed her pain. Loss. Fear. Everything that a person felt? It was in the aura.

Good. Bad. All that crazy stuff in between? In the aura. Madness. Brilliance. All there.

Most auras gleamed with lights. But Adam's had been different. No light for him. Just darkness. So much darkness.

A human would never have an aura that looked like his.

The bright glow of headlights suddenly filled the interior of her car. Automatically, her gaze flew to her rearview mirror. "Jerk," Sabrina muttered, but the word was more reflex than anything else.

If anything, the lights seemed to grow brighter. Or maybe...The other car was just coming closer. Her hands tightened even more on the wheel and her foot pressed down harder on the gas pedal. But she heard a revving growl, and before she could escape, the other car slammed into her from behind.

Sabrina screamed. Again, it was a reflex action.

In the next breath, she was hit again. Even harder. She couldn't keep her car on the road. Her headlights flashed across the nearby trees, and then Sabrina's convertible was slamming into one of those trees. The impact was jarring. Hard and brutal. Her airbag exploded and sent a cloud of white toward her face. The seatbelt jerked against her, and Sabrina heard the sound of shattering glass. Then...

Silence. Just the frantic pounding of her heart, filling her ears. Her breath raced from her. She shoved against the airbag and turned to peer out of her window. The other driver…Was he still there? Was he coming for her?

Adam had taken her knife. She was alone. She'd been hunted for so long. Tonight, she'd made a fatal mistake. She'd run from Adam, fearing what he could do to her. Maybe…Maybe she shouldn't have run from him. Maybe she should have run *to* him.

Sabrina could see nothing in the dark. She didn't hear the other vehicle. Didn't hear the other driver. She grabbed at her seatbelt, fighting to get free. She was a sitting duck in the car, and she knew it. She had to get out. She had to get away.

Did she smell gasoline? Oh hell, she did. And the seatbelt was stuck. It wouldn't unhook. The front of her car was smashed into a tree, and the back had been smashed by that asshole driver. "Help!" Her cry was too low. She tried again. "Help!"

But she feared the only help out there…It might be the other driver.

Was it him? The man who'd made her life hell recently? The man who'd made her so desperate that she'd turned to Luke for help?

Then she heard it. A low, deep growl. One that seemed to be getting closer. Her breath heaved from her lungs as fear iced her body.

The growl died away. Then…

I'm being hunted.

Sabrina wasn't like other paranormals. Most of them could see perfectly in the dark. Not her. When it came to night vision, she was pretty much on a human's level. Probably had something to do with her seeing auras. Since she saw auras, she didn't get any other vision bonuses. So she couldn't see who was out there. Only the dark. The dark terrified her.

Where was a cop when she needed one?

The car shook around her. And then, above her head, there was a low, grinding sound. A ripping. A tearing? She looked up and saw what appeared to be knives cutting through the fabric of her convertible top. She didn't waste her breath on a scream, not then. Sabrina leaned across the passenger seat and strained, trying to reach for her glovebox. She had a big, heavy duty flashlight in there. Not much of a weapon, but it would work. Maybe. It would—

The top of her convertible was torn away. She hadn't reached the flashlight. The seatbelt held her trapped. Oh, dammit, in terms of paranormal strength, she was physically weak. She was—

"Sweetheart, I thought you said I wasn't the man you needed."

Adam's voice. Adam was the one who'd just cut through the convertible's top. Only he hadn't used a knife. He'd used claws. Those same claws were cutting through her seatbelt. They were heavy claws, wickedly sharp.

"*Shifter.*" That was what he was. Mystery solved.

His claws came at her.

CHAPTER TWO

The muse had a scream that would probably break glass. And Adam happened to have extremely sensitive hearing. *Sweet hell. What is she trying to do?* Adam covered Sabrina's mouth with his hand, stopping her mid-scream. "Do you want to burst my freaking eardrums?" he snarled.

Her mouth pressed to his hand. The feel of her lips against him…Damn, this was so not the time to get a hard-on for the muse.

But at least she'd stopped screaming.

Carefully, he lifted her from the car. Cutting through the fabric of the convertible's top had been the easiest way to free her from the wreckage. His claws were gone now, but they would come back later. They always did.

He carried her away from the wrecked car, and then Adam set Sabrina on her feet. But he didn't let her go. He kept his hands around her shoulders as he scanned her body, looking for any sign of injury. "Are you hurt?"

Sabrina shook her head. "Bruises, nothing major."

His jaw locked. "What in the hell happened?"

Her gaze shot around the area, as if looking for a threat. "Some jerk slammed into me from behind. I lost control of my car and hit a tree." She tried to pull away from him. He wasn't in the mood for that shit, so he just tightened his hold on her.

"There wasn't another vehicle here when I arrived," Adam said.

She tried jerking away again. And failed.

Her paranormal strength was really rather pathetic. He'd faced off with stronger humans.

"He *was* here," Sabrina huffed. "It's not like I crashed myself."

"You were drinking at the ball, you had a champagne flute when I first saw you—"

"For show," she snapped, cutting him off. "My metabolism is wonky, okay? I can't handle alcohol, not at all. Bad things happen when I drink."

He filed that tidbit away for later. "Come on." He turned her and pushed Sabrina toward his waiting motorcycle. Time to get someplace safe.

But then the muse dug in her heels.

His eyes squeezed shut as he grabbed for patience. *I've never had much of that shit.*

"I'm not just going to get on that motorcycle and ride away with you into the night! That's not how things work. I *know* you're trouble. I've got enough of that and I can't—"

Sighing, he just bent and lifted her over his shoulder. The woman needed to eat more. He could barely feel her weight. She struggled against him, but he just tightened his grip. Then they were at his bike. He put her on the seat and clamped a hand around her shoulder when she tried to immediately scuttle away. "Do you want to die?"

Her long lashes—seriously, they were insanely long—covered her eyes.

"Because I thought you wanted to live. I mean, wasn't that the whole point of going to Luke? You wanted protection? The best he had?"

Her lashes lifted.

He smiled. "You're staring at the best." Yet she was still refusing him. Didn't make a damn bit of sense to him. "Why go to Luke if you're just going to run from the guy he sends to help you—"

"Your darkness is too strong." She licked her lips.

His cock jerked. Lust rose. The dangerous kind. *I want that mouth of hers on me.*

"When you fall for me, it will be bad. Very bad."

It took a moment for her words to register and when they did…a deep, rumbling laugh escaped Adam. The kind of laugh that shook a man's whole body. The kind of laugh he hadn't experienced in, well, centuries. He could actually feel his eyes even starting to water.

When you fall for me…

He climbed onto the bike in front of the muse. He shoved up the kickstand. Then he glanced back at her. "Sabrina…" He tasted her name. It was the first time he'd said it. Adam rather liked the way it felt on his tongue.

Bet I'll like the way she feels on it, too.

He cleared his throat. "I'm not falling for you."

Her gaze held his. "You won't be able to help yourself. It's who I am…what I am. I'll get into your head. I can inspire you do to great things or terrible things. Since you have so much darkness already…I know which way you'll go." Her lips pressed together.

Terrible things.

"I'll work my way under your skin. At first, you'll feel…strangely good when I'm near. Like you're on some kind of high. Everything will seem better in your life. Like it's all finally fitting together."

They needed to get the hell out of there. The other vehicle was gone, but that didn't mean the driver wouldn't come back. Adam didn't hear

anyone else close by, didn't smell anyone else
but…

It's not safe out in the open.

Yet Adam stayed exactly where he was.
Why? Morbid curiosity. He needed to see just
where she was going with her tale.

"When I leave you, even if it's just for a bit,
even if it's just long enough to go to dinner or
shopping…that's when the cracks will start.
You'll feel like you need me close by. The
inspiration? It will turn to obsession. You'll have
to keep me near. You'll want the rush that only I
can give to you. I'll be your drug, and you will do
anything to have me."

She sounded so confident.

As if all of that had happened to her
before…many times before.

He was partially turned toward her. Her
hand lifted and pressed to his chest. "It will begin
in here. Your heart will beat for me. It's what I
do. I get to my prey. I'm supposed to help them,
but someone like you…the inspiration will be
wrong."

He could feel the heat of her touch even
through his shirt. The drumming of his heart
seemed too loud. And her scent…

Adam cleared his throat. "Obsess a few men
in your time?"

"The obsession is the reason I'm in my
current mess." Her lips twisted, but she didn't

stop touching him. "I inspire certain guys straight to madness." She hesitated, then said, "Some guys just have a hard time letting go of a good thing."

"But you aren't good, are you, sweetheart?"

Her gaze searched his. "Why do you keep calling me sweetheart? You don't know me. I'm nothing to you."

"The way you talk...you could be everything to me." He waited a beat. "In time."

She pulled her hand back. "Just take me to Luke, okay? I'll work out a new deal with him."

"Not happening. Luke's slipped away with his lady, and he didn't exactly leave contact information behind."

Her lips parted. "But...but he knows I'm in trouble! That I need help! I went to him, I offered him a trade—"

"Right. You did." Adam could see the flash of headlights in the distance. "I know the terms." He turned to face the front. The motorcycle revved beneath him. "Protection. Maybe death...you wanted a killer." The bike rocked forward. "And you got one."

"But—"

"Put your arms around me and hold on tight."

Her arms lifted and wrapped around his waist. "I warned you..."

Adam smiled grimly. *Yes, you did.* And then he took off.

*****

He hadn't intended to kill her. Killing Sabrina Lark wasn't part of his plan. But he'd wanted to give her a reminder. Wanted to shake her, to scare her.

I can get to you. At any time. Any place. No matter how far she fled, he could find her.

She would never be free of him.

He'd left the wreckage. Left her. And he'd gone back to the charity ball. Sabrina had been there before, and he liked to retrace her steps. It was one of the things he did. A way to be closer to her.

Sabrina had changed his life. Showed him the brilliance that he'd always possessed, but he'd just been too afraid to really let himself go. *Until her.*

He didn't have fear any longer. He just had determination.

He'd unlocked the power inside of himself.

A woman smiled at him. She had blonde hair. Pale blue eyes. Sabrina's eyes weren't pale. They were bold. Bright. Spell-binding. But the woman's hair was the same shade as Sabrina's.

This woman wore red. A blood-red gown. She held a champagne flute in her hand. Her breasts were spilling forward, pushing the boundaries of that gown.

She was pretty. Sexy.

And coming his way.

He tilted his head and waited. If this was what she wanted…if *he* was what she wanted, then the blonde would get an unforgettable night.

She stopped in front of him. Licked her lips. "Are you here alone?"

No, Sabrina is always with me…just as I'm always with her. That was how it was for some people. A connection that went soul deep.

"I'm alone." Her smile stretched and invited. "But I don't want to be that way."

So he said what was expected. "A beautiful woman like you should never be alone."

Her breath whispered out. Faint color stained her cheeks.

He offered his arm to her. "Why don't we go someplace quiet and talk?"

She took his offered arm, and her breast pressed against his sleeve when she leaned in close to him. "Lead the way…"

He would.

He'd lead her straight to hell, and there would be no going back.

***

"This isn't my place," Sabrina said when Adam finally stopped the bike. He'd taken them down to the beach, to the long line of condos that seemed to shoot straight toward the sky. "I've got an apartment I was using just on the edge of Miami—"

"Yeah, I saw it earlier. Not the safest place." He pointed to the building behind them. "I've got a condo on the top floor. Luke got it for me. All the fucking comforts of home."

Doubtful. Not the comforts of her home, anyway. "I need my place. I need my clothes. I need—"

He drove them toward the parking garage. Paused only long enough to key in his entry code and then they were heading up the ramp. Her hands were still tight around him. Her gown had hitched way up. She'd had to hitch up the damn thing so it wouldn't get caught in the back wheel. She was pretty sure she'd flashed the world during their drive, but Sabrina wasn't overly bothered by that fact.

Modesty was not a big muse trait.

He braked again. She jumped off the bike and hurried back a few steps. The parking garage was cavernous and…well, empty.

"New building," Adam said as he took his time climbing off the motorcycle. "I'm the only tenant."

Her eyes narrowed. "Is this Luke's building?" Because the Lord of the Dark was rich as sin and had holdings all over the world.

"Um, and get this…"

Um…Was that a yes?

"I think he might only rent to paranormals. That's the plan he's considering. He designed the place specifically with paranormals in mind. The building holds extra weight, has windows that don't let the sunlight inside, oh, hell, it's got all sorts of interesting little bonuses." His lips quirked. "Luke thinks having a paranormal-only high-rise condo building is a genius idea. I think it's a clusterfuck waiting to happen."

Her breath heaved out.

"I'm supposed to run security at this building." His gaze swept over her. "After I take care of my new side job."

He'd just called her a side job. Not a side piece, but a side job. She found both titles equally insulting. "I warned you—"

He turned away and strolled toward the elevator. As if he didn't have a care in the world. All la-de-da casual. Did he not get how dangerous she was?

He pushed the button for the elevator. Then he crossed his hands over his chest and glanced back at her. "Did you…or did you not…ask for a guard? I believe Luke called it 24/7 protection?"

"I…did, but—"

"You also wanted someone who wasn't afraid to kill."

She swallowed.

He flashed a smile, and his teeth seemed sharper than before. "I'm not afraid."

No, she got that.

The elevator dinged. The doors opened. He motioned for her to go in first.

After a brief hesitation, she did. *I don't want to be carried over his damn shoulder again.* It was a big elevator, but as soon as he followed her inside, the space suddenly felt tight.

Tense.

Sabrina tried to make Adam see reason. "Look, I needed Luke to send me a paranormal who wouldn't be influenced by me...I figured he'd send a vamp. I mean, they're dead, right?"

He stroked his chin. "I thought the PC term was undead."

"They don't feel as much, not usually. So they'd be in better control with me."

"Or maybe you thought you'd be better able to control *them.*"

Maybe.

He let out a low whistle. "You really think you're going to drive me mad?"

Why was the elevator so slow? "It's a possibility. With your aura being so dark, it's a dangerous risk. I need someone who isn't so tainted..." She needed to make him understand what she was seeing when she looked at his aura. "It's, I swear, it's like you're already under someone else's spell."

He blinked. Then his whole expression seemed to shut down. To turn to pure stone right before her eyes.

Nervous, she backed up and her shoulders hit the elevator's wall. A quick glance at the control panel showed her they were shooting toward the top floor.

He stepped toward her. "No one controls me. Not anymore."

That was what he thought. He didn't get just how insidious a muse's power could be. "I'm holding back on you. I've been holding back since the first moment. If I let myself go…"

His hand lifted and he touched her cheek. Surprised by that sudden tenderness—especially from someone like him—Sabrina stilled. She also tried really hard to ignore the sudden, sharp surge of desire that rose within her.

Wrong time. Wrong place. Wrong guy. Very wrong guy.

"You don't trust Luke, do you, Sabrina?"

Did she look insane? "His business is lies."

"Yet you still made a deal with him."

"Desperate times and all that," she managed. The elevator had stopped. The doors had opened. They should leave or move or something.

"Do you really think he would have sent someone to you who could be so easily swayed by your power?"

Uh...was that a trick question?

His hand slid down her cheek. Down, down...his fingers wrapped around her throat. He had to feel the frantic pounding of her pulse beneath his touch.

His head bent toward her. His lips moved right next to her ear. She could feel the stir of his breath against her. "It doesn't work on me," Adam said.

"What?"

Had she just felt the lick of his tongue along the shell of her ear?

"I'm pure stone, sweetheart. Your power...your inspiration, it won't do a single thing to me."

If only. But she'd heard that line before. People who thought they were so big and so bad, but they'd still been brought down before her. "You wish," she told him.

His head pulled back. His gaze—so dark and deep and unnerving—held hers. "I know."

Okay, did the guy want to play games? She could play. "You want a little test?"

His mouth hitched into a half smile. "Hit me with your worst."

He didn't truly want to see her worst. Sabrina's stomach clenched. Her worst was out there in the world right then...her worst could very well have been the driver who'd run her off the road.

But why just leave me there?

Maybe...maybe he'd wanted to scare her.

She knew he liked fear. To him, it was an aphrodisiac.

That's what I did to him. Her stomach felt leaden. "I don't like games — especially not games that involve people's lives." She lifted her hands and pushed against his chest. "The elevator has stopped. Back away."

He looked at her hands, then up at her. His head inclined. "My floor..."

When he eased back, she shot past him, only to stop short. The elevator hadn't opened into some hallway — it had opened right inside one of the condo units. A big, crazy luxurious place with floor to ceiling windows that looked out over the beach.

She could definitely see Luke's hand in the decoration.

Leather couches. Big screen TVs. Marble countertops. Over the top *everything.*

"I'm guessing you didn't notice that I had to put my key card into the elevator's control panel so we could access this floor," Adam said as he followed her. His steps seemed to echo because the place was *that big.* "The facility is secure, believe me. Video feeds, audio feeds, and if you

don't have the key card, the alarms start
shrieking the minute you try to access a floor that
you shouldn't be on."

She turned around, her gaze sweeping the
high-priced condo. No, not just a condo. A
penthouse. A paranormal paradise.

Or a paranormal prison. Sabrina figured it
was all about how you looked at the place.

He shrugged out of his coat. Yanked off his
tie. Undid the top few buttons on his shirt.

Keep going. She looked away. *Bad Sabrina.
Very bad. You do not need the guy to keep stripping
for your viewing pleasure.*

The leather groaned as he sprawled on the
couch.

Her gaze jumped back to him. Okay, he
hadn't taken anything else off. Just undid a few
buttons. Gotten comfortable. He'd —

"Tell me who I have to kill."

He was cutting right to the chase. She shifted
her stance a bit and kicked off her high heels.
They were damn uncomfortable. And the dress —
she would love to switch into something else.

"Cute toes."

What? She looked down at her toes. The nails
were painted the same blue as her dress. Her
head lifted and she stared back at him.

"Give me a name." He rolled his hand
toward her. "A general description. If you have
something with the guy's scent on it, that would

be even better. I can hunt him down by dawn and have this problem squared away so that we can both go back to our lives."

She wished. Sabrina took a few halting steps toward him. "You think…it will be that easy?"

His face had gone all hard and cold on her again. "I'm very good at killing."

Another reason she should *not* be attracted to him. He was a predator, straight to his core. And his prey? *Humans? Paranormals?*

So she stopped taking those halting steps toward him. She wrapped her arms around her stomach and tried to figure out what she could possibly do next.

"I think I know what happened…" He was all smug. Like he'd just solved a riddle. The riddle of her? "You met some poor jerk. He looked into your eyes and he was lost. That's how it works, right? You have the power in your eyes…"

"No." A quick denial. He wasn't the first to make that mistake. One psycho had once even tried to *take* her eyes from her because he believed that load of bull. "It doesn't work that way. The power is in *me*. Inside. It's not my eyes." She squeezed said eyes closed. "They're just an unusual shade of blue. Muse trademark. Because we see things differently, our eyes appear a bit different."

"Auras. That's what you see?"

"Yes." She made herself open her eyes. "So no one looked into my eyes and got zapped—"

"Then how did you get the bastard so twisted up? Because that's what happened, right? He got obsessed with you. Got dangerous. Got to the point where he'd do anything to have you." Adam's stare was unblinking. "All of those things you warned me about…"

"All of those things and more."

"Am I dealing with a paranormal?"

Excellent question. The problem was…"I'm not sure." She would have once sworn that Eric Foster was completely human but…

He can resist me. Somehow, he'd gotten to the point that he could actually resist her power—she'd learned that particular truth at the wrong time. *When I realized he was a killer.*

He leaned forward, dangling his hands between his spread thighs. "What you mean? You took one look at me and you knew right away what I was."

"You're different." And it was hard to explain exactly how so but…"Your dark aura—"

"Yeah," he said cutting through her words, "I got that part before. So my aura was a dead giveaway that I was something…more."

She nodded. "The man we're after—he isn't who I thought he was." A human? Could a human really be such a beast?

"When you left that ball tonight," his eyes never left her face, "you were followed. I saw the SUV get on your tail the minute you left the parking lot."

"And you came flying to my rescue?" Her words held a mocking edge, but he *had* come to her rescue. Not flying, but racing there on his motorcycle.

"If he'd still been at the scene, I could have ended him right then and there."

She didn't enjoy thinking about someone's death. Sure, she had a reputation for being bad, but people had her all wrong. "I wish I could go back. Change things. Never even meet him." Sadness thickened her voice.

Adam pushed off the couch. He stood to his full, towering height. "There is no going back. Not for any of us. Better to bury that dream now." Bitterness was in his voice and on his face. Bitterness and pain. Whatever secrets were in Adam's past, they weren't pretty. "A name. Give me his name."

When she took this step, when she turned on him, Sabrina knew death would try to come for her. She swallowed the lump in her throat and said, "Eric. Eric Foster."

His eyes widened, and she knew he recognized the name. "The freaking tech billionaire?"

Her shoulders rolled in a small shrug. "What can I say? I'm really good...at inspiration."

***

"You look kind of familiar," the blonde said as she ran her fingers over the front of Eric's tux. "Have we met before?"

"I haven't had the pleasure." They had just climbed into his limo. The SUV that he'd used before? Long gone. It would never be traced back to him. There were some true benefits to having shitloads of money. After he met the blonde—he thought her name was Mary or Maggie or something like that—Eric had called for his driver. His driver knew that Eric valued privacy above all else. Privacy and discretion.

"I swear I know your face," she said as her hand pressed harder to his chest. The scent of her perfume was overwhelming. The driver closed the door and they were alone in the back of the limo. "Are you like a celebrity or something?" She gave a high-pitched laugh. "Maybe I saw you on TV."

He smiled at her. "Not a celebrity." In fact, he made a point of staying away from the limelight. "Something else. Something better."

She pressed her body closer to his. She kissed his jaw. Then she put his earlobe between her teeth and gave a little tug. "Tell me," she whispered, "I'm dying to know."

He caught her hand and brought it to his mouth. Eric pressed a kiss to her palm. "You will be dying," he promised.

Her eyes widened. "What?"

It was his turn to kiss her jaw. Then, just as she'd done, he caught her earlobe between his teeth and tugged. Softly at first, but then harder, letting her feel the edge of pain.

Before the night was done, she'd feel plenty of pain.

"You want to know what I am?" Eric breathed into her ear. "I'm a killer."

Her breath came faster. Her body shuddered. "That's not funny."

"I'm not joking," he replied softly. This time, he eased back and kissed her lips. "And guess what? I'm going to kill you."

CHAPTER THREE

"Was he your lover?" Adam knew he probably shouldn't have asked the question, but he did it anyway. Curiosity compelled him. Curiosity could be a real bitch.

The quick jerk of Sabrina's head told Adam the answer to his question. So did the sudden paleness of her skin.

The bastard was her lover.

Adam forced his hands to unclench. He wasn't exactly sure when he'd fisted them. "You really didn't see what he was, did you?"

She paced toward the windows that overlooked the beach. "Maybe you need a little background on me. A few months ago...well, maybe — maybe it was more than a few months...I-I try not to think about it too often..." Her voice trailed away.

Adam waited. Every muscle in his body was tight with tension. Why did the idea of Sabrina with a lover piss him off so much? She wasn't his. Who she fucked wasn't his business.

I want to make it my business.

He was heading into dangerous territory, and Adam knew it.

"There's a lot of madness in the world." She was staring out of the windows, gazing into the darkness, and definitely not looking back at him. "That madness caught me."

"I don't understand."

Sabrina gave a mocking laugh. "Literally, I was caught by a man named Simon Lorne. A man utterly consumed by madness. Unfortunately, he knew far too much about dark magic and dark paranormals. Simon's wife had been taken from him—killed—and he was willing to do anything in order to get her back."

At that moment, Adam was very glad she could not see his face.

"He had guards...A lot of them. They made sure I never escaped. Simon...hurt me. He was making a collection, you see. Getting everything he needed to cast a powerful spell. Not everything." Her shoulders slumped. "Sorry, I need to be clearer with you. He was getting *everyone* he needed for that spell."

Adam felt rooted to the spot.

"Simon needed the heart from a vampire, the wings of an angel, the lips of a witch, and inspiration from a muse." She gave another rough laugh. Only this one held more pain than mockery. "But Simon mistakenly thought the

power of my inspiration was in my eyes."
Sabrina turned to face him.

Adam made sure his face showed no
emotion.

"He was going to cut out my eyes."

Her beautiful eyes.

"The cavalry came roaring in...and I escaped,
with my eyes still exactly where they belong. I
ran as fast as I could. I was looking for safety. I
was looking for a good life. Instead, I found Eric.
Or rather, he found me." She gave him a weak
smile. "You see, Eric and I had met long before I
was taken captive. We met, and I could see he
was on the verge of brilliance. He just needed
that little push. That bit of —"

"Inspiration?" Adam supplied quietly.

"Yes." She pressed her lips together and then
a few moments later said, "Before my abduction,
Eric and I grew close. When we were together,
things seemed perfect. That wonderful rush of
euphoria. And I thought...Maybe this time will
be different. Maybe *he* will be different." She
raked a hand through her hair. "He was
definitely different."

"Let me guess." He tilted his head and
studied her. "You inspired him to make those
technical breakthroughs. Because of you, the guy
is a billionaire."

"I didn't give him the skills, just the drive to
follow his passion." She swallowed and her gaze

was haunted. "Things went wrong. They often do, if you aren't very careful. I try to be careful. I swear, I do. But when I was taken, Eric…well, he freaked. His obsession with me went to a whole new level. He thought I'd abandoned him, thought I'd left him for someone else. He searched desperately for me, and with every day that passed, he changed more. I should've seen the danger with him. I don't know why I didn't see it." Her eyes squeezed shut. "By the time I was free, by the time I found him again, it was too late. The man I'd known…The man I thought I'd known…was long gone."

"I'm not sure I understand."

Her eyes opened. "Some people say that there is a thin line between brilliance and madness. You ever heard that?"

Adam just stared at her.

"Let's just say that while I was gone, Eric crossed that line. He crossed it again and again. He wanted to punish me, you see. He wanted to hurt me for leaving him."

His muscles were clenched so tightly that Adam's body ached. He could feel the beast he kept chained inside — deep inside. It was clawing at him. It wanted freedom. It wanted blood. Eric's blood. "It wasn't your fault that you were taken."

Her twisted smile made his chest feel odd. "It's not like I could tell him that. I mean…what was I supposed to do? Go up to the guy I *thought* was human and say, 'Hey, sorry for the vanishing act. Totally not my intent to disappear. I was taken by some dark magic wielding psycho who wanted to steal my power to bring back his dead wife. I was held in a prison, tortured for kicks, and prevented from escaping by his asshole guards.'"

Adam raised his brows. "Guess that's not the story you went with?"

"I couldn't tell him I was a muse. That wasn't an option. And when I first saw him again, I didn't realize how much he'd changed."

"Didn't see that in his aura?"

"That's the funny thing." Sabrina hesitated. "I could no longer see his aura at all. For the first time in my life, when I looked at a person, there was no aura. No extra lights or extra darkness. No extra colors at all. Nothing for me to fix. Nothing for me to worry about. It was just him. I thought...I thought that meant we were supposed to be together...or some fated thing like that." Her chin notched up. "Paranormals are big on fate, you know?"

He knew.

"I was so happy to be free of Simon. And Eric seemed happy to be back with me, too. But then...then I found out just how he was punishing me for my absence. How he'd been punishing me every single day that I'd been gone."

Adam knew this part wasn't going to be pretty. "How." Not a question, a demand.

"He hunts. He stalks. He kills." Her voice was soft and sad. "Eric picks women that have some sort of similarity to me…maybe it's the hair color or the shape of the woman's face. Maybe it's the sound of their voices, but each woman possesses some characteristic that reminds him of me. He takes those women. He hurts them. He kills them." A tear leaked down her cheek. "Women are dying in my place because…"

Adam stepped toward her. Touched her. He had to do it. His hand lifted and he wiped away that tear. Then his fingers lingered against her cheek. *I don't fucking like her tears.* "If he's so pissed at you, why not just kill *you*?" Adam hated asking that question.

"He had the chance." Her gaze held his. "The first night I went back to him, he could have killed me then. I was defenseless. Trusting." Her chin notched up. "I slept in his bed."

The beast inside of Adam clawed harder. It wanted freedom.

"He could have killed me while I slept. He didn't. Instead, I woke up and I found myself walking through his house. It was like I was being pulled. It's, uh, hard to explain, but I found myself in his study, and there…that's where I found them."

Shit. She'd actually found the bodies?

"I watch those crime shows on TV," she murmured. "The agents say the killers collect trophies. That was what he'd done. Eric had made a trophy collection. He took jewelry from each woman. He put the jewelry in his safe."

"How did you get into his safe?"

She gave a faint laugh. "The combination was the day we met."

Because you obsessed him.

"Next question," Adam growled. "Just how did you know the jewelry belonged to murdered woman? Maybe the guy had just bought it for you."

Sabrina shook her head. "I took a necklace from the safe, and as soon as I touched it, I had a flash of the victim's aura. For just a moment, I could see it so clearly. It was bright with her pain and her fear. So much fear. I knew she'd been murdered. I touched a ring next. And I saw another woman's aura. Bright with the same fear and pain. Horrible to see. It was the same thing with every piece of jewelry that I touched."

"Did he know what you'd found?"

"Yes. Because I turned around, and Eric was there. Watching me. And smiling."

***

"That is a gorgeous ring." Eric lifted her hand closer so that he could admire the ring. "Topaz...so distinct."

She didn't speak. She did whimper.

"Someone very special to me has eyes that match this ring. The London Blue Topaz...that's what it's known as in gem circles. Did you realize that was what you were wearing?"

She tried to tug her hand free.

He tightened his grip. "It's a very rich and deep blue topaz color. Very, very desirable. Sabrina's eyes are just like this...incredible." He looked up at the blonde. A pale imitation of Sabrina. The woman staring so fearfully at him just didn't burn with the fire — the bright light — that shone from within Sabrina. The light that always seemed to push him to do more. To be more. "I'll be taking that ring."

She whimpered again. Blood had mixed with the red of her dress. He'd been very careful with her wounds. He hadn't hit anything vital, not yet.

"I saw her first tonight, before I came to the ball and met you. I gave her a little scare, just to remind her that I was close. I'm always close to her."

"Pl...please...let me go..."

"Soon." When he was done. "But let's try a few things first." The limo had slowed. A few moments later, the back door opened. If his driver caught the scent of blood filling the car, he didn't so much as blink.

Eric unfurled himself from the back of the limo. He turned back to the woman —

She burst from the car. Shot out, screaming for help.

He rolled his eyes. They were parked in front of a warehouse. *His* warehouse. There was no one around to help her.

The driver didn't move. Eric smiled at him. "Tony, I think I have a runner."

Again, the man's expression didn't alter. Not so much as a blink.

"Gonna be a big night." Eric rolled back his shoulders. The hunger for blood, for violence, swelled within him. He looked down at his hands, and for just an instant, he thought he saw claws where his fingernails should have been. But no, he didn't have claws. He wasn't a monster. "One hell of a night…"

Eric gave chase. There was nothing like the thrill of the hunt.

Sabrina had taught him that.

She had taught him so many things…

CHAPTER FOUR

"How did you get away from him that night?"

Sabrina's lips trembled. "I still hold some sway over Eric. I convinced him that he needed to let me go, but I barely did it. My power over him had weakened, and I don't know why or how. I couldn't control him. I couldn't inspire him." There was no mistaking her fear. "So I fed him a line of bullshit that he bought. I lied my head off. I was able to convince him that by hurting me...by killing *me*...he'd lose all that he'd gained. I was his key. I had to stay safe."

Adam gave a grim nod, but he said, "You were — still are — playing with some serious fire."

"And I've been burned plenty of times. My magic held long enough for me to get the hell out of there but..." She shook her head. "He's been following me. Always following me. Wherever I go, no matter how fast I run or how far, he's there. And he lets me know...just like he did tonight. Attacks that aren't fatal. More like taunts.

But…right after each one…" Her gaze fell.
"Another woman dies in my place."

Adam had his target's name. He could get a
picture of the guy off the Internet. If he had the
man's scent, though, fuck, yes, that would help
even more. He could track Eric Foster so easily.

"He's about six foot two, two hundred
pounds. Eric likes to work out. A lot. Says it
clears his head. He has blond hair, hazel eyes. He
looks…I don't know. Normal. All-American.
Harmless." Her gaze lifted once more.
"Charming."

"It's the pretty faces that hide the worst
monsters."

She sucked in a breath.

Fuck, did she think he'd just called her—

"I didn't mean for him to become this way. I
never imagined…look, the inspiration goes
wrong, okay? I learned that early on. If I'm
around someone who isn't exactly, ah, stable,
then things can get bad." Her hand lifted and she
tugged on her ear. "Like a freaking artist who
thinks his ear is blocking his creative powers and
it has to go."

His eyes narrowed.

"Or a poet who takes so many drugs his
whole world goes dark. Don't even get me
started on the rock star who thought the needles
would help him to feel his music better…"

Adam cleared his throat.

Her shoulders straightened. "I learned the signs to watch for, all right? The cracks in the auras. When I see those, I steer clear."

The same way she'd tried to steer clear of him at the ball? Because she was so sure her inspiration would go wrong with him? His eyes narrowed.

"But you can't see everything," she told him with a sad shake of her head. "You can't predict everything."

Fuck, no, you couldn't. He knew that. *And, sweetheart, yours wasn't the pretty face I was talking about a few moments ago. Your pretty face isn't hiding a monster. That was another woman, a very long time ago.*

A woman who'd made him into a monster, too. "Get some sleep." He turned away from Sabrina.

"Excuse me? That's it? I give you my big confession and you just say for me to 'get some sleep' after that heartfelt reveal?"

"Yes." Because now he had a starting point. He went to his computer, typed on the keyboard, and a moment later, Eric Foster's face appeared.

I see you now.

"Where—exactly—will I be sleeping?"

"Pick a room." Adam paused. "Mine's the first one on the right."

"Okay…are you asking me to sleep in your room? Or telling me not to?"

He didn't fucking know. A muse in his bed…he was sure that would be something pretty unforgettable. *So unforgettable she drove one sonofabitch absolutely mad.*

Madness. Was that a risk he wanted to take?

Adam glanced back at her. The dress hugged her perfect body, her eyes were so deep…

Dammit. He yanked at his shirt, sending buttons flying.

Her eyes widened. "Um, Adam?"

"You might not want to watch this part."

"Watch you stripping?" Her tongue swiped across her lower lip. "It's not so bad…so far."

He dropped the shirt. His hands lowered.

She kept watching.

He stripped in front of her. And maybe he liked it when her eyes were on him. His cock sure liked having her staring. It grew even bigger for her.

"What exactly are you—" Her voice was a bit husky.

He marched for the French doors that led to the balcony. There was a reason he'd gotten this floor. Not just the fucking view. He yanked open the door and the scent of salty air hit him. For just a moment, he remembered sinking so fast beneath those waves…sinking like a stone.

Fuck.

"Adam, something's wrong with your back."

She'd followed him, her steps silent since she'd ditched those sexy heels.

He lifted his hands up toward the sky. The change was already sweeping over him. "Go back…inside." His voice was guttural. Watching a man strip…yeah, she might have liked that part.

Seeing a man become a beast? That was more the stuff of nightmares.

Only she didn't go back inside. He *felt* her coming closer and then her soft hands were on his back, brushing right along his shoulder blades. "Something is growing out of you."

He turned his head so that their eyes met. "Wings."

Her lips parted, dropping into an O. "What kind of shifter are you?"

He hadn't said he was a shifter. He just hadn't corrected the woman. He didn't turn into a werewolf. Or a panther or even a shark.

His beast was a different sort…

"It feels…" She was running her fingers over the growing wing on his right shoulder. "Almost like stone."

Because it was. Because he was. He'd told her before that her power wouldn't work on him…and it wouldn't. Because inside, the heart that she said would get broken? It was stone. He was stone on the inside, but sometimes, that stone came out, too.

"Go back…" His voice was deeper, almost booming. "Inside."

"Adam?"

"I'm…hunting…"

It happened then. He gave a deep, wrenching cry as the stone erupted, spreading to cover all of him. And as that stone spread, his body became something different. His face contorted. His teeth became fangs—a mouthful of razor-sharp teeth. His back arched, curved, and his wings grew spikes along the edges. Soon the man he'd been was but a memory, and a big, stone monster stood in his place.

"*OhmyGod.*"

Adam shot off the balcony, taking flight into the air, and he didn't look back.

He didn't want to see the horror on her face. He'd already seen it too many times with other people.

***

She should close her mouth. Stop gaping. She should step away from the balcony and the thundering waves that she could hear below and she should get her butt back inside.

Sabrina knew that. She also knew that she couldn't take her gaze off the *gargoyle* that had just flown away from her.

Holy hell. Holy sweet hell. Just…*damn*. An actual gargoyle. She'd never seen one of those before. Not in her very long life, and there were few creatures who'd lived as long as she had. Maybe a handful of vamps held that claim to fame…Luke…and his asshole twin brother, Leo. But not many others.

The Greeks had put her on a pedestal so long ago. She'd lived the high life.

Then she'd fallen off that pedestal. Fallen pretty hard. That happened, though, when you inspired the wrong warrior to attack and ransack the country.

A gargoyle. She had not seen that one coming. But it would explain a few things. If the stories were true, gargoyles didn't feel. Their hearts were truly locked in stone. And a heart that was locked away…

Sabrina smiled. Adam hadn't been bullshitting her. She didn't have to worry about her power working the wrong way with him. He'd be immune to her charms.

He'd be safe.

And I'll be safe with him. Finally, someone I don't have to worry about.

Except…the gargoyle had just flown away. He'd said he was going hunting, and she knew exactly who he was after. "Be careful!" Sabrina screamed after him. "Eric is more dangerous that you realize!"

She'd wanted a hunter, wanted a guard but…
I don't want Adam hurt because of me.

Then she blinked. He was made of stone. Literally. What could Eric do to him?

Luke sent me the perfect protector. And she'd doubted him.

Crap. She was going to owe the Lord of the Dark for this. Owe him big time.

***

The scent of blood hit Adam…blood and fear. Fear was a particular favorite of the gargoyle's, and it always drew him close. As Adam circled the city, that scent pulled him away from the bright lights. It pulled him away from the busy streets. It had him turning toward the warehouses.

Not the prey I seek. Not –

He heard a woman's scream. It barely reached him. But his hearing…as the beast, it was so much stronger than all other paranormals. He maneuvered his body toward the sound, and a few moments later, he saw the building. And the name on that big, fat warehouse. *Foster Technologies.*

Well, hell. Was he the greatest hunter in the world or what? A screaming woman, *Foster Technologies*…it didn't take a genius to put those pieces together, not after the story Sabrina had given him.

Eric hurt her…and then he killed a woman in her place.

Looked like the guy was in a killing mood right then. Too bad that Adam was going to interrupt his plans.

Adam slammed his heavy body down, breaking right through the roof of that warehouse. Wood and dust fell around him as he shot straight to the floor.

His wings spread up around him. His gaze swept to the left, to the right.

Guards came running at him. Men who were shouting. Humans with their guns. They lifted them up. They fired.

Idiots. They were firing at stone. What kind of damage did they really think they were going to do? He swung out with his right wing, hitting two men. The impact was the equivalent of those fools running straight into a brick wall. They fell and didn't get up.

The third man kept firing at him. Firing, but backing away.

The guy shouted, "What in the fuck are you?" Spittle flew from his mouth.

Adam locked one claw-tipped hand around the fellow's throat and lifted him high into the air. "I'm a delusion, obviously. A creation of your fear-riddled mind." His voice echoed. "Because you are afraid, aren't you?"

The guy had pissed himself. A rotten odor.

But only to be expected when a human confronted a monster face-to-face.

"L-let me go." A weak gasp. Probably all the human could manage because Adam was squeezing his throat.

"I heard a woman scream. Where is she?"

The guy's eyes rolled to the right. Toward the door there.

"Good job." And he tossed the man back, barely hearing the thud as the human hit a nearby wall. Adam stepped forward and the floor broke a bit beneath him. That shit always happened. As a beast, he was too heavy to maneuver easily in most buildings. Still, he marched toward the door, cracking the floor as he went. Then Adam yanked that door open, ripping it right from its hinges.

The woman wasn't screaming any longer.

And the scent of blood was very, very strong. *Still alive? Or was I too late?* Fuck. He hadn't wanted to be too—

He heard the squeal of tires. Someone was fleeing the scene…someone *thought* he was getting away.

Wrong. Adam whirled toward the squealing tires, ignoring the coppery odor of blood, but he didn't see a doorway or a hall. Just a wall. So

Adam crashed right through that wall. Then another. Then—

Outside.

A limo was fish-tailing away from the warehouse. Driving hell fast, but still not fast enough. *Not fast enough to escape me.* Adam bounded into the air. His powerful wings flapped around him. Stone could fly...yeah, fucking amazing. In seconds, he'd caught that limo. He caught it by landing on its long hood, slamming down into it, and the impact of his body hitting the hood made the limo's rear fly up into the air. A moment later, the vehicle crashed back down with a shuddering impact.

The windshield cracked. The driver's side door flew open, and a man in a black coat and pants—a driver's uniform—burst out. He ran, screaming.

Adam didn't let him get far. Adam flew back into the air and came back down in front of his prey. "Boo."

The human screamed again. Louder. It was the response that Adam expected. "Where's. Your. Boss?"

"I'm right behind you, freak."

Adam spun around, dropping the driver. He hadn't heard Eric Foster approach, but suddenly, the guy was right there. *Impossible. My hearing is too strong. He couldn't have gotten the drop on me. No way. No —*

Eric's gaze swept over him. "Aren't you something new? Made completely of stone? All the way inside? Or is that just some kind of hollow shell?"

Eric's face and voice showed no shock. It was as if he saw paranormal creatures every single day. *What's happening here?* Then...*screw it.* So what if the guy had snuck up on him? Eric was about to die. "Ready for hell?" Adam lunged toward Eric. His hand raked toward the guy, claws out and—

His claws went right through the other man. Right fucking through him. "*What?*"

Eric laughed. "Thanks for the invitation, but I've already been to hell. Happened the first time I lost my Sabrina. I don't intend to ever go back."

Adam tried to grab Eric again, then he realized..."You're not fucking here."

"And you're not very fucking bright, are you? All muscle...I mean, all stone. No brain." Eric stared back at him, but the man's appearance wasn't as clear any longer. "Technology is amazing. An absolute miracle. Science is the new magic these days. Things like you...you're a relic. Nothing more."

Adam was staring at—what? Some kind of fancy hologram?

"Sabrina opened my mind. Anything is possible now. I can create anything. I can do anything. I can go anywhere, anytime."

That was why Adam hadn't heard the guy's approach. Eric wasn't really there. It was just a hologram or projection of the guy.

But the blood…that was real. He spun and rushed back toward the warehouse.

The hologram called after him, "I'd like to know…why did you mess up my good time tonight? I don't know you…and I really hate when strangers get involved in my life."

Adam hesitated just long enough to look back. "I'm going to kill you."

Eric smiled. And then he just…disappeared. Winked away…like a computer, turning off. Adam bounded back into the warehouse. He followed the scent of blood and found a woman…trying to crawl away. A woman in a red dress, with blonde hair that looked far too much like Sabrina's. Adam saw the woman from behind, her face obscured from view and…

Sabrina. Eric picked her because she reminded him of Sabrina.

Adam reached for her, but stilled when he realized he had the hands of a beast. If he touched her, even using care, he could crush her bones. The woman was still alive. Barely, but…

She looked toward him. Blood streamed down her throat. *That's why she stopped screaming.* She stared at him and horror widened her eyes. She opened her mouth, screaming silently now as tears leaked down her cheeks.

He'd seen that horror before.

"I won't hurt you—"

Her eyes rolled back. She passed out even as the blood kept pumping from her wounds. She needed help. But not the kind of help a gargoyle could give.

So he had to turn back into the form of a man.

***

"What in the hell are you?" Eric leaned closer to the computer screen as he studied the bastard who had taken out three of his guards.

Good thing those assholes were there. Gave me time to escape. And his driver had followed the exact escape plan that had been in place. *Drive fast…as if I'm with you. Be the distraction.*

If the guy lived, Eric would give him a bonus.

But for the moment, his attention was completely focused on the stone beast. Only…a hand had just burst through the beast's chest. A human hand. It was punching its way out of that stone.

Like the stone is a shell, and the man inside is breaking his way to freedom. How very, very interesting.

Eric's fingers flew over the keyboard and he directed his surveillance cameras to zoom in closer on the man. The guy was slowly coming out of the stone. Breaking his way to freedom. Breaking out of the stone prison that had been his body. The man emerged fully nude. He was tall, muscled. He had dark hair. Dark eyes. The stone was rubble around his feet as the fellow rushed for the fallen woman. The mystery man put his hands to her wounds, trying to stop the loss of blood.

Intriguing. It would appear that this particular monster wanted to be a hero.

As Eric watched, the man scooped the woman into his arms and ran from the room. Eric tensed. If the blonde survived, she would be a problem for him. A very big problem.

But he couldn't go after them. Not then. When the uninvited guest had come crashing to the scene, Eric had retreated to the safe room hidden on the lower floor of his warehouse. If he left that room too soon, he could wind up as dead as his guards.

Eric was afraid to leave.

He didn't like being afraid.

But that bastard made of stone? *He* scared Eric. That meant Eric had to find a way to end the freak—very, very soon.

He switched video feeds. The mystery guy had loaded the woman into the limo. They raced away from the scene. Dammit. The woman could *not* survive.

And neither could the wannabe hero.

It was a good thing that he'd put a GPS tracker on the limo. The hero thought he was getting away, but he wasn't. Not really.

Eric reached for his phone. He dialed quickly, and when his call was answered, Eric said, "I need a clean-up crew at the warehouse. And I'll need my force team to tie up some loose ends." His force team...that was the guards he kept armed to the teeth. They did the grunt work for him. After a few more terse instructions, Eric hung up. His fingers tapped on the keyboard, and just like that, he could see where the limo was going.

"You'll be sorry that you ever interfered with my business." Eric smiled. He had a plan, and he wasn't afraid any longer.

CHAPTER FIVE

She'd stripped out of the evening gown. It wasn't as if she could wear the thing to bed. But Sabrina hadn't wanted to priss around the penthouse naked. So she helped herself to one of Adam's shirts. The thing pretty much swallowed her, not surprising really, given Adam's size. The bottom of the shirt hung to the middle of her thighs. It was a soft, cotton T-shirt, and it smelled like Adam. A rich, subtly masculine scent.

She liked wearing his shirt.

Sabrina had discovered there were three bedrooms in the penthouse. All nice bedrooms, with big beds and killer views. But...

Sabrina found herself curling up in Adam's bed. His scent lingered in the bed, too. It was a faint thing, but oddly, it reassured her. Being in his bed made her feel safe. Ridiculous, she knew that. It was just a bed.

His bed.

She wasn't in his bed as some sort of invitation. Really, that wasn't it at all. The penthouse was just so empty. So big. And it felt cold. Or, rather, the other rooms felt cold. She was warm in his bed.

A clock sat on the bedside table. The glowing numbers were easy to see in the dark. Two hours had passed since Adam left her. Two incredibly long hours. She squeezed her eyes shut. Sabrina knew she should try to sleep, but—

The faint squeak of the wooden floor had her eyes flying right back open.

He was there. Standing beside the bed. A big, hulking shadow. She jerked upright, breath catching in her chest.

"Easy." Adam's voice was quiet, but rough. *Sexy.*

She jumped from the bed. Easy was the last thing she felt. Her hands grabbed his shoulders. That wasn't good enough. Suddenly she was yanking him close and holding him in a tight hug. Had she been afraid while he was gone? Yes.

She'd been afraid something would happen to him.

Adam tensed in her hold. Then his hands came up and curled around her hips. He held her a moment, his grip almost painfully tight, but then he was pushing her back.

"He's not dead," Adam told her grimly. "You don't need to thank me yet."

Her lips parted. He'd thought—She felt heat stain her cheeks. "Asshole," she snapped, "I was worried about you, okay? I hugged you because I was glad you were back. Nothing more."

"And you're in my bed because…?"

She glared at him.

Adam gave a low laugh. "Right. Why don't you hold that thought while I go wash the blood off?"

He turned away from her.

Wash the blood off? It was so dark in the bedroom that she hadn't noticed any blood. He was in the bathroom now, and he'd just flipped on the light in that space. Sabrina hurried after him. "Is it your blood?"

He stood in front of the marble sink. With the light shining down on them, she could see that he was wearing clothes that were too tight, too small. A black shirt and black pants. And was that blood on them? She *did* see what looked like darker spots on the shirt.

"Not mine, hers." He jerked on the shirt and it seemed to rip apart beneath his hands. She saw the blood then — dried blood on his chest, on those powerful muscles. On his chiseled abs.

"Hers?" Sabrina repeated even as her heart seemed to drop in her chest.

Adam stalked toward the shower. A quick twist of his wrist and water shot out from the shower head. From both gleaming showerheads. Then his hands went to the top of his pants. He stripped out of them and they hit the floor.

The guy didn't even seem to notice that he was giving her a perfect view of his ass. Maybe he just didn't care.

"Yeah, hers." His voice was rough and angry. He didn't look at Sabrina. "A woman with your blonde hair. A woman that your buddy Eric stabbed over and over again. Then he left her to die. It was her blood, her screams—that led me to his warehouse. Only when I got there, he was gone and his guards were left. His guards and his driver. When they fought me, they didn't survive." His laughter was a dark rumble. "At least the bastard driver had back-up clothes in his car. So when I left the blonde at the hospital, I wasn't naked."

She shook her head, a denial of his words, of the attack on that other woman. A denial that this was happening at all.

But it's what Eric does. He hurts me...like he did tonight in the crash...and then he kills someone in my place.

Adam slid into the shower. She lunged forward and grabbed his arm, stepping onto the tiled floor and feeling the water rain down onto her. *"No!"*

His gaze met hers. "Fucking, *yes*. I counted nine stab wounds on her body...that was before he cut her throat so she wouldn't be able to scream any longer. A human. He was playing his torture games on a human. If I'd gotten there just a bit sooner…" His lips twisted in fury. "He would have been the one with the wounds. He would have been the one lying in a pool of his own blood. *Choking* on the blood."

Her racing heartbeat shook her whole chest. "Did you see him? Did you see—"

He twisted his hand, and, suddenly, he was the one holding her. He'd yanked her even closer to his naked body. The water from the shower head on the right had already soaked her hair and the T-shirt she wore. The cotton clung tightly to her body.

"You didn't tell me just how much you'd inspired him." His mouth was less than an inch from hers. His words were angry, so was his expression. "Just what did you help him to do? What all techno tricks did you teach him? Because I thought I had the sonofabitch. Then it turned out he was just a hologram. He wasn't even there."

"Yes, he was." Her body trembled. "If the woman was still alive, he was there. He must have just hidden from you. Did you search the warehouse?"

His jaw locked. "She was dying. I left to get her help." He let her go. Moved back. Put at least a foot of distance between them. "I could have searched, or I could have saved her. I made the choice." His lips flattened. The water pounded down on them both. "I'm sure you think it was the wrong fucking choice, but she was bleeding and helpless and—"

Once more, she surged toward him. Once more, her hands wrapped around his shoulders. "I don't." Dammit, why did everyone think she was so selfish? So evil...oh, right.

Because I'm a muse, I'm supposed to be bad.

Some days, she was. She liked to give out punishments to those who pissed her off. She liked to deal her brand of payback but...

An innocent woman? Tortured?

What had Adam said before...? *She had your hair.*

"I took the limo. I took the dead driver's clothes that were inside, and I dropped her off at the nearest hospital." A muscle jerked in Adam's jaw even as water beaded down his cheek. "And I let the bastard get away. Next time, he won't be so lucky."

"Thank you."

"What are you thanking me for? I just told you, *I* let him get away. I—"

She rose onto her toes and pressed her lips to his, stopping that angry tide of words.

She'd thought he was dangerous.

He was.

She'd thought he was dark.

He was.

But...

He'd saved a woman that night.

That hadn't been in his aura... A goodness...a sliver of light. She hadn't seen that.

At the touch of her lips, a long shudder worked over his body. His hands were at his sides. His mouth was open and her tongue snaked out to lick his lower lip before dipping inside. She kissed him with skill, with sensuality. After all, Sabrina knew how to kiss. When it came to sex, no bragging, but she was pretty much a rock star.

She'd had plenty of centuries to practice. And to seriously inspire.

But...

He wasn't kissing her back.

She was using her patented-bring-him-to-his-knees inner lick on his mouth, and he was stone still.

Stone still. Fitting but...

But he wasn't kissing her back. He was holding his control so casually when desire had tightened her breasts and made need heat between her legs.

And for once, she wasn't so sure. Uncertainty swept through her and her mouth slid away from his. Sabrina blinked up at him. Water clung to her lashes.

"You like playing with men?" he growled. "Seducing them, getting a rush of power?"

She shook her head. But...

His head lowered. His eyes narrowed. "You should be careful with me. I don't play."

He also hadn't kissed her back. Not even a bit. Embarrassing. Depressing. Because…

I really wanted him. Not because he was strong and big and bad. Her normal attraction requirements. No, this time, she'd been drawn to a potential lover for an entirely different reason.

Because he was good. Because he saved a life, not took one. Because he helped a stranger when there was nothing in it for him.

Sabrina whirled away from him. The T-shirt clung to her like a second skin. Her breasts were aching and tight—because *she* had been turned on by the kiss. But he…he'd been stone cold. She should have known better. What in the hell had she been thinking?

He caught her before she stepped out of the shower. He whipped her around and pinned her to the glass wall. "No, sweetheart, you don't get to tease and leave."

Now anger pulsed through her. "I wasn't teasing." Her chin notched up. "Just making the mistake of touching stone that doesn't feel."

He moved his body closer to her. His *lower* body this time.

And she realized that he felt plenty.

Talk about hard as stone. His cock was erect. Fully erect. Long and hard and oh, so ready. She hadn't looked down at him before. She'd been exercising some extreme restraint—and when they'd been kissing, their upper bodies had been close. Not the lower parts…

"That's why you don't tease. Because when I want someone, it can be a dangerous thing."

Those words should have been a warning. They should *not* have turned her on more. It just went back to her slightly shady inner wiring. A bad girl wanted what a bad girl *craved*…

"If you kiss me again, I won't hold back. I will take you."

She blinked away the water that had dripped from her lashes. "Maybe I'll be the one taking you…"

He gave a ragged laugh. "You do like the fire."

Even though she'd been burned.

She'd been burned…and other women were paying the price for her last mistake.

Pull away from him. Get your shit together. You're feeling vulnerable and mixed up and you need to back away. Back away! "I want out of the shower now." Sabrina spoke slowly, clearly. "Let me go."

He stared into her eyes. She could only see the darkness in his gaze. Nothing else.

But there was more to him than the dark.

His hands fell from her. Her breath whispered out. She hurried out of the shower, stepping onto the lush rug and immediately creating a puddle of water on top of it.

"The shirt looks good on you."

His gravelly words reached her.

"But I bet you'd look even better without it."

A bit more confident now that she was away from him, Sabrina nodded. "You're right. I absolutely would." Then, because he'd done her the favor of showing her his ass, she decided to be fair. She turned away from him and yanked that wet T-shirt over her head. Then she dropped it, and walked away.

She didn't let the shaking start until she had closed the bathroom door behind her. Then she locked her arms around her stomach and rocked forward, her confident pose absolutely gone.

I counted nine stab wounds on her body...that was before he cut her throat so she wouldn't be able to scream any longer.

It was good that her face was still wet from the shower. This way, her tears would stay hidden.

***

She'd left him wanting. Fucking *aching*.

He'd gone to her with blood on his body. And she'd kissed him.

He'd failed. He'd let her tormentor get away. And she'd rubbed that luscious body of hers against his.

She had the best ass he'd ever seen. Heart-shaped, full. Perfect for grabbing and holding tight during one rough ride.

He yanked the handle on the shower, making the water go ice cold. He needed that icy blast because he was *not* going back to her with his dick at flag-pole level. She liked manipulating him, he got that. Manipulation was part of her make-up.

But she wasn't going to play him. He wouldn't let her.

So he stayed beneath that shower. He let the icy blast do its work. Or tried to let it. But images of her kept sliding through his mind.

And the way she'd used her tongue when she kissed him…

The water just couldn't get cold enough.

Next time, sweetheart, you put your lips to mine…and I won't hold back.

***

Eric was back in his Miami mansion. He had homes all over the U.S. now. When you were richer than God, you got perks. He had a lot of perks. When he'd first been with Sabrina, his home had been in California. And after she'd left him…

I didn't have a fucking home. Not for too long.

He liked the Miami place, though, because he knew Sabrina liked to hide in the Miami crowds. He'd bought the place just so he would be close — but not *too* close — to her.

His clean-up crew had arrived at the warehouse in record time. They'd taken care of the bodies, no questions asked.

Eric made a mental note to get a new driver. The last guy...well, he hadn't survived. But his sacrifice had been appreciated. Maybe Eric would send the fellow's mom some money. He thought she might have cancer or something...the driver had mentioned something about her once. Tony had been desperate to get money for her.

So desperate that he'd been willing to overlook the things that happened inside that limo.

Desperate people are the best employees.

When the clean-up crew appeared, they'd come with more guards. So Eric had seized his opportunity and gotten the hell out of the warehouse.

A knock sounded on his study door. He looked up from the screen in front of him, frowning. "What?"

The door opened. His visitor was Raymond Banner, his head of security. The guy was former Black Ops, an ex-Mercenary for hire, and he had a definite talent for giving pain.

Eric had hit gold when he'd found that guy.

"The cops still haven't appeared at the warehouse."

Eric grunted. "That's because our hero didn't call the cops. He dropped off the woman and he disappeared." He'd already tapped into the hospital's video feed. He'd seen the mystery fellow rush in, carrying the woman. The hero had put her on the nearest gurney, bellowed for a doctor, then rushed out.

And where did you go?

Eric looked back at his computer, tapping, tapping with his fingers. The GPS signal on the limo had gone dead. Odd. It should have still been sending him a signal. He'd counted on using that signal to lead him back to his new prey.

"What about the woman? What do you want me to do with her?" Raymond asked.

"She's in surgery now. If she survives, we'll evaluate then." *And we'll kill her.* Raymond would handle that job. The guy was absolutely brilliant at an up-close stealth attack. He could slip into that hospital and bam...*Dead.* "Don't make any move until we see what happens next. If she dies on the operating table, then the cops will just think the man who brought her in...they'll think he's the one who hurt her. They'll focus on him."

Raymond walked closer and the floor groaned beneath his feet. "You haven't told me much about the guy."

"Not true." The printer hummed behind him. "I'm even giving you a picture of him right now. Go take a look. And I'm running that picture through every facial recognition program that I have. I'll soon have his name, his home address...his every secret."

Raymond picked up the printed picture. "How'd he know you were at the warehouse?"

"He must have followed me." Obviously. But Eric considered this point carefully. "From the charity ball." Eric nodded. *Must have been tailing me all along.* "I'll pull up the security footage from there, too. See who he talked to...see if anyone there knew him..."

Raymond had just pointed him in the right direction. Eric gave a low hum as he worked. His whole body was revving up. There was nothing quite like the thrill of the hunt. He worked silently, his fingers flying. He always loved hacking, it was a basic skill he'd possessed since he was twelve years old. Computers were his world.

When he accessed the security footage from the ball, his muscles tensed. It was easy to spot the mystery man...And it was also too easy to see the man watching Sabrina.

My Sabrina. That bastard had followed Sabrina out onto the balcony. There were no cameras out there, so there was nothing for Eric to see. Since he couldn't see what was happening on the balcony, Eric stared at the timeframe on the video feed, counting the seconds that passed as the mystery guy stayed out there with Sabrina.

Too long. Far too long.

Rage wrapped tightly around his heart and taking a breath? It got a hell of a lot harder.

Then Sabrina was running back into the ballroom. Fear was on her face, and he knew Sabrina did not fear easily. And the man she left behind? *He'd* scared her. Interesting.

Eric sped through the footage, but he never saw the other man leave the balcony. Obviously, the guy found another way to slip away from the party.

Raymond cleared his throat. "Learn anything new?"

Sabrina. It was always about her.

A new admirer? Was that who this fellow was? Another fool who had become obsessed with her? If so, then it would be Eric's job to end that obsession.

"I think I know how to find him." Eric smiled as he turned to face Raymond. "Wherever she is, he will be close by."

Raymond's brows shot up. "She?" he repeated.

"Sabrina. Sabrina Lark." Her name was an endearment as it slipped from his lips. "He'll be close to her." And if there was one thing Eric knew how to do, it was find Sabrina. He could find her anywhere, anytime.

Eric would never lose her again. He'd taken steps to make absolutely sure of that fact. Eric nodded toward Raymond. "Get your men ready. I'll have her location for you within the next five minutes."

***

The bathroom door creaked open behind her. The bedcovers were wrapped tightly around her body. She cleared her throat and called out, "This doesn't mean anything, so don't go getting all excited. I just happen to like this bed. The others were either too soft or too hard, and I guess I'm just a Goldilocks because they didn't work for me. There's plenty of room here, so I'll be sleeping in this bed tonight. If that's a problem for you, feel free to go crash somewhere else."

She had her back to him so she couldn't see his expression, but there was definite tension in his voice as he replied, "You're kicking me out of my own bed?"

Not kicking him out, not exactly. "I said there's plenty of room. You just have to stay on your side of the bed."

"The whole thing is fucking mine." Now he was disgruntled. She almost smiled. The floor creaked and then the mattress dipped as he slid

onto the bed. Immediately, Sabrina could feel the heat from his body. She also realized —
immediately — that she hadn't taken into account just how big he was. Adam definitely took up more than half of the bed. She inched closer to the edge, not wanting to touch him.

She liked it too much when they touched.

The room was dark, she'd made a point of turning off all the lights. Sabrina had always found it easier to hide in the dark. She could hear the sound of his breathing, deep and even, and for some reason, that sound reassured her. It reassured her enough that she found the courage to ask, "Will the woman survive, do you think?"

Silence...Then he said, "I'm not sure. She was pretty bad. Obviously, your ex wanted her to die."

Even though it was dark, she still squeezed her eyes shut. "No, he wants me to die. He's just afraid if I do, all that wonderful inspiration I gave to him will die, too. He doesn't want to go back to being ordinary. He doesn't want to go back at all."

"But if he's after you," Adam's voice growled, "then why doesn't he have you? Tied up, locked up, and secured safely where he can always have you close by?"

"Because he doesn't like to get too close to me. He's afraid of what I might convince him to do. The last time I tried to work my magic on him…I failed, but I could see him struggling. He's worried I might be able to get in his head." Her lips twisted. "He doesn't even let his guards get too close to me." She thought of her past. Of the hard choices she'd been forced to make. Of the choices most would never know about.

Under the right circumstances, she could inspire her prey to do just about anything. Kill a friend, family member, a stranger…Or she could get that prey to take his own life.

"So that's why he hit you with his car, so he didn't have to get physically close to you."

Probably. "Eric likes to remind me that he is always waiting nearby."

More silence. She should sleep. Sabrina knew she should close her eyes and just try to rest. Instead, she rolled toward him. *Don't ask him. Let it go. Don't push for what you don't want to know.* She figured that was the weak voice of her conscience, trying to stop her from making a bad decision. Too bad for her conscience, Sabrina had been ignoring its voice for a very long time.

"The stone surprised me. I didn't expect…" Her words trailed away.

"You didn't expect me to turn into a nine foot tall beast with wings and claws? Oh, sorry, a nine foot tall *stone* beast."

"I thought you might be a wolf shifter. Maybe a panther. But, no, I wasn't expecting a gargoyle." Sabrina paused. "That's what you are, right? A gargoyle? Kind of hard to mistake that, you know, what with the whole stone beast thing that you had going on."

"Yes," he rasped. "I'm a gargoyle."

"Your kind—they're made, not born. I mean, I've been around a really long time, and I heard the stories, even if you are the first gargoyle that I've ever actually met." Her words came faster. "Is it true? Were you once a man? A knight? Doing the whole wearing armor and riding a horse bit?"

"Go to sleep, Sabrina."

"You were a knight, and a witch cursed you. She put you under a spell, and basically made you her slave, isn't that how the story goes?" Her words wouldn't stop. Her conscience was yelling at her to be *quiet*, but her conscience just wasn't strong enough.

"Go. To. Sleep."

Okay. The guy obviously didn't want to share. She understood. Normally Sabrina didn't share anything about herself. She just felt…different…with him. "I thought all the gargoyles were dead. That the witches used them up until nothing was left."

"*Sabrina…*" A warning edge blasted in his voice.

"I think I'm the only muse left. Once, I had two sisters. We lived together in Greece. The people there treated us as if we were gods—

goddesses. It was really nice, at first. But things went wrong. They often go wrong. My sisters were killed, and I was left alone."

"You get chatty at bedtime. I'll have to remember that."

"Do you know what it's like to go through centuries and centuries alone? To always watch what you say and do? To be so careful, but to still make so many mistakes? If you don't know, let me just tell you. It sucks." Then, Sabrina flopped back over, giving him her back.

"So you're trying to tell me that you aren't as bad as people think?"

Her eyes were closed. "No, I am bad. Don't ever forget that." Then she stopped talking. Not because she'd given into her conscience, but because if she said anything else, it would hurt too much.

***

The man before Sabrina should've been a perfect king. He was young and strong and smart. So smart. He sat on the golden throne, his long legs stretching out before him. A cold smile curved his lips. His eyes were on the sight before him.

The sight of a dead body. One of his own guards. The new king had killed him. Just run him through because he'd suspected the guard hadn't been loyal.

Or just…not loyal enough.

Sabrina stood behind the curtain, watching and waiting. The king gave the order, and everyone swept from the royal chamber. The dead body was left behind, per the king's request. When everyone was gone, the king rose. He walked toward the dead. He still held a bloody knife in his hand. As Sabrina appeared from her hiding spot, he knelt and begin stabbing the man, over and over again.

"He's already dead." Her words were soft, but the new king heard her. He always heard her. She'd been the one whispering in his ear for the last year. Telling him that he was meant to be more, telling him that he should rule. Telling him that his power was meant to be.

But she could see the cracks now. Cracks in this aura. Cracks that told her…The madness that had fueled his father's blood — that madness had also passed to the son. The more power he gained, the more the madness had grown. Had it strengthened because of the battles? Because of the bloodshed that didn't stop? War could drive any man to the brink.

Only this king…He'd gone beyond the brink.

He was mutilating the dead. He was unraveling before her eyes.

But he looked up at Sabrina and he smiled at her. "My muse."

He knew what she was. In this wondrous land, the humans loved their gods and goddesses. There had been no need to hide from him. He'd seemed so perfect.

"This isn't the path you want to take. This is a dark and twisting path, and at the end, you will only find the same madness that claimed your father." She moved closer to him, sure that her heart was breaking. "There's time to stop. There's time to change."

He rose, moving away from the dead man and stalking toward her. "I am king. I do what I want. No one can stop me." He paused right in front of her, and his left hand rose to touch her cheek. "I think the time of gods and goddesses should come to an end. People don't need to worship you any longer. They need to see that you are no different from humans. That you live, that you breathe…" He lifted the hand that held the knife. "And that you bleed."

He was going to stab her. Sabrina knew it. He was going to murder her just as easily as he'd murdered the guard.

"No. You don't want to kill me." She smiled at him, a sweet, gentle smile. "I am not your enemy. I'm a friend. I'm the one who helped you. I'm the one who led you here."

The tip of the knife pressed just above her heart. "I don't need you any longer. I don't want the people worshiping you. They should worship—"

"You?" Sabrina finished, her voice husky. "Is that what you want? For the humans to see you as their new god?"

"That is what I shall become."

He thought he would kill her. He was wrong. Sabrina rose to her toes and she put her mouth beside his ear. "You need to eliminate the biggest threat to the throne. You should not hesitate, you should not stop. You must protect the throne. Always. The biggest threat is so close."

He'd gone still before her. "Biggest...threat?"

"Yes." She curled her hands around his wrist and moved the knife away from her heart. "That threat is you, Akin." For the first time, she used his name, and just speaking it—*it hurts.* But the tip of the knife now pressed to his chest. Her whole body had turned icy. "Eliminate the threat. That is what a good king would do."

His eyes were emerald green. So deep, so pure. His eyes were staring into hers when the knife pierced his heart.

***

"Don't! Stop! I take it back!"

Sabrina's scream woke Adam. He jerked upright and immediately reached for her. His hands curled around her as Adam pulled her close. "Sabrina?"

She drew in a deep, shuddering breath and her eyes opened. "I did not want that particular trip down memory lane."

Adam had no idea what she was talking about but—

An alarm started beeping. *Security alarm.* "What the hell?" He jumped from the bed. He was naked, so he paused just long enough to grab a pair of running pants and then he was rushing toward the bank of security monitors in his office. He heard Sabrina rushing after him.

"What's happening?" Sabrina demanded.

He sat in a chair before the monitors, his gaze flying over the screens. He saw two black SUVs parked in front of the building. Men in black— clothes and ski masks—were trying to break into the front entrance. Trying, not succeeding. "We've got company."

"They found you. Eric and his men—they must've followed you!"

"Doubtful. I'm a hard guy to follow. I took your ex's limo, but after I dropped off the victim at the hospital, I made sure that limo got ripped apart. I have a few friends who specialize in the dismantling business." He slanted her a hard glance. "No one followed me. You're the one who

said Eric always seems to know where you are."
But now Adam wondered…just how did Eric
keep tabs on Sabrina? Adam's gaze swept over
her and he tensed. "My shirt? Again?" Her firm
breasts — breasts he'd been dreaming about
before her scream had brought him crashing back
to reality — pressed against the front of the white,
cotton T-shirt.

Sabrina leaned against him, moving to get a
better view of the monitors. Her hair fell forward
and brushed over his arm. "I was wearing an
evening gown, remember? You popped up and
decided I had to take a ride on your bike. Not like
I had a lot of pajama options. So, yes, I'm
borrowing your shirt. Deal with it."

His gaze had dipped to her legs. Long, bare
legs. Those legs had been in his dreams, too.
They've been wrapped tightly around him.

"Those are Eric's men." Her scent was about
to drive him crazy. "I've seen the type before.
They think that they are bad asses, wearing black
gear, covering their faces, and always keeping
their guns at the ready. I think they're ex-
military." She exhaled angrily. "Eric is trying to
surround himself with a powerful force."

Adam turned back to the monitors, and he
tried to ignore the appeal of her sweet scent.
"They aren't powerful enough. Humans never
are. And their bullets? They don't do anything to

stone." He rose, sending his chair rolling back. Adam headed for the door.

Sabrina grabbed his arms. "Wait—are you just going down there? Seriously? I counted at least half a dozen men, all with some really big guns."

"Yes, I'm going down there. And I don't really give a shit how big their guns are."

Her lips parted. Beneath her hands, he was already starting to change. His skin was hardening, thickening, as flesh became stone.

"Adam." What could have been fear appeared in her eyes. "Let's think about this. What if it's a trap?"

He held off the change, with an effort. An effort that made sweat break onto his body. "Stone, sweetheart, remember? They can't hurt me when I'm a gargoyle. No human can hurt me then." It was only when he was in the form of a man that he was vulnerable. Adam inclined his head toward her. "Besides, this is my job. I take out the stalker on your trail, and then I'm out of your life. The deal is done."

She didn't look reassured. Her gaze darted to the monitors. He followed her stare. The men in black were now using some sort of saw to try and cut through the building's main door. Nice try, but that wasn't going to work.

"Stay here, Sabrina. You can watch all the action on the screens." But he hesitated, because he wanted—

Her.

Adam wanted her. He wanted to kiss Sabrina. He wanted to taste her again. He wanted to claim her. To possess her completely.

Leaving her there? It felt fucking wrong. Very, very wrong.

His head was bending toward her. Their mouths were close. It would be so easy to eliminate that distance. So easy to take what he wanted. But he stilled. If Adam put his lips to hers, he wouldn't stop. He would take and take and take.

There were asshole humans waiting outside. He had to deal with them first. But then he would be back for Sabrina. He stepped around her and marched for the door.

"Be careful!" Sabrina yelled after him. "Everyone has a weakness! Everyone! Be careful, dammit!"

Adam didn't stop walking. He maneuvered through the penthouse and a moment later, he headed onto the balcony. The wind whipped against him. And he let the stone consume him.

CHAPTER SIX

Adam could've at least kissed her good-bye.
Hell, would that really have been too much to
ask? Sabrina's breath heaved in and out, and her
heart raced as she stared at the computer screens.
The men in black were still at the front of the
building. They were so intent on getting inside
that they didn't even notice when a giant
gargoyle appeared right behind them.

Her whole body tensed. "Seriously, Adam,"
she whispered, "be careful." Because she'd seen
the mighty die during her life. Seen gods perish.
Seen dragons fall. Everyone and everything *did*
have a weak spot.

It was just a matter of finding that spot. A
matter of working the weakness.

The gargoyle grabbed one man and hurtled
him into the air.

Now they all see you. So much for a sneak
attack. But when you were as big as he was, it
was probably hard to stay hidden for long.

Darkness still hung heavily around them. A
glance at the clock to her right told her it was

nearing three a.m. The street outside was empty — except for the men in black and the very pissed off gargoyle.

Her hands curled around the arm rests of her chair as she leaned forward.

Two guards down. He'd taken them down easily and as she watched, he was swinging his arm toward a third. He was...

The phone on her right rang. The sound was so sudden and jarring that she jerked in surprise. Then her gaze shot to the phone.

It kept ringing. Not a coincidence. No freaking way. She swiped up the phone and shoved it to her ear. "What?"

Laughter. *Familiar* laughter. "Are you enjoying the fight as much as I am?"

Eric's voice. Unmistakable. The stuff of nightmares. Because, right, she wanted to add more to her already busy nightmare realm. *As if it weren't already overflowing.*

"I've got a camera on one of the SUVs that is parked near your building. It lets me watch everything perfectly." He gave a whistle. "The building you're inside does have good security, I'll give you that, and I'm betting you're locked away tight in a safe room, watching the scene unfold."

It wasn't a safe room...was it? Her gaze darted around her. *No windows. Only one door.*

"What *is* your new friend, Sabrina? I've got to say, I'm curious about him. So I thought I'd watch him in action a bit so that I could see just what his strengths are."

"Leave me alone." She made her voice ice cold. "How many times do I have to tell you—"

"You should never have walked out on me. I...I think I loved you, Sabrina."

She should hang up the phone. Slam it down. "How did you even get this number?" It was a landline in the building and—

Eric laughed. "Seriously, love? It was child's play for me."

Yes, dammit, it probably had been. He'd probably tapped on his computer and gotten the number in mere moments.

Another guard had fallen. As she watched, the gargoyle picked up a different man and held him with one claw-tipped hand wrapped around the human's throat. *Is Adam strangling him?*

"And you say I'm the monster." Now Eric was disgusted. "I don't know where you found that freak, but the guy is worse than I am. At least I'm human..."

Are you?

"Here's how this will work, my dear. While the stone freak is busy, you're going to leave your safe room. You're going to slip away. I made the distraction for you—you're welcome. You're going to exit the building, and you're going to run away from him. Just run. You know I'll find you."

How? How does he keep finding me?

She'd wondered before. She'd even thought that maybe he'd put some kind of tracking device under her skin. She'd looked, but hadn't found any sign of cuts or implants. And she would remember him doing something like that, wouldn't she?

"I'm curious…I saw the video feed of you with him at the ball. Is he forcing you to stay with him? Is he another fool who took one look at you and became obsessed?"

Not obsessed. I'm supposed to inspire. To bring out the good in people.

Only she didn't do that. All too often, her power had the exact opposite effect.

"You were afraid in that video. You were afraid of him. I know when you fear a man. After all, I've seen the way you look at me."

Adam had stopped choking the human. He'd dropped the man in black, and the fellow lay sprawled on the ground. Was he dead? Sabrina leaned forward, straining to see better, but the video feed just wasn't letting her get a close enough view.

"Is he holding you prisoner?"

They were shooting at Adam, and she could see chunks of stone breaking away. Then his big, powerful wings stretched behind him. He leapt into the air, dodging the bullets.

"If he is, then run. Run to me, Sabrina. You know I can protect you from him."

She gave a broken laugh. "You don't protect me from anything. You think I don't know you were the one in that SUV last night? You sent me crashing off the road!"

Silence. "I just wanted you to know I was close…"

"You wanted me to know you were a psychopath," she muttered. "But guess what? I had already figured that out."

"*Sabrina*. I'm not a psychopath. You know I'm a genius. I can make anything happen. I can change the world, I *have* changed it. And it will keep changing. You and I together — we create our reality."

That was one of his favorite new catchphrases. *We create our reality*. Sounded like BS to her. "You want to know what my *reality* is right now? The guy you called a stone freak? I'm choosing him. I'm not his prisoner. I'm with him willingly, so your plan for me to just waltz out of here while his back is turned —"

"Margaret Lacy."

"What?"

"That's the name of the woman your *freak* dropped off at the hospital. And if you don't get your ass out of that safe room and out of that building—right the hell now—I'll have one of my men carve her into a hundred pieces. Do you remember Raymond Banner, the head of my security team?"

Like she could forget that guy.

"He's already in her hospital room. Security at that place is really a joke, isn't it? He's standing at the foot of her bed, just waiting on a text from me. Oh, don't worry, he's dressed like an orderly so no one will suspect that his intentions are foul."

She leapt to her feet.

"But if you don't move, right now, she won't be a survivor. Poor Margaret will just be dead."

She didn't see Adam on the monitors. There were four armed men still standing, searching for him. But Adam had flown away. "You're bluffing…"

"Am I? Well, I guess we can just wait and see. I mean, it's not your life on the line. It's a stranger's, and I've always suspected that you don't really care much for others. Not in your nature, is it?"

"Why are you doing this?" Sabrina cried.

"Because you left me. And when you did, you took something with you."

"I took *nothing*."

"You took my control. I was lost without you. The urges I'd kept inside for so long? I couldn't contain them. And then once I started, once I got a taste for the blood and the pain, there was no going back. I saw my true potential."

Wonderful. She'd inspired the asshole to become a serial killer.

"I still see it." His breath rushed over the line. "Uh, oh, guess he's back. You need to choose, Sabrina. Tick, fucking tock. You know I won't kill you. I would never do that. But I won't let that freak keep you. You will stay mine."

He wasn't even shocked that Adam was a gargoyle. Just how much had he learned about the paranormal world?

"Fine." Another sigh from him. "It's as I suspected. Humans don't matter at all to you, do they?"

Humans. It was the first time he'd made a distinction.

"I'll get Raymond to start cutting."

"No! Dammit, stop! I'm leaving the building, okay? But I'm on the top floor and it's going to take me a while to get down. *Give me some time.*"

"You have five minutes. If you're not out of that building and running fast by the time those five minutes are up, Margaret Lacy is dead."

He hung up on her. She threw the phone across the room. Then she was running for the door. Sabrina yanked it open and stumbled into the hallway. She didn't go change into her gown. *Five minutes. Just five.* There wasn't time to change. She raced toward the elevator, banging on the button to get the doors to open. They dinged and opened, and Sabrina jumped inside. She hit the control panel, pushing the button for the parking garage but...

The elevator didn't move.

She hit the button again. And again. And she was cursing and swearing but the elevator wasn't moving.

Adam had used a key card before. So where in the hell was that card?

She rushed back into the den. Her gaze flew frantically around the room, but she didn't see the key card. She went into the office. Not there.

There had to be another way down. *Stairs.* She could take the stairs. Provided that the staircase door didn't require some key card.

I'll never get down them in five minutes. She'd already lost valuable time.

But she still ran to the stairwell. Only the damn door was sealed.

Adam had locked her in. She shot to the bedroom, ripping through the drawers there. No key card.

How much time has passed?

Eric would be watching the building. She didn't think he'd been bluffing at all. If she didn't get out of there before the time ran out, the woman — Margaret Lacy — would be sliced apart in her hospital bed.

Sabrina burst out onto the balcony. The balcony wrapped around the entire top floor, overlooking the crashing waves, and then circling around to the front of the building and the street below. She ran to the side that hung over the street. *"Adam!"* Sabrina screamed. *"Help me!"*

She climbed onto the edge of the balcony, hanging on for dear life. Oh, shit, it was high. She could see Adam, a big, hulking mass below her. He was still fighting and she could see guns, but she couldn't hear the blast of bullets. *Silencers?*

"Adam!" Sabrina yelled again. "I need you!"

He looked up at her. Then he shook his head.

He shook his head. One claw-tipped hand pointed imperiously as she strained to see him, and she knew the guy was telling her to go back inside. He didn't get it. That wasn't an option. "Catch me!" Her voice echoed back to her.

Then she leapt off that balcony. *Hellhellhellhell*...The wind whipped around her.

Was Eric watching? Did he see that she was trying to get down to him? That she was trying so hard she was risking her own life?

Catch me. Catch —

It felt as if she'd been flying forever before Adam caught her. Before those stone arms locked around her and yanked her against his chest, holding her in an unbreakable grip. Her eyes opened. She didn't remember squeezing them shut, but it made sense. She hadn't wanted to see herself slamming into the ground below on the off-chance that Adam hadn't flown his stone ass up to save her. "Thank you," she whispered. Her arms wrapped around his wide shoulders — giantly wide. "Now if you could just gently put me on the ground…?"

Instead, he sent them soaring higher.

"*No!*" Sabrina screamed.

"What in the fucking hell…" Wow. His voice was deep and hard. Boomy. "*What in the fucking hell were you thinking?*" The monster before her snarled.

The very, very angry monster.

But he was dealing with a very, very desperate muse so he wasn't going to frighten or intimidate her. "You have to put me on the ground. I have to walk away from this building. If I don't, he's going to kill Margaret Lacy!"

He was still lifting them higher. "Who?"

"The human female you saved! She's in the hospital, but one of his men is in the room with her. Eric is watching us right now. He has a camera on one of the SUVs. If I don't walk away from you…*now*…he will order his man to cut her up." Her eyes were watering. From the wind and the jump and not from tears. *Not from tears.*

His eyes were glowing. No, not glowing so much as burning. With a red fire. Red in the face of all that hard stone. His face wasn't a man's. It was some weird thing that appeared to be a blend of a wolf and a lion. He had some crazy big, wickedly sharp teeth bursting from his mouth. "Please," Sabrina said. She was begging and she didn't care. "Just put me on the ground. His men won't shoot me. I just have to walk away and she lives."

"You...can't trust him." Each word sounded as if it were being torn from him. "You...can't..."

"I can't let that woman die. And I know you understand this because you're the one who took her to the hospital." She released a rough breath. "Put me on the ground. I'll walk away. She'll live."

His eyes seemed to burn even brighter. Those massive stone wings shook behind him. Then he was flying down and she could feel the wind whipping against her. Relief made her almost dizzy. Or maybe that dizziness came from the fact he was flying so fast. Either way, Sabrina kept her arms clenched tightly around him. He seemed to be heading straight toward one of those SUVs. The men with guns weren't firing any longer. She suspected that Eric had told them not to shoot. He wouldn't want one of their bullets to hit her.

Adam didn't slow down when he neared the SUV. In fact he slammed right into it. Sabrina screamed even as metal groaned and glass smashed. Then he was flying toward the second SUV and crashing into it, too. He shielded her completely with his stone body, making sure that she wasn't hurt.

"No more camera," he growled. Then he was shooting back into the sky.

"You were supposed to put me down! No, Adam, stop! You know he has that woman! He'll kill her! You have to —"

"Trust…me."

With her twisted life, trust wasn't easy for her. But the gargoyle was flying too far and too fast, and it was already too late to go back. She didn't have a choice.

He'd taken away her choice.

Margaret, I'm sorry. Sabrina twisted and heaved in Adam's grasp, but he wouldn't let her go. The gargoyle was too strong. They flew into the night.

***

The last thing that Eric saw was that fucking stone freak flying right at the camera. Sabrina had been trapped in his arms, and, once more, the fear on her face had been unmistakable. Then the feed had ended, courtesy of that asshole.

Eric had his phone pressed to his ear. "Where are they?" he snarled. "I don't have a visual. Tell me where they are." His fingers flew over his keyboard as he tried to track Sabrina. The problem was that she was moving too fast for his system to follow.

"We lost them, boss. That guy…" Eric could hear the fear thickening the man's voice. "He caught her in the air. The woman jumped. Did you hear what I said? She jumped from the building. From the friggin' top floor. I don't know if the camera picked up that part. She jumped and he caught her and then they flew away. I have no clue where they are now."

She jumped. No, Eric hadn't seen that. The camera had been positioned at a different angle. Sabrina could have died falling from that height. He pushed away from the computer.

You were willing to risk yourself for a stranger? Oh, Sabrina, that just isn't like you.

"Didn't sign on for fighting a monster," the disgruntled voice of the guard muttered in his ear.

Eric stiffened. "You want out? Then you just walk away right now." It wasn't that easy of course, it never was.

Silence.

"I thought so." Eric eased out a slow breath. "Clean up the scene outside the building. Then get your ass *inside*. I want to find out what's inside." Because the building was a mystery to him. He'd tracked and tracked online, but he hadn't been able to trace the owner, not yet anyway. The building had only recently been completed. Top-of-the-line and extremely pricey. "Report back when you gain access."

"Two of our men are dead. What are you going to do about them?"

Dump their bodies. What the hell did the fool think he was going to do? "A clean-up crew is on the way." Or it would be.

Eric hung up on the fellow and tapped his fingers against the side of his phone. A moment later, he was making another call. This time, he was calling the guard he'd placed in Margaret Lacy's hospital room. Not just any guard...but the chief of his security team. *Because I trust Raymond Banner the most.*

Raymond answered before the first ring was even finished.

"Is she awake?" Eric fired at him.

"No. The doctors still aren't sure that she will wake up."

That will make things easier. "I think company is coming your way." That was the only thing that made sense to him. For Sabrina to jump...That meant she was desperate to help Margaret Lacy.

How disappointing. Eric had expected more from Sabrina. Or maybe he'd expected less. Either way, this would give him an opportunity. He'd seen Sabrina's mystery freak fight when his body had been covered in stone. But what about when the guy was just a man? Eric was betting the bullets wouldn't bounce off him, not then.

"Listen, boss…" Raymond's voice was quiet. "Margaret Lacy is still in the intensive care unit. At least three nurses are constantly in that unit. If I go in, they'll be able to ID me."

Eric had lied to Sabrina. His man hadn't been standing at the foot of Margaret Lacy's bed. Raymond was in the hospital, yes, but he wasn't killing close. Mostly because Eric hadn't sent him to the hospital in order to kill Margaret Lacy.

I sent Raymond there to wait for Sabrina.

"Forget Margaret and the nurses, for now." He didn't want a bloodbath in the middle of the hospital. "Get to the parking garage. No, get to the roof," Eric immediately corrected as he thought about the situation. "That's where they'll land." Eric smiled.

"What?"

"Sabrina and her new friend are incoming. I want you up on the roof waiting for them. When you first see them, don't make the mistake of firing your weapon. The guy she's with is using some sort of stone body shield. Your bullets won't penetrate the stone, and one might ricochet and hit Sabrina. Wait until the guy transforms." And he *would* transform. Eric was really good at predicting. He spent his whole life making predictions. He ruled the tech world because of his ability to predict what would happen next.

What people would want. What the next big thing needed to be. "They'll land on the roof because Sabrina will want to see Margaret Lacy for herself. The freak with her will transform and when he does, I want you to shoot him. Kill him and when it's done, report back to me."

"Back up a minute," Raymond muttered. "Can we cover that transform bit again?"

Eric locked his back teeth. "You know monsters are fucking real." One of the things that he enjoyed about Raymond — there was no need to bullshit with him. Raymond was aware of the paranormal score. Back in his mercenary days, Raymond had taken out two vampires. He still had their teeth on a necklace. *And* the guy's step-brother was a witch. The fellow's connection to magic had come in handy before, and Eric knew he'd be using it again, too. But for now…"This guy is a monster. Eliminate him."

CHAPTER SEVEN

They landed on the roof of the hospital.
Sabrina was still just wearing a T-shirt and it had
ridden up high on her legs. She pushed it down,
trying to stop flashing Adam, as he stood before
her. He was still made of stone, a giant beast
that—if she was honest—scared her. He was over
nine feet tall, made of absolute rock, and he had
razor-sharp teeth and claws. What woman
wouldn't be scared when facing off against him?
But...

He'd flown straight to that hospital so they
could try and save Margaret Lacy. That was
good. She was starting to think that *he* was good.

"You need to transform," she said, eyeing
him nervously. "It's not like you can just waltz
around the hospital corridors..." She gestured
toward him. "Not the way you are. Not without
freaking everyone out." He needed to transform,
and then they needed to get to Margaret Lacy. If
they weren't already too late. "He could be
killing her right now."

The stone before her seemed to harden even more. The color of the stone changed a bit as she watched and the bright red of Adam's eyes? The burning light faded and became a perfect black.

A shiver slid over her. "Adam?"

He didn't answer.

She turned around, her gaze sweeping over the hospital's roof. Stars glittered overhead, and in the faint light, she didn't see anyone else. The roof appeared deserted. The city waited beneath her, oddly quiet. And Adam? She focused on him again. He just looked like a statue. She crept toward him and lifted her hand. Her fingers skimmed over his chest. "Can you hear me?" What was happening? She'd seen shifters transform back into the bodies of men before. It was a brutal change. Bones popped and snapped and the fur melted from them until their flesh was revealed. But this…this was different. Adam was different.

She couldn't just stay there, waiting and wasting time, while Margaret Lacy might be getting sliced apart. She rose onto her toes, trying to better peer into the darkness of his eyes. "I'll be right back, I promise. I have to find Margaret Lacy and make sure—"

A door was opening. She could hear the creak of hinges. Someone else was coming onto the roof. Sabrina spun away from Adam and rushed toward the opening door. She nearly collided with a man — he was wearing green scrubs, and he was carrying a big backpack. His left hand curled around the strap of the backpack while his right hand shoved open the door.

He blinked at her, seemingly surprised, and then his gaze was sweeping over her. "You got here first."

You got here first. His words sank in and goosebumps rose along her body because she recognized the tall, fit, and definitely menacing human before her. *Raymond Banner.* His right hand flew toward the backpack and she knew his weapon was inside it. Sure enough, in the next second, his hand was coming up again and she could see the edge of a gun.

Sabrina backed up as Raymond kicked the door shut behind him.

His gaze darted over her shoulder. "Still stone. Guess we'll wait together."

She kept her hands at her sides as she tried to figure a way out of this mess.

He raised the gun and aimed it right at her head.

Sabrina swallowed. "Since Adam was flying, Eric knew we'd land on the roof. He told you to come up here and wait for us."

Raymond didn't speak.

"Margaret Lacy. Is she still alive?"

"Don't worry about her. You're the one in my sights. If I squeeze the trigger, a nice hole will appear right between those gorgeous eyes of yours."

She retreated another step.

"I'm not obsessed like Eric. Your life doesn't particularly matter to me." He gave her a cold smile. "So this is how things will go down. You will do what I say, when I say it. You'll stay out of my way, and you'll get to keep living. We'll wait for the freak over there to become a man and then—"

"Then you'll shoot him." She knew exactly what would happen. Sabrina's head turned toward Adam. Still a statue. But...A fist suddenly punched through the wall of stone that had been his chest. A man's fist. *He doesn't shift back into the form of a man.* He *was* a man, trapped inside the stone. He was fighting his way out. And the moment Adam was free, the jerk in front of her planned to kill him. Sabrina couldn't let that happen. "Stop."

Raymond lifted one brow. "Stop?"

She took a deep breath, squared her shoulders, and walked toward him. She made herself smile. "I want you to do something for me. I want you to take all the bullets out of that gun." He was human, or at least, Sabrina certainly hoped he was. If Raymond was human, then her power would work on him. She could influence him.

"You're fucking crazy. As crazy as Eric. No wonder he wants you so badly." He shook his head. "But like I said before, I'm not Eric." And he pressed the barrel of the gun right between her eyes.

Sabrina could hear stone breaking behind her. Falling to the roof. Fear dried her mouth, but she wasn't backing down. She couldn't. Her life was on the line and so was Adam's. "You're meant for so much more." Her voice was soft, gentle. Her heart was about to burst right out of her chest, but she kept her face expressionless. "You're meant to be far more than what Eric is."

"Tell me what I don't already fucking know." But Raymond's face didn't look as hard and his eyes had begun to gleam.

"What you don't know is what you *can* become." His aura was gleaming behind him. Bright with red, like streaks of blood. But there was a shade of green there, too…and green usually meant…*change?* "It's not just violence," she whispered. And her words were the truth. There was more to this man than just violence and death. She could see it. "You know that? You're good at what you do. Being a soldier was second nature, but after the missions ended, you still needed that adrenaline rush. The rush drives you. It can help you become even stronger."

He licked his lips. "How do you know about my missions?"

She could see them, in his aura. There was so much to see in his aura. Pain and pleasure. Fear and hope. Desperation. Destruction. *This man can do terrible things.* But there was also light in his aura. Glimpses that flashed and showed her what he could be. "I know a lot about you."

More stone crashed behind her.

"I know that you don't want to be on this roof. I know you want to be more than Eric's hired hand, obeying his twisted orders. You wanted to be your own boss. You were born to be a leader, but you're following someone like him?" The gun muzzle was still pressing into her forehead. "You're letting him taint you. You're letting him rip away the potential that you have."

His eyes were boring into hers. She amped up her power. He was harder to inspire than she'd suspected. Some gave in with just a few whispered words—almost as if she were a siren and they were helpless but to follow her commands. Others were different. Others—like this man—had locked their dreams deep and she had to fight in order to find the right key and let them out.

"*Sabrina!*" Adam bellowed from behind her.

Raymond jerked at the shout, and she knew he was about to shoot Adam. The gun flew away from her forehead. It moved to aim at Adam—

She stepped into the path of that gun. "No." Her voice was still low and calm. "You want to be a leader. You go lead. You turn around and you walk off this roof. Out of this hospital. You tell Eric to fuck himself." She didn't usually have the chance to influence Eric's men. He typically kept them away from her. *You made a mistake this time, Eric.* "You start your business. Don't follow his orders any longer. You use your strength and you *help* people. You don't hurt them. You don't watch, hating it, while the blood flows. You don't do that anymore."

Adam's hand curled around her shoulder. "You fire that gun," he growled at Raymond, "and I will rip off your head in the next second."

Raymond blinked, as if he were confused. He *was* confused. He was twisted up on the inside and she was using that confusion. "Walk away, Raymond. Right now. Go find your own path."

And it happened. She could see it in his face. His expression slackened. His eyes widened. Her power had gotten to him. Sweet, hell, yes, it had worked. Raymond lowered the gun. He turned away. And he took a step toward the closed door that would take him off the roof. But that step was all he got to take because in the next second, Adam had grabbed the guy. Adam's fingers locked around the back of Raymond's neck and then Adam slammed the fellow — face-first — into that still shut door. There was a very solid *thunk* on impact, and then Adam let Raymond go.

So much for him starting on that new path.

"I had that covered," she muttered.

Adam's hands curled around her arms. But, oddly, his touch was…gentle. Ever-so-careful. As if he were afraid he'd hurt her. Her gaze darted over him. The guy was totally naked — *mental note, he needs to keep extra clothing handy* – but he was back to being in human form. What a fine human form it was.

And a well-endowed one. *Another mental note.*

"Don't ever do that again." His voice was low, lethal, and it had goosebumps rising on her arms. She forgot her mental notes.

"I was trying to save your life," she told him, notching up her chin. "Raymond is one of Eric's guys—"

"I figured that part out."

She jerked away from him and backed up a quick step. Or three. "Did you? Did you also figure out that he was waiting for you to become a man again so that he could shoot you? Raymond had no intention of shooting me—"

His hands wrapped around her again — curling around her shoulders this time, but his grip was still careful. "That's not what it looked like to me. When I broke out of that stone prison—"

Stone prison. Interesting word choice. Mental —

"He had a gun to your head. It looked to me like he was about to blow your brains out all over this rooftop."

She flinched. "Okay, well, granted, it *could* have looked that way."

Adam growled.

"But I had him under control! He's just a human. I was inspiring him, okay?"

"You put yourself between me and his gun."

She bit her lip. Now she wanted to tread extra carefully.

"Not exactly typical 'Bad Thing' behavior," he continued in that still-growling voice of his.

They were in the middle of a waking nightmare, and she actually found that voice of his sexy. Her timing was awful. "Don't go making a big deal of this, all right? It wasn't like I was doing some epic sacrifice routine. That's not my gig. Like I said before, I had him in my control." *I think I did, anyway.* "Raymond wasn't going to shoot me. Eric has standing orders for me to stay alive."

Adam just kept staring at her. He may as well have been shouting "*I don't believe you!*" over and over again.

"I need you, okay, Adam? I need you alive because *you* don't fall under my control." She still wanted to test that one a bit more, but it seemed to be the truth. "Luke sent you, and I doubt I'd get a second guard if you wound up dead.

Instead, I'd be on my own again, and I don't want that to happen. *Not* until Eric has been taken care of." She licked the lip she'd bitten a moment before. Adam's gaze dropped to her mouth. "Maybe you can just toss Eric into that prison that Luke has on his island? Toss him in and throw away the key?"

His mouth took hers. Not the response she'd expected, but she'd take it. Her emotions were all over the place. Desperate fear. *That guy could have shot me in the head!* Heady relief. *The human hadn't hurt Adam.* And desire…because the desire she felt for Adam always seemed to lurk beneath the surface when he was near.

"Never," he gritted against her lips, "risk yourself like that for me." Then he was kissing her again. Hard and wild. Rough and deep. He was making her toes curl right there with an unconscious human near and—

She surged back. "There could be more of Eric's men inside the hospital. We—we need to see about Margaret."

His breath heaved out. "We'll see to the female human. And then I'm getting you out of here. I'm getting you far away." His eyes gleamed. "You and me, Sabrina. We'll be together, safe, and I'll be putting my mouth right back on you."

"Promises, promises." The taunt slipped out before she could give it a second thought. Being flippant was her nature. She didn't know how to turn off that part of herself. And in stressful situations? *I get worse.*

He smiled at her. "Count on it."

***

Margaret Lacy was unconscious. She was in the ICU, and at least four nurses were working in the area. Machines beeped and whirred near her. Her eyes were closed. A tube led into her mouth.

"She looks like hell," Sabrina whispered from her position beside Adam. She'd "borrowed" an outfit from one of the nurses' lockers. As he'd watched, she'd even taken the woman's name tag from the locker so that she looked all "legit" as she'd told him.

Meanwhile, Adam was wearing the scrubs he'd stripped off the human male who'd been fucking dumb enough to put a gun to Sabrina's head. *I should have killed him. I should have ripped his head off and tossed it over the edge of the roof.* He'd actually planned to do that very thing. Adam had stripped the scrubs from the guy first. No sense getting them bloody. Then he'd gone in for the kill.

Sabrina had stopped him.

Since when had the muse developed a conscience?

"Stay here," she ordered quietly, "I'm going in to look at her chart." She tapped her name tag proudly. "See, told you being legit would pay off."

Stay here. Here was in the hospital corridor. Before she could walk away, his fingers closed around her wrist. He put his mouth to her ear. "Be careful." They hadn't seen any sign of other goons who were on Eric's payroll, but that didn't mean those fellows weren't lurking nearby. "Keep yourself on guard."

She gave a quick shiver. Maybe it was because he'd licked the shell of her ear when he spoke that last word. He hadn't meant to do that.

Fucking lie. He totally had meant to lick her. Adam had a serious hard-on for Sabrina. She was sexy as all hell, but the fact that the woman had protected him? *Him?*

He couldn't remember the last time that anyone had stood between him and a threat. That bullet could have torn through her head. She'd risked herself…

For me.

No way was he going to be able to keep his hands off her now. With that one act, she'd sealed both their fates.

His fingers slid along her inner wrist. Her pulse was racing. He wanted to lift her wrist to his mouth. Kiss the skin. Lick her.

If he had his way, he'd be licking her all over.

But first…

Adam forced himself to let Sabrina go. She straightened her shoulders, smoothed her hair — not that it needed smoothing, she still looked freaking perfect, probably some muse thing — and then she headed into the ICU. She walked with authority, even making some light bit of chit-chat with the other nurses. As if she'd done this routine a thousand times.

Then she was thumbing through the charts. Nodding as the others talked. Glancing slyly over at Margaret Lacy. But as she stared at the human in that hospital bed, pain flashed on Sabrina's face.

No, don't get closer to her. Don't —

Sabrina was striding right to Margaret Lacy's bed.

Hell. His hands clenched into fists. This was going to be a problem. He glanced down the hallway and spotted a cell phone that someone had left on a waiting room chair. He could actually see the phone's owner, heading for the coffee pot in the corner.

Sorry, buddy, but I need to make a call. Adam swiped the phone and slid out of sight. He quickly dialed Luke's private line. To his surprise, the Lord of the Dark picked up on the second ring.

At close to four freaking a.m.

"I don't know this number, but you have just asked for death," Luke said, voice hard and ominous. "*No one* wakes me up—"

"It's Adam Cross."

"Oh. Well, Adam, *asshole,* you just messed up my beauty sleep, so you'd better be calling to say that a certain job is done and a lovely muse is about to inspire the ever-living hell out of—"

"The job isn't done," Adam cut through Luke's words. *Lord of the Dark.* When the guy had talked about Sabrina, something fierce and twisted had flared inside of Adam. Something angry. Something wild.

Oh, wait. Is this shit jealousy? It had been a very long time since he'd tangled with that particular emotion. He'd almost forgotten what it felt like. "We have a problem."

Luke's sigh drifted to him. "Didn't I send you there to fix the little muse's problem?"

"A human is being targeted—a human female. She's been brought into the crossfire." His hand tightened around the phone. "Sabrina's ex-lover thought it would be fun to use his knife on her, and now the lady is fighting for her life in the ICU."

Silence.

"Sabrina's ex—a real dick named Eric Foster—is using the human against Sabrina. He's blackmailing Sabrina with the woman. The jerk contacted Sabrina tonight and said if she didn't come to him, then he'd finish what he started on Margaret Lacy." He'd gotten the full story from Sabrina during their flight to the hospital. *The bastard called on my damn phone line.*

"Margaret Lacy," Luke repeated. "I'm guessing that's the human's name?"

"Yes. And she needs help."

Luke laughed. "Since when am I in the business of helping humans? Oh, right, since never. You must have me confused with my brother, Leo. I understand your confusion, given that we're twins and all, but let me clarify things for you. Humans are his deal. The dark paranormals?" Luke's voice hardened. "They are mine." Possession was thick in his voice. "So what I want you to do is protect the muse."

"The muse," Adam stressed the title, "is going to sacrifice herself in order to protect the human. She jumped off the damn penthouse balcony today because she was so desperate to save the other woman."

"Then it's fortunate that a gargoyle was there to catch her, am I right?"

Smug asshole. What if I hadn't been there?

Another sigh drifted from Luke. "Oh, very well. If this is such a big deal, then I'll contact Leo and get him to show up at the hospital. He can handle the human." A pause. "So…which hospital is it again?"

"Our Lady of Grace." His voice was flat and brittle. "Just so you know, when I see your brother, I will be punching his face in."

More laughter came from Luke, only this time, the laughter held real humor. "I'd almost forgotten. You did have a bit of an incident with my brother, didn't you? I'm guessing you two still have a bit of bad blood between you?"

An incident? "He fucking tore off my wings and let me sink to the bottom of the ocean." That counted as more than an "incident" in Adam's mind.

"Then I guess it's only fair that you take your turn punching his face. Enjoy yourself," Luke murmured. "I know if I had the chance to hit him, I'd sure have myself one hell of a good time." Another small pause. "He'll be there in five minutes."

Adam smashed the phone in his hand, turning it into dust. Not like he could leave it behind. The Lord of the Dark wouldn't exactly like it if his telephone number wound up in the hands of a human.

"Adam?" Sabrina was steps away, frowning at him. "Is everything okay?"

He shook the dust from his hands. "I called Luke. Protection is coming for your human."

Her shoulders seemed to relax. "That's good. She's got a lot of recovering to do, and as she is now, Margaret Lacy is a sitting duck for anyone who might want to hurt her." She crept closer to Adam. "Who is Luke sending for her?"

"Leo." He couldn't keep the disgust from his voice.

Her eyes widened. "Tell me you're kidding."

"I don't kid."

She raked a hand through her heavy mane of hair. "Yes, I noticed that." Her hand fell back to her side. "Leo. Jeez, that guy and I don't exactly have the best history."

Neither do we.

"But he will take care of the human." Sabrina nodded briskly. "Leo may have his faults — a whole freaking truckload of them — but he does try to protect humans."

There was another problem with Leo's involvement in this mess, a problem the Sabrina didn't know about. When she'd been held and tortured by Simon Lorne, Leo knew that Adam had been one of the guards at Simon's makeshift paranormal prison. He knew Adam had been part of the force that kept Sabrina captive.

I didn't have a choice. There was nothing I could do. He'd been under a spell — hell, for too many centuries, he'd been spellbound. Would Sabrina understand that? Would she realize that he'd been a prisoner, too, just in a different way? He hadn't wanted to follow Simon's orders...there'd been no fucking choice.

When she learned about what he'd done, would she still look at him with desire and hope in her eyes? Or would he see disgust and fear in her gaze? Dammit. Adam had hoped to hide this particular truth from her. As far as he'd been concerned, she'd *never* needed to know about his past with Simon.

That knowledge will just hurt her and I don't want her hurt.

But if Leo was incoming…fuck…Maybe Adam should tell her now, while there was still time. *It will be better if that part of my past comes from me…and not from him.* "Before Leo gets here, there's something you should know…"

A whoosh of air filled the corridor and then Leo was just…there. Tall and dark, his face hard, his eyes gleaming. An exact duplicate of Luke, only Leo didn't rule the dark paranormals. This twin was the Lord of the Light.

He was also the biggest asshole in the world.

"It's too late," Leo announced dramatically as he lifted his hands into the air. "Here I am." His gaze swept over Adam. "I think I remember you." His lips pursed as he studied Adam. "Shouldn't you be at the bottom of an ocean somewhere?"

Adam locked his back teeth and a rumbling growl vibrated in his throat.

"And you..." Leo's attention shifted to Sabrina. "Doing your usual routine? Driving humans mad? Causing chaos? Destroying lives?"

"Oh, Leo, always a nightmare to see you." But there was something in her tone...And something in the way Leo was staring at her.

There was history there. A lot of it. Adam studied them carefully.

"You still pissed because of what my cousin predicted?" Sabrina crossed her arms over her chest. "Even you can't change fate, Leo."

His eyes narrowed. "I make my own fate." The tension in that narrow corridor thickened as Leo's expression tightened with what appeared to be disgust. "You're the one with the fucked up choices, Sabrina. Just look at your new choice of companion." One hand waved toward Adam. "After what he did, I can't believe you even want him near—"

Sonofabitch. Leo needed to stop talking. He also still deserved to have his face punched in so...Adam attacked. He rushed forward and drove his fist right to the side of Leo's face. Adam might not be currently covered in stone, but he still had plenty of paranormal strength. When Adam hit him, Leo's head whipped to the side. Then Adam hit him again and again. He drew his hand back for another hit, and that was when he realized...

Leo wasn't fighting back. He also wasn't defending himself.

Why the hell not?

Sabrina grabbed Adam's arm. "Enough." Her voice was flat as she quickly scanned the corridor, obviously searching for humans. Then she exhaled. "Look, I get it, okay?" She positioned her body right in front of Adam. Right between him and Leo. "You think I don't have the urge to pummel him, too? But this isn't the place, and we need him to help the human." Her hand was still around Adam's arm. "No more punching. Not now, anyway."

Adam nodded grimly. Not now. He wouldn't make any promises about later.

Sabrina's hand fell away from Adam as she turned to face Leo. "Can I count on you to help Margaret Lacy? A man named Eric Foster hurt her. Badly. She's completely vulnerable. She's a human, one of yours—"

Leo straightened. "No one will touch her. I guarantee you," he said, his voice quiet and oddly subdued all of a sudden. *Maybe the punches made him subdued.* "She will be safe."

"Thank you." Sabrina's body was still tight with tension.

"You two should get out of here," Leo muttered as he rubbed at his jaw. "Dawn is coming. Soon the streets will be full of humans."

"Right." Sabrina reached back and grabbed Adam's hand. "Margaret Lacy is in the ICU, she's—"

"I'll find her," Leo cut in, waving vaguely in the air. "*Go.*"

She turned away from him, and keeping her hold on Adam, Sabrina hurried down the narrow corridor.

Adam spared one last look for the Lord of the Light. Adam had stopped Leo before the guy spoke too much and revealed the truth about Adam's past with Simon Lorne. *This time,* Leo had been stopped. What about next time?

Guess I'll just have to keep punching the sonofabitch.

***

Raymond groaned as he opened his eyes. His whole face hurt. His face and his head. And he was damn cold. He stood up and realized why he was cold.

He was fucking naked. Someone had stolen his clothes. Well, damn. He was buck naked, on a hospital roof. The sun was starting to rise.

He had shit for luck.

Raymond surged toward the nearby door. He grabbed the knob and turned, but nothing happened. Nothing freaking happened because the door was *locked.*

Shit. For. Luck. Raymond didn't see his weapon. It was long gone, along with his clothes. And he was stranded on the damn roof.

Sabrina had done this. Sabrina and the freak of a lover that she had. He would make them pay. He'd enjoy it while Eric took his time killing—

"You tell Eric to fuck himself." Sabrina's voice whispered through his head. *"You start your business. Not follow his orders. You use your strength and you help people. You don't hurt them. You don't watch, hating it, while the blood flows."*

Raymond looked down at his hands. There was so much blood on them.

"Find your own path."

His shoulders straightened. Maybe he'd do just fucking that.

CHAPTER EIGHT

"We're going back to the penthouse?" Sabrina asked, the worry obvious in her voice. "Is that the best plan? What if Eric's men are still lurking around there? What if they've managed to get inside? What if they are waiting for us? We already know he wants to kill you—"

"Let him try." Adam's hands tightened around the steering wheel. It was a car that he had "borrowed" from the hospital. One that belonged to the dumbass he'd left naked on the roof. In addition to taking the clothing that fellow had been wearing, Adam had also taken his gun, his wallet, and the man's car keys.

Raymond Banner would have to find another way home from the hospital.

"You aren't made of stone." Sabrina gave a frustrated *hmmm* as if realizing what she just said. "I mean, you aren't made of stone at this particular moment in time. You're vulnerable now."

"Am I?" He could see Luke's building up ahead. "Somebody did a good clean-up job." The wrecked SUVs were gone. Traffic drifted normally on the road. There was no sign of Eric's team. "And don't worry, no one is waiting inside the building." He drove forward and turned into the parking garage.

"How can you be so sure of that?"

"Because Luke locked this place down. He's got plenty of protection spells in place. No humans can get inside."

She seemed to mull that over for a moment. "No humans, but that means paranormals *can* enter the building. What if Eric is using a paranormal, what if he—"

Adam had gotten past the parking garage's security. "The place is set so that only certain paranormals may enter. I'm one of those paranormals. You're another." Others had access, too, like Luke and a few of the Lord of the Dark's chosen inner circle. But that was it. "Luke set this place up to be a safe house for you. If you hadn't left, you never would've been in danger."

He turned off the car.

"If I hadn't left," Sabrina told him curtly, "Margaret Lacy would be dead. You saved her before. This time, it was my turn." Then she exited the car, slammed the door with some extra force, and marched toward the waiting elevator.

Taking his time, he followed her inside. Adam didn't have the key card on him, so he typed in the sequence code that would let him access the top floor.

A moment later, the elevator was rising.

"You locked me in." Her voice was accusing.

Adam turned to face her.

"I couldn't use the elevator. I couldn't use the stairs…"

Adam took a step toward her. Then another. He saw her tense as he closed in. He lifted his arms and pressed his palms flat against the mirrored wall behind her head. "You weren't supposed to leave." That part still pissed him off. "You were supposed to stay inside where you were *safe*. You *weren't* supposed to jump from the top floor, screaming my name."

She licked her lips. Those utterly delectable lips. "I screamed your name…"

Sweetheart, you'll be doing that again. But under an entirely different set of circumstances.

"I screamed your name…because I knew you'd catch me."

He blinked. "Say that again."

She gave him a slow smile. Sexy as fuck. Then she leaned up on her tip toes, bringing that red bow mouth of hers closer to his. "I knew that you'd catch me."

"That's a fucking lot of trust to put in a man."

She rolled her shoulders in a little shrug. "You had wings. I was counting on you to use them."

It struck him then—"You aren't afraid of me. Not even a little bit."

The elevator was rising fast.

"Not even a little bit," she agreed. Her lashes lowered. She seemed to be staring at his mouth. "So when are you going to stop talking and actually kiss me? A girl can only wait so long…"

His mouth took hers. There wasn't any kind of controlled skill in his kiss. No seduction. No finesse. He just pretty much attacked her like a starving man. Kissed her too hard. Too rough. Too wild.

But her hands wrapped around his shoulders and her nails sank into his skin, sliding past the fabric of those stolen scrubs. She pushed her body against his, and he could feel the warmth of her breasts, the tightness of her nipples.

Her mouth was just as wild on his. Her kiss just as hungry.

She's not afraid of me. She wants me.

And he'd warned her what would happen if they kissed again.

We both want this. We need this. The elevator dinged and the doors slid open behind him. Adam considered not moving at all. He could rip off her clothes. Could shove his garments out of the way. He could take her right there, in that elevator, against the wall.

The pleasure would hit them in moments and —

There's a security camera in the elevator.

Fuck. He pulled his mouth away from hers. His breath heaved out. He stared down at her. Her lips were swollen from his kiss. Her mouth wet. Her cheeks were flushed and her eyes gleamed.

He couldn't look away.

"Why did you stop?"

He could still taste her.

"Adam? Why did you stop?"

He picked her up and she gave a little gasp. He carried her carefully, holding her close, and she looped an arm around the back of his neck. He took her to the bedroom. *His* bedroom. The bedroom they'd shared the night before. He lowered her onto the floor until her feet touched the lush carpeting, and then, with her standing in front of him, he stripped her.

And he tore some of the clothing in the process. *Want her too badly. Can't hold back.*

But…would she be able to handle him, all of him? Since he'd stopped being a human and become a gargoyle, his sexual needs had changed. They'd turned darker, deeper. He liked sex rough, and he liked it wild. He liked—

"Like what you see?"

She was totally naked before him. And every inch of her…utter perfection. Curved hips. Full breasts. Legs that seemed endless.

"I'll take that as a yes." Sabrina's hand trailed down his body, no shyness in her at all, as she stroked right to his crotch. His dick jerked at her touch. He could feel her touch so well through the thin scrubs.

But I still want these damn things gone.

"Skin to skin is better," Sabrina said, as if reading his mind. "Don't you think?"

Hell, yes.

He ditched his clothes and then he tumbled her back onto the bed. She gave a little laugh, but then he was kissing her and there was no more laughter. Not from either of them. The kisses were rough and deep, and he was touching her, stroking every single inch of her body. She felt like silk beneath his hands. Hot silk. He kissed his way down her neck, down to her breasts. He licked her nipples. He sucked. He had her moaning and arching beneath him.

His hips were cradled between her spread legs. His full cock shoved toward her sex. She was wet, so warm, and he knew that when he sank into her, she'd feel like heaven.

But…

Get her ready. Get her there first.

His hand slid between their bodies. He stroked her, working on her clit, then he drove two fingers inside of her.

Sabrina's nails raked over his back. A hard, long scratch.

The beast he'd chained inside let out a deep growl.

I like her.

"Screw the foreplay," Sabrina gasped. "I want you inside of me...*now.*"

His head lifted.

"Second time," she whispered. "We'll go slowly then, okay?"

He wasn't going to argue. His cock pushed harder at the entrance to her body, Sabrina rocked her hips against him, and then he was inside her.

Fucking heaven. She was tight and so hot and wet. He lost a bit of his sanity at that first plunge into her, and Adam feared he might never get it back. The ferocious need burst out of his control then, and he was driving into her and withdrawing. *Thrust. Withdraw. Thrust.* Again and again. No control was left. There was just a wild battle for pleasure.

And she was still with him. Arching up against him. Moaning. Urging him on. Her legs had wrapped around his waist. Her sex was totally open to him. He sank into her, going as deep as he could, and then pulling back, making sure to stroke over her clit with each thrust.

Her body tensed beneath his and Adam knew her climax was close. His own was barreling at him, full speed. He put his mouth on her neck. Sucked the skin, bit lightly, even as his fingers plucked her nipple. He rocked back down against her, plunging — if possible — even deeper into her. He felt her sex clench around him, holding him so fucking tight, and then she was calling out his name, her voice rich with pleasure and passion.

She came for him, and he had to watch her — she was such a thing of beauty. Her eyes went blind with pleasure. Going even brighter than before. Her lips parted as she said his name, and her hips pushed hard up against him. He wanted to stay still, to keep watching her, but her sensual movements pushed him over the edge. Adam drove into her once more and erupted. The wave of release burned through his whole body. So much pleasure that the beast inside of him was howling and snarling with joy. So fucking good.

The best he'd ever had.

The drumbeat of his heart slowly eased. Sweat covered his body, and Adam realized that he'd locked his hands around her wrists, pinning her hands to the bed. He didn't quite remember doing that.

His breath heaved out as he gazed at her. Worry nagged at him. *Too late. I should have used care before.* "Sabrina…?"

Her eyes had closed, but at his voice, they opened. Still so bright. Still shining with pleasure. "That was fun." She smiled at him. "Let's do it again."

Oh, the hell, *yes*.

And his own mouth curled into a smile. A real one. He hadn't smiled and actually meant that shit in longer than he could remember. But suddenly, his heart wasn't feeling quite so heavy. The stone wasn't weighing on him. The beast that he kept inside was quiet, content, and Adam had to lean forward and kiss Sabrina. His tongue licked over her bottom lip, then swept inside the sweetness of her mouth.

His cock was rising again. Thickening eagerly inside of her. Her hips squirmed against him.

Wish I'd found her sooner. The thought, unbidden, slipped through his mind.

His head rose.

And her smile was back. "I'm guessing that's a yes on the second round?"

He let go of her wrists. Her hands flew up to immediately curl around his shoulders.

"A definite yes." He withdrew, then thrust slowly into her. He wanted to think that — since he'd taken the edge off — he would have more control this time.

But that was probably just bullshit. When it came to Sabrina, he was a desperate, starving man. He knew his hunger for her would soon grow to be just as voracious as before. To try and hold onto his control a little longer, he curled his hands around her hips and rolled them over so that she was on top. She gave a sexy little gasp at the movement. *Hell, I think everything she does is sexy at this point.* He was beneath her on the bed, and his view was phenomenal. She pushed back her long hair and stared at him, her eyes wide. "Oh, this is nice." Her knees were on either side of him, and she pressed them down—sending her body up—only to slide back along the length of his cock a moment later. *"Very nice."* She gave him a wicked smile. "How did you know I liked a bit of control?"

His hold tightened on her. "Something we have in common." He fucking loved being in command. And to show her, he lifted her with his grip, then brought her down even as he surged his hips up in a hard thrust.

Her lips parted. *"Did I say nice?"*

He did the move again. Again. And this time, he brought one of his hands to the front of her body. He found her clit and stroked her even as he thrust inside of her.

"Way…way better than nice…" Her head tipped back. Her breasts thrust forward. Her nipples were tight.

He had to lick and taste them.

Adam shot up. He kept his hand on the center of her need and he took one breast into his mouth. He bit her lightly, scoring her with his teeth and then his tongue rasped over her nipple.

"Adam…*Adam!*"

She was coming again. Already. Hell, yes. Her sex was squeezing his cock, contracting all along his length, and he loved the way she felt when she climaxed. Her body shuddered. Her breath trembled out.

He'd never seen a more beautiful woman.

He let go. He thrust fast and hard, driving into her as she came. Then he was with her, his climax erupting as his cock jerked deep inside of her.

He held her tightly. He kissed her while they both climaxed.

And knew that he would be wanting so much more from her.

***

Okay, that had been intense.

Adam had closed the blinds and turned off all the lights. Even though day had finally come, they were in total darkness in the bedroom. Sabrina was grateful for the dark. After that last climax, she was pretty much in pieces. Pleasurable pieces but…still, pieces.

More than sex. Way more. Something is happening between us.

And she wasn't exactly sure what that *something* was. Sabrina just knew that she was…scared.

She didn't want him to see her fear.

He pressed a kiss to her shoulder. She was still naked. So was he. Dressing when the sex was so good just seemed pointless. But they needed to rest. She was pretty sure she hadn't slept more than a few minutes in the last twenty-four hours.

"I see why they get obsessed."

His voice was a low rasp in the dark. Sexy. Deep. But...she frowned at his words. "I don't understand." The fear she felt? It got a little worse.

"Having you in his bed...you'd obsess any man."

She didn't want obsession. She never had. Sabrina didn't want a lover who was so caught by her power that he couldn't let go. Sabrina had to blink right then. Several times, real fast. Because...maybe...tears were filling her eyes.

"Is the sex with you always that good? Is it...part of the inspiration deal?"

What. The. Actual. Fuck? "Stop talking."

Silence.

No, him just being quiet—that wasn't good enough.

His bedroom had made her feel safe before, but right then, she felt as if she were suffocating. She needed to get out of there. She needed to get away from him.

"I...meant that as a compliment." His voice was halting. "You're fantastic in bed. You've got to know that."

"Stop the talking!" His voice had been halting, and hers was angry. Coldly, furiously angry. "This isn't what I —"

"You don't want to know that you're great in bed?" Now he sounded confused.

Sabrina pulled in a slow, deep breath. Then she rolled to face him. In the dark, he was a big shadow. "Do you know what I have been for most of my life?"

"Inspiration."

No, he didn't get it. "I don't think you quite understand just how long I have been roaming this earth." Probably because she looked down right incredible for her age. "Let's just say, I was born into a time of savagery, a world of blood and power. To the men of that time, I wasn't inspiration. I was a trophy."

"Sabrina…"

"Powerful rulers wanted me at their side. Warriors wanted me close when they were battling. Sailors heading out on the high seas? They wanted me there showing them the course to take. I was a tool for them. I was kidnapped, I was held captive, I was given no choice. They wanted my magic, and they would do anything to possess me." Her breath whispered out. "I didn't want to be an obsession for any of those men. I *don't* want to be an obsession for anyone. It's not a choice I have. And it's not a fucking joke. It's my life. So it's not exactly a compliment for you to talk obsession right after we're intimate. The last thing I ever want to do is obsess a man again." They were still dealing with the fallout from her last obsession.

The slightly calloused tips of his fingers stroked her cheek. "I'm sorry."

His apology caught her off guard.

"I don't exactly have a lot of experience talking to a lover." His voice was gruff. "I didn't mean to hurt you. I would never want to do that. I only meant…"

She waited, but he didn't continue. Seriously, the guy was going to leave her hanging? No, not happening. "You meant what?"

"I've never had sex that good. It was almost too good."

Was that some kind of insult? Sabrina wasn't sure.

"The pleasure was the best I've ever had. You are the best lover I've ever had."

Her cheeks began to warm. *You're the best, too, and —*

"So I just wondered, if you being that good, if it was part of —"

Sabrina put her fingertips over his lips. "No, it's not part of the muse deal. Just so we're clear. That's just me, and that's just you. It is not always this way with a lover."

His tongue lightly licked her fingertip.

Her heart jerked in her chest.

"Good to know. Because…the idea of some other lucky bastard being with you that way…it really pisses me off."

She opened her mouth to reply, but then stopped. Sabrina paused for a moment, and considered how she would feel if another woman enjoyed that much pleasure with her gargoyle.

I'd want to claw her eyes out.

This was new. This was jealousy. This was possessiveness. This wasn't her usual M.O. Confused, Sabrina didn't speak again. Her heartbeat slowed, and her breathing evened out. Her lashes drifted shut, and she was almost asleep when she heard him say…

"I promise, no one will hold you captive again. You won't be a trophy any longer. This time, I won't make the same mistake. I won't stand by while you suffer. I swear, I won't."

This time? What an odd word choice…

***

Sabrina was back at the high-rise on the beach with her stone freak. Eric stared at the computer screen. He'd traced her movements. She'd gone to the hospital, then returned to the fucking impenetrable mystery building. His team had worked and worked there during the hours of darkness, but they hadn't been able to get inside the place.

Magic. He knew some kind of spell was keeping his team out. Eric hadn't even known about magic, not until Sabrina. Or rather, not until Sabrina's disappearance. He hated magic. He hated the paranormal monsters out there. He hated everything that defied the natural order.

Science. Technology. The future lay in his hands. The paranormals? They were the past. He was working to eliminate them. All of them.

Except Sabrina. He would never eliminate her.

He hadn't thought she'd return to the high-rise building. Raymond should have gotten her at the hospital. Raymond was his best damn man. Raymond should have killed the stone freak and immediately reported back to Eric. Only he hadn't. It had been hours, and Raymond still hadn't checked in. Did that mean the guy was dead?

Probably. "Where the hell are you, Raymond?" Eric muttered. He had a tracker on Raymond's car. He had a tracker on the cars of all his inner security team members. Paranoid? Yes, but it was also smart.

"I'm right here."

Eric's head whipped up. Raymond, sporting dark bruises all over his face, stood in the doorway. He was wearing mismatched clothing that was far too tight. As Eric stared, Raymond let out a long, rough sigh. "It was one hell of a night."

Eric jumped to his feet. "What happened?"

"The target nearly killed me." He shuffled wearily inside. "I think you're right, though. About his vulnerability. When he's human — or at least, in human form — the guy can be hurt."

Excitement heated Eric's blood. "You hurt him? Did you shoot him? Did you see him bleed? Did you —"

"Your Sabrina was afraid."

His excitement dimmed. A snaking cold took its place.

"Your lady was so worried about me shooting him while the dude was in human form that she stepped between him and my gun."

Eric shook his head. No, that wasn't right. Sabrina hadn't been protecting the freak. "*You're lying.*" He reached into his desk and pulled out the loaded gun that he kept in the top drawer. Eric aimed that gun at Raymond. "Why would you lie about her?"

Raymond lifted his hands. "Easy there, boss. I'm on your side. You know that. Haven't I always followed orders? I've never given you any reason to doubt me." He kept his hands up even as his face paled. The darkening bruises were in sharp contrast to his stark white skin. "I'm not lying to you now. Sabrina wanted to protect him. She was willing to risk her life for him. And the reason my face is smashed to hell and back? It's because of the big bruiser. He was furious that she'd been in danger."

"So the fuck am I. Sabrina is *never* to be placed in mortal danger." *I'm the only one who can hurt her.* "You know that rule. It's my number one rule. Rule number two? You don't get close to her. None of my guards get close to her. Because if you get close to her, then she can get in your head." His breath was ragged. His heart was racing. Sabrina had been in front of a gun? What if she had been shot? What if she'd been killed?

"They beat me to the roof, okay? When I got up there, the guy looked like a freaking statue. Sabrina jumped in front of me. I think she was trying to buy him some time. The guy literally had to break out of the stone. When he came out, he was a man. That's when I could've shot him. That's when she was so desperate to protect him." Raymond's face was grim. "You're not going to want to hear this, but I think they're involved. Intimate, you know?"

He fucking knew what intimate was.

Raymond slowly lowered his hands. "They left me on the roof. Unconscious. By the time I was able to get back inside the hospital, they were long gone. And so was Margaret Lacy. Only none of the staff there remembered exactly how Margaret Lacy had left. They were running around like crazy, desperately searching for her. It was as if she'd just vanished into thin air."

Another problem. Eric put the gun back in the desk drawer. "I know where Sabrina is, and I know where her new...lover is, too." The trick was getting to them. They were using magic to keep him out. He began to think and to plan. "I made her leave before, and I can do it again." He just had to find the right motivation. Something that would make her care.

"He's going to come after you," Raymond warned quietly. "I mean, he's already come after you once. You were lucky to escape him at the warehouse. The guy is hunting you, and now we know why. He's taking your place at her side. A possessive lover, a protective lover, and he wants to eliminate any threat to Sabrina."

Eric blinked in surprise. "I'm no threat to Sabrina."

"You ran her off the road yesterday," Raymond reminded him, eyes narrowed and face hard. "You don't see that as a threat?"

He straightened his shoulders. "I was playing, just reminding her how close I was. I wasn't going to kill her. That has never been my intention." He would not live in a world that didn't include her, he couldn't. Eric looked down and realized that his hands were shaking. They did that sometimes. Kind of made him feel like a drug addict who'd missed his fix.

Is Sabrina my fix?

"Well, maybe the new guy doesn't understand your intention." Raymond took a step toward him. "Look at the timeline, man. You force her off the road, and he immediately attacks your warehouse. He comes gunning for you. It's obvious he's not gonna deal with your shit. He wants to take you out."

Eric realized exactly what he needed to do. This new man, this new lover of Sabrina's—Eric had to discover all of his secrets. He had to learn everything that he could about the stone freak. He sat back down at his desk. His fingers started to type.

"Uh, boss?" Raymond cleared his throat. "What are we going to do now? If magic is keeping us out of that building, you want me to use magic to get us in?"

Because Raymond had been the man who introduced Eric to the paranormal world. Raymond had a step-brother who was a witch. Or a warlock. Whatever the hell it was supposed to be. Interesting family dynamics. The witch—a guy named Kevin—had scryed to find Sabrina. The scrying itself had given Eric an idea for tracking Sabrina...for always knowing where to find her.

I made his magic into my science. He'd also taken the liberty of getting the guy to run a protection spell on him...a spell that was supposed to block Eric from any outside influences. *Because I don't want Sabrina in my head.* Even as he'd performed the spell, though, Kevin had been telling him that it probably wouldn't hold. That someone like Sabrina would eventually break through the spell...

And that's why I don't get too close to her. It's why I've stayed physically away. Even though keeping his distance was fucking hard.

"Want me to call Kevin?" Raymond pushed. "And see what he can do?"

Because for the right price, Kevin would use his magic for anything.

Eric's fingers had stilled over the keyboard.

"I know you don't like magic," Raymond continued as he rocked back on his heels. "But this is different. I mean, he's made of *stone.* Kevin can tell us more about him — or, if he can't, then I'm betting he knows who to talk with in order to get information."

Eric knew there would be a price for that information. "See what the witch knows and report back to me immediately. If the intel is good, I'll pay you."

"Just how much will you pay?"

Eric glanced at him. "What do you want?"

"If the info pans out, fifty grand."

Greedy bastard. But Eric just inclined his head. "*If* the information pans out."

"Thank you." There was almost a hum of satisfaction in Raymond's voice as he turned for the door.

The door shut a moment later, and Eric dismissed the man from his thoughts.

Raymond could call the witch, but Eric had another plan, too. He pulled up an image he'd taken of Sabrina's new lover…in the man's human form. He zoomed in on that photo. When he'd been trying to research the guy before, he hadn't been thinking in the right way.

Or maybe…maybe he just hadn't been thinking in the right time.

Let's use the facial recognition software again. Let's search deeper into history. Let's see where you've been, asshole.

Not just within the last five years or ten years.

The last thirty. The last forty. He'd access archived newspapers, he'd search every inch of the web. He'd find that guy.

You can't hide from me. He had the most sophisticated software out there. If the fellow's identity was anywhere online, Eric would find him. It was just a matter of time.

CHAPTER NINE

When Sabrina woke up, she was in bed alone. She stretched slowly and her fingers reached out to touch the pillow near her. Cold. Just as the sheet beside her was cold.

Adam had been gone for a long time.

She rose from the bed and started to grab one of his T-shirts, but then she saw the bags at the foot of the bed. Bags from pricey, high-end, designer shops. Curiosity pushed her toward those bags, and she felt a wide smile split her face when she saw the clothing inside. *Finally*. Sabrina dressed quickly, sliding into a pair of new jeans and a soft-as-silk shirt. Both the shirt and the jeans fit her like a glove. There were even shoes waiting for her. Cute little boots that were sexy as hell. She combed her hair quickly and borrowed Adam's toothbrush. When she was finished, she started hunting for him.

Her hunt didn't last long.

Sabrina found Adam standing on the balcony. He was staring down at the waves far below them.

His back was to her, and he didn't turn at her approach, but Sabrina saw his shoulders stiffen slightly, so she knew that he was aware of her. Taking her time now, she moved to his side. For a time, she just stared at the crashing waves, too. Then she cleared her throat, and she said, "The sun is already setting? I can't believe I slept the whole day away."

"You needed the rest." He paused. "I hated to wake you."

She turned to him, tilting her head slightly. "So you went shopping instead? Thanks for the clothes, by the way. They fit perfectly."

His eyes seemed to heat. "I learned your body pretty well, so it was easy to pick them out."

Her smile stretched a bit more. It felt almost normal to be out there with him. To be standing on the balcony, as the sun slowly sank beneath the waves of the ocean. It was a romantic scene for two lovers.

"When darkness falls, I'm going after Eric again."

And just like that, normalcy fled. So did her smile. Because they weren't just two lovers enjoying a romantic view. He was the hunter sent to eliminate the threat to her. And she…she was the woman who'd created a serial killer. She pulled her gaze away from Adam and stared once more at the ocean. "You ever make mistakes, Adam?"

"I've made my share."

The deep rumble of his voice seemed to roll right through her. "I bet that my mistakes are worse than yours."

"Don't be too sure of that." A growl. This time, his words were a definite growl. Very animalistic. Almost savage.

She glanced at him from the corner of her eye. "You know, we're not quite equals in this relationship of ours."

"Relationship? Is that what we're calling it?"

Sabrina had no idea what to call it. They were lovers. He was her protector. He was her guard. But when the threat out there was finally gone, when Eric was eliminated, Adam would disappear from her life. She knew that.

Sabrina just didn't like it.

If he's just going to vanish, then I guess, no, we don't have a relationship. Did they have anything? And why did her heart ache? "I want you to tell me about your past." The words slipped from her as the wind blew back her hair. "I already know that you're not like most shifters."

"No, I'm not." His shoulder brushed against hers.

She looked back at the setting sun. It seemed as if streaks of fire were falling into the ocean. "I'm guessing you weren't born as a gargoyle, huh? You were made into one. At least, that's what all the rumors say. Over the years, I've heard my share of whispers about gargoyles."

"What did those whispers say?"

"That gargoyles were once knights. You know, the shining armor variety. Riding horses, carrying lances, and, in general, saving the day." *Humans.*

He didn't speak.

So, Sabrina kept talking. "But then you were cursed. I mean, the knights were cursed. A powerful coven of witches put a spell on the knights. The witches wanted unstoppable warriors, and who could possibly defeat a stone army?"

More silence from him. The guy didn't want to share. Obviously. He wanted her secrets, but it appeared that he wanted to keep his own hidden from her. Hardly fair. She turned away from the sight of the ocean and headed for the doors. "I'm starving," Sabrina mumbled as she tucked a strand of hair behind her ear. "I can't even remember the last time I ate." True story. But her hunger was also an excuse to get her off that balcony so that she could escape his silence.

Her hand lifted to reach for the door, but his fingers flew out and curved around her wrist. He'd done that quiet, stalking thing, and she hadn't even realized that he'd followed her.

"That's not exactly how things happened."

Her head turned, just a bit, and she met his gaze. "Then how, exactly, did they happen?"

"I was the leader of those knights. Those men were my friends. They trusted me. And I fucking let them all down. I sent us to hell." A muscle jerked along the hard line of his jaw.

She waited to hear more. But he just stared back at her. Sabrina gave a rough laugh. "You don't get to just drop a bombshell like that and say nothing more. Tell me. *Tell me what happened.*"

He stared into her eyes, and then Adam gave a grim nod. "I made a mistake. I fell for the wrong woman."

Her stomach clenched.

"Meredith seemed so innocent. She was being persecuted, you see. Hunted. An insanity had swept across the countryside back then. Families were turning against each other. Friends were becoming mortal enemies. It was a true hysteria. And many good people were being punished for no reason."

Uh, oh. *Hysteria.* "Witches." She remembered that time all too well.

"Meredith was accused of being a witch. She was going to be burned. I couldn't let that happen."

No, a knight in shining armor wouldn't let that happen. Not to the woman he'd fallen for.

"I helped her to escape her prison, but then she wanted me to go back for her friends. She told me they were all innocent, that they had never done anything wrong. My men and I — the five best friends that I had, the five best warriors I knew — we broke into their dungeon cells, and we got them out. We thought that we were doing the right thing."

She waited for him to continue, but when he didn't, Sabrina prompted, "When did you learn they were real witches?"

"When they burned that village to the ground." His eyes squeezed shut. "I could hear people screaming. The fire was everywhere. We couldn't stop it, no matter what we did. Children were burning, and those witches were just there, chanting, watching it all happen. Men, women, kids — the flames took them all. The people we had rescued? They were evil. They were dark. They *deserved* to die."

She had a best friend who was a witch. All witches didn't exist for destruction. Some could help humans. Some were on the side of good. Or, semi-good.

Some…weren't. "I'm surprised you didn't kill the witches right then and there."

His eyes opened. They'd turned red, hinting at the dark power he held in check. She could almost see the burning town in his red gaze. "I tried to kill them. But Meredith had put up some kind of force field to protect herself and the others. Our swords couldn't get to the witches.

We couldn't stop the fire, and we couldn't stop them. You see, the witches needed to be together in order for their power to work. They'd been separated in the dungeon. My men and I...we brought them back together. We were the ones responsible for the fire and the death. The witches were laughing while everyone burned." He released a ragged breath. "My parents burned and so did my little sister."

"I'm so sorry." She wanted to wrap her arms around him and hold Adam tight.

"My men and I battled the flames with our bare hands. Burns covered our bodies, and I thought for sure that we would die, too. But Meredith had other plans."

Meredith, you are one serious bitch. If our paths ever cross, you'll be the one who burns. "She turned you into a gargoyle."

He nodded, a stiff, jerky movement of his head. "It actually seemed as if she was healing us, at first. The burns faded, but then the stone grew to cover our flesh. Meredith and her witches wanted guards that they could control. They cursed us, and we had no choice but to follow their orders."

"I...don't understand."

His hand lifted and pressed to his heart. "We were her guard dogs. She commanded, and we followed. And how the fuck did she do it? Easy. She held our hearts in her hand."

Automatically, her hand flew up and touched his chest, resting right over his heart. She could feel it beating beneath her fingertips.

"She didn't hold the heart of the man, but the stone heart of the beast. When the spell was first cast, I swear, we are two separate things, Sabrina. There was the man, and then there was the gargoyle. When the stone beast took over, the man was trapped inside of him. Back then, I couldn't control him. I couldn't stop him. Not while she held his heart." His lips twisted. "Over the years, her power just grew. She was able to control all of us, completely — whether we were in the form of men or beasts — because the gargoyles eventually became part of who we were."

She pretty much hated his back story. It sucked. "Tell me this witch is dead."

"She's nothing but ashes, courtesy of me and Luke Thorne."

"She's dead, but the spell remains?"

"It's hard to break some curses. They survive even after death. I found that out, too late."

"What happened to your friends?"

Pain flashed in his eyes, and she knew there had been no happy ending for them. *I'm sorry.* She'd already said that once, hadn't she? Sabrina inched closer to him. "And the stone heart? Do you have it?"

"No one is controlling me right now."

That wasn't exactly an answer to her question. Her lips parted.

"Others have controlled me over the years. Djinns and gargoyles…we have the same weakness. You control our hearts, and you control us. I've been forced to do things that I never wanted to do." So much emotion was there, blazing at her from his burning gaze. "I wish I could take back the past. If I could, I would've left Meredith to burn." Then he squared his shoulders and walked slowly back into the penthouse.

Sabrina drew in a deep, bracing breath. She attempted to school her features before she followed him inside. She found him in the kitchen. The guy was pulling out food, as if he were about to cook a meal. As if he hadn't just dropped a serious bombshell on her.

Sabrina nibbled on her bottom lip. "They're not all bad, you know."

He'd just put on a pot of water to boil. Adam raised one dark brow at her.

"Witches," she blurted. "They're not all psychotic. They're just like everyone else. Good, bad, some crazy mix of both in between."

"So says a 'bad' paranormal." His fingers tapped on the countertop.

Had he really just thrown that back at her? Her chin lifted. "I happen to have a really close friend who is a witch. She doesn't curse knights, she doesn't burn children, and she doesn't spend her days trying to hurt people." Cordelia wasn't like that. Cordelia was powerful, almost scarily so once she got to spell-casting.

The woman had even *married* a human. Didn't that say something about her non-scary-witchiness?

Adam's jaw tightened. "I'm sure she's fabulous." But his tone said otherwise.

"Maybe she can help you." Okay, those words had just blurted out. "Cordelia could try to break the curse. She can stop you from turning to stone. I mean, if you want to be human again…"

He turned away from her and put spaghetti in the pot. His shoulders were tense and his broad back was ram-rod straight as he prepared the meal. Sabrina hopped up onto a barstool and watched him. Watched and waited. When the silence got too much for her, she asked, "Do you want to be human?"

The spaghetti was ready. He grabbed two plates and brought the spaghetti toward her. He even poured her a glass of wine. Not that she had any intention of drinking it—wine never worked for her. *He does not want to see what happens to a muse when she drinks.*

Adam sat next to her. "Sometimes, you can't go back."

"That's not an answer. You either say yes or you say no. Do you want to be human again?"

After she asked the question, Sabrina realized she was holding her breath.

He lifted his glass of wine and stared at the dark liquid. Almost blood red. "Do you think I haven't gone to other witches and tried to get this curse broken?"

"But Cordelia—"

"I get that you think your friend is all that—"

Because she was.

"—but some curses last forever. I know what I am, and I know what I will always be." His gaze held hers. "But what about you?"

Her trembling fingers reached for her wine glass. "What about me?" She was so nervous that Sabrina almost took a gulp of the wine. *Almost.*

"Do you like being a muse? Or do you see it as a curse?"

Her heart raced faster.

"If you could, would you want to be human?"

"Why waste time wishing for something that can never be?" She forced a smile to her lips and then she lightly tapped her glass against his. "How about we just toast...to bad things?"

His eyes gleamed. "To bad things."

She held his gaze and put her wine glass back on the table, never tasting a single drop.

***

Raymond had known that his step-brother Kevin was different—he'd known it from the moment they met. Raymond had been fifteen and Kevin had been thirteen. Just how different, though? That part hadn't been revealed until much, much later.

Raymond glanced over his shoulder, looking back into the narrow apartment hallway. He wanted to make sure that Eric hadn't sent anyone to follow him. He didn't trust Eric, mostly because Raymond wasn't a fool. When he didn't see anyone lurking in the shadows, Raymond lifted his hand and pounded his fist against the door. "Kevin! It's me!" He pounded again. "And I need to talk to you, right the hell now."

The door swung open. Kevin stood there, blinking a little owlishly behind his glasses. His black hair was smoothed back from his forehead, and he was dressed casually, in jeans and a T-shirt. As always, the guy was paler than death. "What's the emergency? Don't you just know how to pick up a phone?"

Some conversations needed to be held in person. Raymond shouldered his way past Kevin, and his step-brother closed the door with a soft click. "Anyone else here?" Raymond demanded.

"Okay, you're weirding me out. No, no one else is here. Just us." Kevin pushed up his glasses, even though they were already perfectly in place.

The guy did things like that, though, a lot. Moved nervously. Always seemed to be twitching.

Raymond blew out a heavy breath. "You know I don't usually like your magic bullshit."

Kevin stiffened. "It's not bull —"

"A gargoyle. I need you to tell me how to handle a gargoyle."

Kevin's mouth dropped and nearly hit the floor. "What?"

"I didn't fucking stutter." Raymond raked his hand through his hair. "A gargoyle. A made of stone, super strong, damn gargoyle. Tell me everything you know about the beast. All weaknesses. All strengths. Everything."

Kevin licked his lower lip. His gaze was suddenly bright and avid. "Have you truly found yourself a gargoyle? Because I thought they were all gone. I mean, it's not like they're easy to make. From the stories I've heard, only one coven ever could create them. A seriously, badass, dark coven. That coven turned humans into their freaking pit bulls."

"Keep talking…because Eric Foster is throwing around lots of money for this info." Raymond crossed his arms over his chest and waited to hear more.

"How much?" Kevin gnawed on his lower lip.

"Eric said if the intel is good, he'll pay fifty grand."

"Fifty...*fuck me*." Kevin ran toward the large bookshelf in the corner. He pulled out a heavy, encyclopedia-like book. Then he was flipping through the pages, muttering to himself. Mostly talking about what he could do with fifty grand.

Raymond kept waiting. "I don't have all night."

Kevin looked up at him. He swallowed. "Look, I love money. *Love it.* And fifty — shit, I could use that cash, but...if you are really dealing with a gargoyle, then my best advice to you is this...Run. Run fast. Run hard. If this gargoyle is after you, if his master has set him on you —"

Whoa. Back up. "Master?"

Kevin nodded. "Gargoyles are like the attack dogs of the paranormal world. They're controlled by a master. Back in the day, the leader of that dark coven, Meredith LaShay, she controlled them. But then that witch got herself burned..."

Kevin was missing the important parts. "How?"

"No one is really sure how they were able to get the jump on her. I mean, Meredith was supposed to have been the most powerful witch of all time. And a serious looker, by the way, but she was still burned until only ashes remained and —"

"No," Raymond snapped. He didn't give a shit about how she'd burned. "How is the gargoyle controlled?"

"Oh." Kevin frowned and went back to the book. "There's supposed to be some kind of magic stone that is tied to each gargoyle. The story says that the stone is the gargoyle's heart." He seemed to wave away that notion. "Probably just the original rock that was used in the binding spell. Whoever holds the stone, controls the beast. You get that stone... And you got yourself one serious killing machine. Because gargoyles? They don't have weaknesses. In beast form, they *cannot* be killed. They feel no emotions. They just do what their masters order."

Interesting. "What about when they're in human form?"

"The stories say they still have enhanced strength and speed then. Superior vision and hearing, but their bodies can be hurt. When flesh covers them and not stone, that's when they bleed."

So Eric had been right with that suspicion.

"Was that...you think that info will be worth the fifty grand to your boss?"

Raymond offered him a slow smile. "I think I can convince him to pay. I mean, he fell for that bullshit spell you gave him months ago, didn't he? The one that you said would help protect him from Sabrina Lark's influence. If he bought that, then he'd buy —"

"That wasn't a bullshit spell." Kevin appeared insulted. "I used a fucking angel feather in that spell. Do you know how hard it is get one of those? And that spell is the only one that can stop a muse's power, it just doesn't work forever. Nothing stops her forever."

Raymond thought about his little roof-top chat with Sabrina.

"Uh, bro? You haven't...you haven't been near her, have you?" Kevin raked his hand through his hair. "You haven't let her get close? I swear, if I had another feather, I'd do the spell on you, but I don't have—"

"I'm fine," Raymond cut in flatly. "Don't worry about me."

Kevin's eyes lowered. Nervous energy seemed to bounce off him. "But I do worry." His voice was low. "Because you're the only family I have. We're brothers, right? Not blood but, hell, blood has never mattered anyway."

No, it hadn't.

"I've got your back. You've got mine. Always, right?"

Always...ever since Kevin's mother and Raymond's father had been killed by a drunk driver.

Kevin started nodding, fast jerks of his head. "If you're serious...if this is all real...holy shit, but do you know what we could do with a gargoyle? With him at our side, no one would be able to touch us. Not Eric Foster. Not *anyone*. The world would fear us."

Yeah, but they had a problem. "He's not at our side right now. And the stone that you talked about, the one that controls him? I have no clue where it is."

"Find out who he is working for and then you find the stone." Kevin's hands closed around his shoulders. The guy was practically vibrating. "I'm tired of being on the bottom of the paranormal totem pole."

Kevin's mother had married a human, so Kevin's powers were weak. That was how he had been able to pass as human for so long. "I already know who he's working for. Or at least, I know who he is screwing. And you're not going to be thrilled…"

"Why do I care who he screws?"

"Because it's Sabrina Lark. It's the same woman that has Eric so obsessed."

Kevin's eyes widened. "Sabrina?" And if possible, he became even paler. "The muse?"

"She's involved with the guy." Raymond nodded grimly. "So that makes me think she's the one with the stone."

"If she does have it, then we have to tread very, very carefully with her."

Damn straight they did.

"We can't let her get into our heads," Kevin whispered. "We can't…"

And Raymond just pressed his lips together, saying nothing else. *She's already tried to get in my mind.*

Kevin swallowed. He blinked a few times and said, "If she has the stone, she'll be keeping it close. You take it from her, and that gargoyle will be on your side. You'll have the power. *We'll* have it."

Raymond thought it was time that he stopped taking orders from other people. Maybe it was time to start giving the orders.

CHAPTER TEN

Eric saw Raymond bound out of the apartment building. *It's about time.* He'd started to feel bored. Eric slowly exited the limo. "Escort him over to me," Eric muttered to the guards who came to his side. He'd made sure to bring plenty of guards along for the ride. After the discoveries he'd made that day, Eric wasn't going to take any chances. He knew exactly how dangerous Sabrina's new lover was. And he knew *who* the man was. *Adam Cross.*

He'd gone back twenty years, thirty years, forty…and his searches had yielded a great deal of information about the other man. Adam Cross had been around for a very long time, and he'd fought in a great many wars. The man had taken out the enemy, again and again…

Sometimes, he'd been a hero.

Sometimes, he'd been a villain.

But always, he'd been surrounded by blood.

Raymond glanced up, and his gaze unerringly landed on Eric. Eric smiled at him, even as he wondered if Raymond would run.

Because something had changed with the other man. Eric knew it.

He was alone with Sabrina. She got to him. I know she did. Sabrina got to everyone.

"We need to chat, Raymond," Eric called out. "Why don't you come get in the car?"

Raymond tensed.

Get in the car, or I'll have my guards throw you in. They won't hesitate. You might have acted as their supervisor, but I'm the man who pays them. I'm the one with the money.

But then Raymond started walking toward him. Eric glanced at the guard to his right. "Go inside and bring out the brother. If he gives you any trouble," he said softly, keeping his voice low enough that Raymond couldn't overhear him, "then just knock his ass out and drag him to the limo." The guard nodded and strode toward the apartment building.

Raymond threw up his arm, stopping the guy. "Where in the hell do you think you're going?"

Eric clapped his hands, pulling Raymond's attention back to him. "Before, you seemed so certain that your step-brother could provide us with assistance. So certain you wanted fifty thousand dollars."

Raymond glared at him.

"I decided you were absolutely right. We do need paranormal assistance on this one...and I want your brother with us. *Now.*" He paused and stared straight at Raymond. "Don't you think that's a good idea? I mean, *I* thought it was brilliant. That's why I came here to pick up you and your brother."

Raymond seem to consider his options.

You don't have any.

After a moment, Raymond nodded. "You're right. We haven't been able to get inside that high-rise yet, and maybe one of Kevin's spells can help us." But his voice was guarded and Eric saw the anger burning in his eyes.

Sabrina got to you. You were a good guard, a good leader to the men under you...now, you're a waste of my time.

***

"I'm going after him tonight."

Sabrina glanced up at Adam. Dammit, her eyes seemed even brighter. Would he ever get used to them? Every single time that he looked at her, Sabrina's beauty unnerved him. He'd had sex with her. He'd watched the pleasure wash across her perfect face. Having her should have cooled his desire. It hadn't. Adam wanted her again. He wanted her right then. He wanted to shove aside the plates and spread her out over the countertop. He wanted to pour wine on her sweet skin and lick it away. He wanted —

"I want to come with you," she said.

Adam immediately shook his head. "I told you before, you're safe here. Eric can't get inside to you. This place is impenetrable. He can't get—"

Suddenly, the balcony doors burst open, propelled by a powerful burst of wind. Adam immediately jumped to his feet. He grabbed Sabrina's hand and pushed her behind him. He faced the threat coming, a snarl on his lips.

A man strode into the penthouse. His steps were heavy. His dark hair blew back from his head, and his jaw was locked tight. His gaze swept over Adam, and a faint smile curved the man's lips. "Still in protector mode, I see."

"Leo!" Surprise filled Sabrina's voice. She wasn't standing behind Adam any longer. Instead, she'd hurriedly moved to his side. "What in the hell are you doing here?" Then, in the next breath, she turned an angry stare on Adam. "So much for this place being impenetrable!"

"My powers are just as strong as my brother's," Leo muttered as he shrugged. "So getting past his protective barriers? Not exactly a challenge for me."

"I don't remember inviting you here." Adam's body was braced for an attack. He was sure one would be coming from the Lord of the Light.

"Don't remember inviting me?" Leo's mouth tightened. "You two are the ones who called me before. You wanted help with a human, remember?"

As if they'd forgotten so soon. Calling the guy to the hospital had been one thing. *No one invited you to bring your ass here.*

"She's safe, by the way. Healing nicely, far, far away. And just to show how extra kind I am, I'll make sure that all memories of Margaret Lacy's attack are wiped away from her mind. It will be as if it never happened." He waited, but when no one said anything, Leo frowned at Sabrina. "I did that as a favor to you."

"I never asked you to take away her memories. You shouldn't play with the minds of mortals." She was obviously seething.

A muscle jerked in Leo's jaw. "That's a lesson that you should have learned yourself, Sabrina. But instead, you spent more centuries than I want to count screwing with humans." Leo's eyes narrowed. "Though it would appear that you changed your game a bit." He looked pointedly at Adam. "Screwing with beasts now, are you?"

Adam lunged toward the guy. His hand flew out and locked around Leo's throat. "You don't say shit like that to her."

A burst of raw power shot straight into Adam's chest, sending him hurtling back.

"And *you* don't hurt her!" Leo snarled at him. Real fury was on his face. "You don't hurt one of the few people in this world that I consider to be a friend." Fire began to dance around his raised hand. "I remember you, gargoyle. You really should have just stayed at the bottom of that damn ocean."

There were a lot of weird things happening right then. First, had Leo just called Sabrina his *friend*? Second, that sonofabitch was about to send a blast of fire flying at Adam. *Fuck me.* Adam called for this beast, knowing that he had to change to stone if he wanted to survive, and Adam *had* to survive. He had to protect Sabrina. He—

"Stop it!" Sabrina yelled. "Don't even think of burning him." And just like that, she'd put herself between him and Leo.

"You think he's here to keep you safe," Leo said as he shook his head. "He's not, Sabrina. He's just another trick that my brother is playing on you. You don't know the truth about him. Adam Cross is not on your side. He's not on anyone's side, but Luke's. Adam can't even think for himself. He's being controlled. He's—"

Leo's going to tell her about my past. About my time with Simon Lorne. "Get the hell out of here," Adam snarled. Claws burst from his fingertips and the stone began to surround him.

"No one is controlling Adam!" Sabrina shouted. "Look, yes, *I* made a deal with Luke." Frustration boiled in her words. "It wasn't as if I saw you hanging around trying to help me out, *friend*. You weren't anywhere nearby. You haven't been near me, not for a very, very long time. Not since—" But she broke off, looking back at Adam and her eyes widened. "No, don't change! Not now!" Then she reached for him, grabbing the stone that covered his hand. "Stay with me!"

"You don't even know what he did," Leo announced, his words pulling her gaze back to him. "I think I pity you, Sabrina. *Pity*. That's why I came back. At first I was going to wait and see how the game played out, but then I thought back to how we once were. To the secrets we shared so long ago."

Secrets? Fuck, there was some serious intimacy in Leo's voice. And that pissed off Adam *and* his beast. Sabrina had said that she'd never slept with Leo, but...

"He held you captive," Leo told her, his voice stark.

At those cold words, Sabrina blinked. Her bright gaze held Adam's for just a moment longer, but then her head turned back toward Leo.

And Leo kept talking. Damn him. "When you were in the Everglades? In that hell-hole prison that Simon Lorne created? Well…when you were there, your new lover was close, too." Leo's voice was cold and hard and he just wasn't shutting up.

Adam bellowed his fury.

Sabrina's hand slid away from him.

"Adam was one of the guards in that nightmare place. He was at Simon's beck and call. Adam helped to collect the prisoners. He helped to keep them there. He helped to keep *you* there."

Sabrina shook her head. "No, you're lying." Her words were for Leo, but her stunned gaze was on Adam once more. And in that gaze, he could almost see her begging…*Tell me it's not true.*

"Lying? No, not this time." Leo's voice turned harder. "Don't believe me? Summon Luke. He'll tell you the same thing. I saw your gargoyle at that prison. When I was trying to break in to free the prisoners, I fought him. I ripped the bastard's wings off, and I dropped him into the ocean. I'd hoped that attack would kill him, but I'd forgotten that a gargoyle can't die, not in stone form."

She shook her head again, harder this time. "No, he wouldn't—"

The beast had taken over. Stone covered him and the great, hulking wings had just burst from his back.

"It's not like he had a choice." Leo would *not* stop talking. "I told you, he never does. He was being controlled then — controlled by Simon Lorne."

Adam had tried to explain to her before…his curse…his heart…

"Just as," Leo continued grimly, "he's being controlled now. Only this time, Luke is the one holding his leash. You think that Adam is your protector, but he's not. Luke is playing a game with you. He's using you because he knows about our past. They're going to hurt you, Sabrina. Luke and Adam. And I can't let that happen." He opened his hand and reached out to her. "Come with me now. Let's get out of here before it's too late — "

It was already too late.

You will not take her.

Adam let out a roar that seemed to shake the walls of that penthouse. Sabrina stared at him in shock. Shock, and yes…fear. He could see the fear on her face. Her lips had parted and her eyes had widened. He reached out to her, just as Leo had, but Adam's hands were covered in stone and his scarily sharp claws seemed to slash toward her.

"*See? I warned you!*" That was Leo's bellow. The asshole grabbed Sabrina and pulled her away from Adam. "You can't trust him." His arms locked around Sabrina as he seemed to tuck her against his body.

Adam — the beast that he was — stilled. "Let. Her. Go." His voice was guttural. The voice of the gargoyle, not the man. Deep. Echoing.

"Turn back," Sabrina whispered, and she gazed at Adam as if he'd just broken her heart.

I am so fucking sorry.

She lifted her chin. Leo's arms were still around her. He was holding her intimately close, and Adam *hated* that. "Turn back right now, and talk to me as a man," Sabrina ordered even as her voice broke.

But the beast was in control. Adam couldn't think clearly. The man he was — that man was trapped inside, pounding against the stone prison.

"He's cursed," Leo said softly. "I told you. He doesn't have a choice. His beast is in control. And the guy guiding the beast? I'd bet money it's my brother. Luke is playing some game with you. Probably offered you one of his trick deals, didn't he? You thought he was helping you, but all along, they've both been scamming you."

His wings stretched behind him as Adam shook his head. "No…protect her." Were those tears in Sabrina's eyes? It sure looked that way, dammit. He took another lunging step toward her, but Leo hauled her back — fast — retreating with her until they were at the edge of the balcony. Beneath them, the waves pounded against the beach.

"Were you there?" Sabrina demanded as she stared at Adam with pain etched onto her face. "Adam, were you there when that bastard held me in his prison?"

He wanted to lie to her. He could tell by the smirk on Leo's face that the guy was expecting him to lie. "Yes."

The pain deepened on her face—and mixed with betrayal.

"I had no choice." He had to force out each word. Speaking as the beast was so hard. The gargoyle liked to fight. To destroy. Chatting wasn't exactly his strong suit but...

Wings are growing from Leo's back. Adam could see them. Long, covered with what looked to be scales...

He's going to take her away.

Adam's right hand was still extended toward Sabrina. "Won't...hurt you again."

Her lips were trembling.

"Don't trust him," Leo chided her. "Sure, I can buy that he might not *want* to hurt you, but the big fellow doesn't get a choice in the matter. It goes along with the whole being cursed bit. He doesn't have control. How many times do I have to say that line? Whoever holds his stone heart— hell, it's not even a heart, not really, just a stone that the witch Meredith used to bind to his very soul—whoever holds that stone controls him. He can't fight the orders that he's given. Adam Cross is a puppet on a string. A dog being jerked on a leash." He gave a rough laugh. "And my brother holds that leash right now." His eyes burned with fury as he told Sabrina, "If Luke decided he wanted you brought to his island, if he wanted you tossed in one of the cells he has hidden away down there, all my brother has to do is snap his fingers…and your lover will change before your eyes. You could beg him, you could plead with him until you were blue, but he'd always follow the orders of the hand that holds the stone."

A tear leaked down her cheek. "You were there," she said. "One of Simon's guards…"

The gargoyle's hand pushed against his stone chest. The stone was starting to crack, busting from the inside as the man fought to get to her. *Sabrina is hurting.*

He'd done that. He'd hurt her.

Leo's head lowered so that his mouth was right next to Sabrina's ear. He probably thought that Adam couldn't hear his murmured words.

You're wrong.

"Come with me, muse, and I'll make sure the latest obsessed human can't get his hands on you. I helped you before, remember? Back in Greece when your lover was dying at your feet. I can help you again. And we'll make our own deal.

You come with me, I save your sweet ass, and then you give me Fate's location."

Her eyes squeezed closed. "No."

"Okay," Leo growled. The tenderness was suddenly gone from his voice as if it had never been there. "Second choice. I'll just take you. I won't watch someone I care about get hurt again. I *won't*." His wings spread behind him. He lifted into the sky, still holding tight to Sabrina. She screamed then. A loud, angry scream as she fought against his hold. She screamed, and it was—

My name.

"Adam! Adam, help me—"

He flew right after them. His wings beat against the air and a snarl broke from his lips. Leo was fast, but Adam was just as damn fast. They rushed over the crashing waves, heading deeper into the darkness of the night. Sabrina was twisting and punching against Leo, but the Lord of the Light wasn't letting her go.

Adam's claws slashed into Leo's wings. He ripped them wide open and Leo immediately began to plummet. Adam grabbed Sabrina, wrenching her from the Lord of the Light's grip as the guy went down.

Learned that trick from you, asshole.

Sabrina locked her arms around Adam. She was shaking in his arms and he whirled, ready to get them the hell out of there. Leo had disappeared beneath the waves.

The Lord of the Light wouldn't die down there. It would take a whole lot more than a little swim to stop Leo. He'd regenerate — and attack again.

The penthouse isn't safe, not when it comes to Leo. He can get in too easily.

So Adam didn't take her back to the penthouse. He flew forward into the night, holding her carefully. And knowing that her trust in him...It had just been shattered into a million pieces.

CHAPTER ELEVEN

He was there. He was there. He. Was. There. The words wouldn't stop replaying in Sabrina's head and the pain in her chest seemed to grow worse with every minute that passed. By the time Adam put them down on top of a dark building on the edge of Miami, her whole body was shaking.

As soon as her feet touched the roof, she backed away from Adam. He stared at her a moment, his eyes doing that burning thing that they did, and then the stone around him hardened even more.

She was staring at a beast.

An attack dog on a leash.

She pressed her lips together and swiped her hands over her cheeks. She knew Adam was preparing to transform. He'd break himself out of that stone. Bust his way to freedom. But that process took time. Very, very precious time.

Time enough for her to escape? *Maybe.*

Because she didn't feel like facing him right then. She didn't want to hear lies from him. She'd told him about her imprisonment by Simon

Lorne, and Adam hadn't said a word about having been there at the time. He'd kept that from her.

What others secrets was he holding back?

She saw a door to the side. She ran toward it and started yanking on the handle. Either she was desperate and extra strong or the door was just old and weak, but it groaned and opened beneath her hand. She stared into the cavernous darkness that waited for her, and then she ran forward, rushing down the stairs. She nearly slipped and fell — twice — but her claw-like grip on the railing kept Sabrina on her feet. Soon she was at the bottom floor. She shoved open the door there and found herself in another big, dark room. Faint light poured in from the windows, those that were positioned near the street. Just enough illumination for her to see that she was inside some kind of old restaurant. Maybe a bar? There were tables and chairs. A small, wooden stage. The place was deserted, obviously closed down. Adam had picked an abandoned place for them to seek temporary refuge.

Adam. *No, stop it. Don't think about him. Not right now.*

She rushed toward the doors that she knew would lead her to the street. But even though she pulled and pulled on them, they wouldn't open. Frantic, her gaze shot to the windows once more, and that was when she realized they were boarded up. Only a small amount of light was drifting inside the place...*because someone put boards over the windows.*

Shit.

But there had to be another way out. Another exit. She just had to find it. Sabrina spun away from the useless windows and started searching. And even as she did...

"Sabrina!" His roar seemed to echo around her.

***

"I don't...I don't quite get what's happening here," Kevin said. He was in the back of the limo. Seated right next to his step-brother. And they were both trying to look innocent and feed Eric a pile of pure BS.

He smiled at them. "We're going for a little ride, that's what's happening." His two armed guards were also in the back of that limo. One guard pointed a gun at Kevin, and the other had his weapon aimed right at Raymond.

"I *work* for you," Raymond reminded him quietly. "You don't need to get all paranoid and pull weapons on me. Not necessary."

Paranoid was his middle name. "I'm afraid the guns are necessary." Eric gave a sad shake of his head. "You were alone with Sabrina. You know the rule. No one ever gets to be alone with her." He tapped his index finger to his temple. "When you're alone with her, she gets in here. Sneaks her way right into your head, and then in a blink, you're doing what she wants."

Raymond didn't look afraid. The guy looked pissed. "She didn't get in my head. She *did* get in the way of my shot. She put herself between me and the target. I *told* you this shit already."

Yes, yes, he had. Eric reached for his laptop. He needed to check on Sabrina. That was a habit now. Always checking to find out where she was.

Because one day, I woke up...and she was just gone.

"You both were going to team up together, weren't you?" Eric mused. "You and your brother. I realized that was the plan, right after you made that push to get my fifty grand. You want my money *and* you want Sabrina for yourself. You're trying to take her away from me."

"I have no interest in your girlfriend," Raymond said flatly. "Truth be told, she creeps me the hell out."

Those words paused Eric's fingers. He narrowed his eyes and peered back at Raymond.

"And I have no interest in Sabrina!" Kevin spoke quickly as he raised his hands. "I mean, hell, I know just how dangerous she can be. She's a muse, man, a muse. Do you even know what that means?"

He had a fucking clue. "I know everything about her."

"Doubt it," Kevin mumbled. Then his Adam's apple bobbed as he swallowed. "She's trouble. Big, scary trouble." He pushed up his glasses as his body rocked forward. "I mean, look at what she did to you."

What she did to you.

"She's got you messed up, man," Kevin added, sympathy in his voice. "She's like a drug, right? And you're jonesing for her. Because I bet you think your mind doesn't work as well if she's not near. You don't get all of those great tech ideas if she's not close. She got beneath your skin, fucking intoxicated you, and now you need her to function, don't you?" His lips twisted. "You aren't the first bastard this has happened to, and, believe me, you won't be the last. A muse is a very dangerous beast, more so because you don't see the danger when you look at her. You just see the beauty."

Eric positioned the laptop on his thighs. "Sabrina showed me my full potential. I've quite enjoyed myself since I met her...but it wasn't technical genius that she inspired in me. I've always been gifted—"

"Keep telling yourself that," Kevin cut in.

Eric's heartbeat slowed. *It's not because of Sabrina. Everything I do...it's because of me...because of what I have always been capable of doing.* He felt heat flush his face and a growl of fury built in his throat.

"Uh…easy there, buddy." Kevin was sweating. "Didn't mean to, um, upset you."

Then you should have shut the fuck up.

"I-I've got news on your girl, okay? That's what me and Raymond were talking about. I found out some stuff. He was going to report back to you on it. No one was going to cut you out of anything." A pause. "After all, you're the money. Money talks, right?" Kevin laughed, but the sound was a bit nervous.

A bit desperate.

"The first time she left you, Sabrina didn't do that of her own free will."

Eric felt his heart stop.

"She was kidnapped." Kevin inclined his head toward Eric. "Remember that hell-hole you found in the Everglades? She wasn't hiding from you there. That place was her prison. She was held inside, against her will, by some bozo who wanted to use her magic. She escaped…she fled, and I'm pretty sure after that escape, the first thing she did was come back to you."

Eric's shoulders straightened a bit. *Sabrina.*

"She came back…but then she got scared. She ran *from* you the second time. No abduction, no force. She *chose* to leave the second time." Kevin paused. "And we think she chose to hook up with the guy who's her protector now."

Eric tried to pull in a deep breath.

"A gargoyle," Kevin blurted, but then he frowned at the two men with guns. "Do they have clearance to hear all this?" He waved his hands toward them. "They aren't going to freak out because they just found out monsters are running around Miami, are they?"

"They're fine," Eric snapped.

"Are you sure?" Kevin's doubt was obvious.

"Shoot him in the shoulder," Eric ordered his guard. The witch with his twitchy movements and his too fast talking was getting under Eric's skin. *No one doubts me.*

The bullet blasted from the gun on Eric's right. The bullet thudded into Kevin's shoulder. He screamed. Blood spattered.

"The next shot will be your heart," Eric told him flatly. "Now *you* shut the hell up. I want to hear from Raymond." Because maybe Raymond hadn't been turning on him after all. Maybe Raymond was still the best right-hand man he had. Raymond hadn't even flinched when his step-brother was shot. The guy was freaking cold as ice.

Something I do admire about him.

Raymond swallowed. "Kevin said the guy...we're looking at a gargoyle, okay? That's what her protector is. An honest-to-shit gargoyle. Kevin knows about gargoyles..." He glanced at his step-brother.

Kevin had clamped his lips shut. He wasn't saying a word. Finally.

Raymond cleared his throat. "Kevin told me that gargoyles can be controlled. It's like they're puppets on a string."

Now he was curious. *"How* are they controlled?"

Raymond hesitated.

"How?" Eric pressed.

"A stone," Raymond confessed. Then he hurriedly added, "I know, sounds too easy right? Sounds like BS? But Kevin knows his stuff, and he said a magic stone is tied to each gargoyle."

Each? So there were more out there? *Interesting.* Eric pointed at Kevin. "Speak. Tell me how they were created."

"Th-they were knights. Witches made them so they'd have strong armies, unstoppable forces."

He'd seen the bullets ricochet off the stone.

"I think…" Kevin's voice was definitely subdued, and he was holding tight to his bleeding shoulder. "I think the stones…were originally used in the binding spell. Meredith LaShay — she was this *insanely* powerful witch — she cast the spell. She held the stones, according to legend, and she bound those stones to the knights, bound them through flesh and straight to their souls. And as long as she held those stones in the palm of her hand…she could control her beasts."

Eric just stared at him. It sounded like some kind of fairy tale. Pure make believe. But…*I saw the gargoyle with my own eyes.*

"Meredith was taken by flames." Kevin spoke haltingly. "And the stones were held by others over the centuries. Each stone is tied to a different gargoyle. You get the stone, you get control of the beast linked to that stone." As soon as he finished talking, Kevin immediately clamped his mouth shut once more. And he looked nervously toward the guns.

"Interesting." Eric cocked his head as he once more focused on Raymond. "You think my Sabrina has this gargoyle's stone?"

"I think she has it cradled in the palm of her hand." Raymond nodded. "I'm sure of it. She was afraid of you, so she went out and got herself the biggest, baddest paranormal protection that she could find. And then she got the guy to come gunning for you. You're the gargoyle's target. He's going to be hunting you."

Eric opened his laptop. "I wonder when they met…" His voice had turned musing as he rolled over possibilities in his head. "How did those two come together…?"

"I have no fucking clue," Raymond said flatly.

Eric began typing on the laptop. He expected to see Sabrina, all nice and snug at that mysterious high-rise but...

She was somewhere else.

He smiled and then he leaned over and lowered the privacy screen that separated him from the driver. "Change of plans," he announced. "We have a new destination."

***

Every door on the ground floor was *locked*. Sabrina wanted to scream in frustration. She needed to escape, but she was trapped. A prisoner, once the hell again.

She yanked as hard as she could against the back door. She'd found it after snaking through the remains of an old office, but despite straining with all her might, the door wouldn't open.

"*Sabrina*."

She stiffened. Her breath hitched out.

"Sabrina," Adam continued carefully, his voice that of a man and not a beast, "we need to talk."

She let go of the door knob. Slowly, she turned to face him. Then she blinked. "Where in the hell did you get jeans?" A pair of faded jeans hung low on his hips.

"It's my building. I keep extra clothes nearby." He shook his head. "All of the doors and windows are well secured down here. Access is only via the roof because, you know, I — "

"Fly in. Yeah, I get it." *It's my building.*

He took a step toward her.

Her hands immediately flew up. "*Don't.* Do *not* come any closer right now."

"You're angry."

"Angry doesn't even begin to come close to describing what I'm feeling." She was...hurting. Her chest was burning and she'd actually cried over the guy. He'd gotten to her. The man of stone had made her weak.

Damn him.

"But...you chose me." He was staring at her in confusion. "You were fighting Leo. You wanted to stay with me."

"Okay, look, first of all...it's not like you just won some big contest, all right? It was you or it was Leo. Not exactly win-win. Leo and I have issues that go back a long time. If I'd stayed with him, well, he would have forced me to reveal something I didn't want to share with him. So right then, you were the lesser of two evils. You weren't my choice. You were what I had to take." Big, big difference.

His expression became guarded. *Man. Of. Stone.* "I see."

"No, I'm not sure you see anything." Her hands fisted at her sides. "You were there."

His head lowered.

"*You were there.* In the Everglades. While I was held in that stupid cell for *months.* You were one of the guards." *Deny it. Deny, please —*

His shoulders straightened. His head lifted right back up and his gaze met hers. "Yes."

A knife right to the heart. That was what his one word answer felt like to her.

"I didn't have a choice. Simon had the fucking stone." Tension rolled from Adam. "Do you think I wanted to follow his orders? I was as much of a prisoner as you were."

"He was going to cut out my eyes."

His lips parted. Adam took a fast step toward her, then seemed to catch himself. He shook his head.

"Yes, he was. Simon mistakenly thought that a muse's powers were tied to her eyes. So he was going to cut out my eyes. He was working some stupid magical spell, and I was one of his ingredients. He was going to kill me. And you…you were a guard there. If I hadn't gotten out, you would have been there when he took my eyes."

He stared back at her, and his hard expression broke apart. Pain flashed on his face. Pain. Horror. Grief?

"I'm so fucking sorry." His words rumbled from him. "I *hate* the way I am. I hate being tied to the stone. I hate that a twisted bastard like Simon Lorne can use me to do his bidding. And you know what? He isn't even the first one. There have been others over the centuries. Those who forced my hand. Who used my power. I hated it every single time, but no matter how hard I tried to fight, the result was the same. The gargoyle takes over. The man is trapped in the stone, and I am fucking *helpless.*"

A tear slid down her cheek. Only this time, that tear wasn't for her.

What would it be like to be trapped in stone? Helpless? To watch while the gargoyle attacked? While he killed?

"There's a reason that gargoyles fall under the 'Bad Things' category," Adam continued in that same rough and ragged voice. "They don't exactly have a morality compass. Whoever holds the stone…that person controls the beast. I'm just along for the fucking ride."

Another tear slid down her cheek.

"*I'm sorry.*"

She couldn't stop the tears. He'd been like that for centuries? All because he'd been a human who'd had the bad luck to be cursed…

"Stop, Sabrina, please."

She couldn't stop. Just like he couldn't fight the magic that bound him.

He rushed toward her. His hands lifted and then he hesitated, as if afraid of what to do next.

Damn him.

"Put your arms around me," she snapped at him. "Pull me close. Hold me. Then lie to me and tell me that everything is okay." Wasn't that simple enough? Obvious enough? Wasn't it—

He locked his arms around her. He pulled her as close as possible. Then he held her. His body was warm and strong against hers. His lips moved against the shell of her ear as he whispered, "Everything is okay."

A choked sob slipped from her. Part sob. Part desperate laugh.

Just...desperate.

"It's not a lie. I *will* make everything okay for you. I'm going to eliminate Eric. That was my mission. I'll do it, I swear. "

She wanted to believe him. "Who's in control of you?" Her head lifted so that she was staring up at him.

He gazed into her eyes. "I am."

"Who has the stone?" Her heart jerked in her chest. "Is it Luke?" It had to be Luke. Luke had been the one to send Adam to her. He must be the one—

"I don't know where the stone is. I hope the fucking thing was destroyed."

Her eyes widened.

"The last time I saw it, Simon had it. But we both know what happened to him..."

He's burning in hell right now.

"I searched that prison once I hauled my ass out of the ocean. See, I didn't choose to vanish when the big battle was going down there. Leo grabbed me, snapped off my wings, and dropped me into the ocean."

"And now you dropped him the same way."

His lips stretched into a cold smile. "Payback is a bitch."

Her breath caught. "Do you think he could have the stone?" No, no, if Leo had it, he would have used it on Adam.

"I'm hoping it was destroyed when Simon's prison was attacked. I couldn't find a trace of it there when I returned. So either it's gone…"

"Or someone else took it."

But he shook his head. "If someone had it, they would have used it by now. They would have summoned me. You don't just keep a gargoyle waiting. No, I think it's gone…"

She wanted to believe him. But Sabrina was very much afraid he was doing exactly what she'd just asked him to do. *Hold me. Then lie to me and tell me that everything is okay.* "If someone does have it…if someone uses it…what happens to you?"

A muscle jerked along the hard line of his jaw. "I go back to being a mindless puppet."

Her heart hurt even more. *Luke, if you've got his stone…* "I want to help you."

Adam blinked.

"There has to be a way to break the curse. Let me call my friend Cordelia. She's the most powerful witch I've ever met. If anyone can break that spell, it's her."

"You...you really want to help me?"

"You didn't ask for any of this." She was pushing past her own pain right then because *his* pain was so strong. She could feel it, nearly bleeding from his pores. "You were trying to help someone." *Meredith.* She'd be hating that woman for eternity. "You didn't deserve this as payment."

"And you didn't deserve to have some psycho terrorizing you."

"I want him stopped not because of what he's done to me...but because of what he's doing to the other women out there." That was why she'd finally broken and gone to Luke. "Eric will keep killing, I know it. He has a taste for blood and pain, and he isn't going to stop. He's too smart, you see. Too smart for the cops to ever catch. Too smart for his victims to escape before he cuts them. He's got all the power, and Eric loves that."

"Then we take his power away."

She licked her lips. He seemed so certain. So strong. Her hands rose and pressed to his bare chest. "Are there any other secrets that I should know about?"

He shook his head.

"You sure?" Sabrina pushed. "I mean, your witchy ex Meredith isn't going to appear and come gunning for us both, is she?"

"Meredith is ash. After she…after she had me and my best friend Toren fight to the death, I killed her while she slept."

Oh. Oh, *shit.*

"Luke was at my side. He made sure she didn't wake. He also made sure the fire was hot enough that even a witch of her power wouldn't survive." He paused. "She burned the same way my sister burned."

She was about to start crying again. No, wait, too late. She *was* crying. What was happening to her?

His hand rose and he wiped away her tears. "I thought a muse was supposed to be cold. That you lived to drive mortals to the brink of madness, and then you walked away."

"That's not who I am." But it was *what* she was. She did bad things without intending to do them. Darkness followed wherever she walked. She eased back and took a long, hard look at Adam. "That's why your aura looks the way it does. The shadow…it's the gargoyle. And it covers the man completely. I can't see you because he's so strong." *I'm calling Cordelia. Whether he wants my help or not, he's getting it. He's suffered long enough.* "There has to be more for you out there."

"I think I'm looking at more."

And he was staring at her. His gaze had heated. His face—she could see his need. The desire for her.

"Adam..."

He bent his head and kissed her. At first, the kiss was soft and tender. He could be tender. He was asking, not taking.

Her hands were still pressed to his chest. She could feel his heartbeat beneath her touch.

His tongue slipped between her lips. Thrust inside. Tempted her to respond to him. Tempted her to want him.

The way he wanted her.

Her eyes had closed. Her breasts—they tightened. They ached. Her hips moved restlessly against him. It was dangerous to go down this path. Sabrina knew it. Wanting him, giving in to that desire—the pleasure would just bind them together.

I already feel bound to him.

"I've never wanted a woman," he whispered against her mouth, "the way I want you."

Not even Meredith?

"Sabrina?"

She loved the way he said her name. He rasped it. Desire curled around the word. He made her name sound sexy and beautiful.

Her lashes lifted. Time for her turn to give him a truth. "I've never wanted a man the way I want you." She wasn't stroking his ego. Wasn't trying to spin some web of seduction around him. Her words were the flat truth. His touch ignited her. His strength turned her on. And his pain…

It wrecks me.

Sabrina stood on her tip toes and kissed him. But she wasn't gentle or tender. She was passionate. Demanding. And she wanted him the same way. His hands closed around her waist and he lifted her up, moving to pin her against the back door.

Strength…turn on.

Her legs locked around his hips. She could feel his cock pushing against the juncture of her thighs. Big, long, hard. She needed him to plunge inside. She was on a sensory overload, her emotions were careening out of control, and the fire of a powerful orgasm would blast everything out of her mind.

Pleasure…she could live in the moment. She could forget everything else, just for a short time.

Her shirt flew across the room. Had she taken it off? Had he? Didn't matter. His mouth was pressing to her collar bone. He was kissing and licking her, and his powerful hold — seriously, he was lifting her with one hand — pushed her up so that he could better access her breasts.

She still had on her bra, but he kissed her through the soft fabric. Her nipples were so sensitive, and a surge of heat flew straight down to her sex. She was getting wet for him. Already. She'd been furious with him, she'd been hurt, and now...she needed.

Her reaction to him wasn't normal. Sabrina knew that. She knew she should probably be scared of the way she responded to Adam.

But there wasn't any time for fear. Her nails raked over his shoulders. "Fuck me, Adam. Right now."

He growled. Animalistic. Hot.

Then he was easing her onto her feet. Wait— *what?*

He'd better not be stopping. But, no, he'd just lowered her so that he could strip away the rest of her clothes. And he did strip her, in pretty much record time. Then he was lifting her up again. Holding her and positioning her, and his jeans were open and the broad head of his cock came toward the entrance of her body.

He didn't thrust inside of her. The head of his cock waited, stroking over her core but not plunging inside.

"Adam!" She squirmed against him. "What are you doing?"

"Look at me."

Her gaze flew to his.

"I want you...the way I have never wanted another."

Her breath heaved. Her sex quivered. Her body was so tight, her muscles aching. She was wet and ready and she wanted him inside of her...

And the way he was talking...the way he was staring at her as if she were the only thing that mattered in his entire world...

Sexy.

"I will never want another this way. Just you."

Oh, wow, that was sweet, that was—

He thrust into her. Adam sank balls deep and a moan broke from Sabrina because he felt so incredibly, wonderfully *good.* Her legs locked tightly around his hips, and he used his hold on her waist to lift her up and down, moving her quickly, and every move seemed to push right over her clit. She was panting and pretty much clawing at him. He was driving into her with relentless force, and it was too much.

It was everything she'd ever wanted.

"Never...another..."

She kissed him. Sabrina came as she kissed him. Her sex contracted around him and the pleasure was so strong that she thought her heart might just stop. She thought the whole world had stopped spinning because the release just blasted straight through her...and seemed to destroy everything in its wake.

He pushed her back against the door, pinning her there with his body. His thrusts became even wilder, even harder, and she realized he was driving her toward another climax. The first hadn't even ended, not fully, but she could feel another building. He was so big and thick inside of her, filling her completely. She couldn't catch her breath. She couldn't slow him down. She couldn't slow herself down. She could only feel and feel and…

She came.

So did he. A hot tide of release that spilled inside of her. She squeezed him tight, holding him right there. She wanted that moment to last and last. Their time together, safe. So much pleasure.

Control was gone for them both. They were both fully exposed and as she stared into his eyes, she caught a glimpse of the man he'd been.

Tender. Kind.

A protector.

A literal freaking knight in shining armor.

Too bad that something bad had changed all that for him.

He pressed another kiss to her lips.

And too bad that she was just another bad thing that had happened to him, too.

CHAPTER TWELVE

"What did the binding stone look like?" Sabrina's voice was soft, but curious.

Adam glanced back at her. Struck, as always, by just how freaking gorgeous she truly was. Why couldn't he get used to her beauty? To the brightness of her eyes? The full curve of her lips?

He rubbed his hand over his chest. They'd moved into the main section of the club—*his* club. He'd bought the place just a month ago, and he had such big plans. He wanted to renovate it all. Turn it into a safe nightclub for the paranormals in the area. Hell, maybe he'd even let in humans, too. He wanted to put down roots in Miami. Wanted a home...

I want her.

She'd put her clothes back on. Covered the body that he loved to see. And he'd gotten the rest of his clothes, too. But his twitching dick told him that leaving the clothes off would have been a killer idea. Because he could have kept right on making love to Sabrina—

"Adam?" She waved her hand toward him. "Did you hear me? What did the binding stone look like?" She bit her lower lip.

He rolled back his shoulders. "Nothing special about it, appearance-wise. Had a red tint. Small enough to fit in a person's fist. But it...I heard Simon say once that the rock was always warm. Always hot, like it had a charge to it." He'd thought that Simon might have left the stone secured in the safe that the guy had at his prison in the Everglades, but, by the time Adam had returned, there hadn't been any part of that safe left behind.

Her expression had turned determined. "I'm going to see if Cordelia can find it."

Now he stiffened. "Sweetheart..." The endearment slipped from him. "I get that you're trying to help me, but the last thing I want right now is for any witch to be anywhere near me *or* the binding stone that's linked to my gargoyle."

She took a tentative step toward him. "I understand but...she's not like Meredith. Cordelia is—"

"No witch." He wasn't budging on this one.

Her eyes narrowed.

"The mission isn't me. It's you." And he needed to focus on that. "I told you before that I'd be hunting Eric tonight, and that's precisely what I intend to do. This place isn't locked down to keep Eric and his goons out, not the way that the penthouse was, but with Leo flying around out there, hell, this seems like the safer bet." They had enemies closing in from all directions. "I can transform into the gargoyle, and I'll track Eric's scent." He tracked better as the gargoyle. Always. "I'll hunt him down, and he'll be dead by dawn." One problem eliminated.

"Let me come with you. I can help."

He shook his head. "If you come with me, you'll just distract me."

A furrow appeared between her brows.

Hell. He hadn't meant his words as an insult. "I'll be worried about you. Focused on protecting *you*. I need to be focused on—" Why not just say it? "Killing."

Her long lashes swept down to hide her eyes. "I'm not so different from her, am I?"

Now he was lost.

"Your Meredith."

First, she isn't my anything.

"She wanted you to kill for her. To hunt for her. To protect her." Her lashes lifted. Her eyes were so big and so deep. "And here I am getting you to do the same thing."

But Adam shook his head. "You are nothing like her."

"I'm bad, Adam. Believe me, I am."

Okay, if that was the game she wanted to play. If she really wanted to try and pretend that she was a creature of darkness when he had started to see the truth about her…when he'd started to see her for *exactly* the woman that she truly was…"Tell me the worst thing you've ever done."

She hesitated.

"Come now," Adam chided. "You know my secrets. Shouldn't I know yours?"

Sabrina eased out a slow breath. "Yes, I guess that is fair." She swallowed. "The worst thing I ever did? I stared into a lover's eyes…and I made him stab himself in the heart. I made him kill himself while I watched."

Not what he'd expected. "Sabrina?"

But she'd turned away from him. "Like I said…" Her voice drifted back to him. "I'm not so different from your Meredith." Her shoulders were stiff. "I'll stay here. I won't try to run away again. Just…go. It's time for all of this to end."

All of this…

Did she mean it was time for them to end? Because he wasn't ready to end things with her. Not even close.

But he did have her psycho ex to deal with…and he'd sworn to take care of that problem. So Adam didn't say another word as he headed for the stairs. He climbed them slowly, and his mind should have already been focused on his prey.

Yes, he *should* have been thinking about the coming attack.

But he kept thinking of Sabrina. And the pain that had been in her voice when she'd told him about her dead lover.

***

The nightclub's windows were covered with boards. The front entrance was chained shut. From the outside, the place appeared deserted but...

"I think I see a light on in there," Raymond murmured.

They were still in the back of the limo. The guards were still armed. Kevin was still bleeding. And Eric...

I found my Sabrina.

"We can't just go storming in the place." Raymond shifted in his seat. "Because if she's in there—"

"She is," Eric was certain. Her tracking signal had led him straight to that old club.

"Well, if she's there, then so is the gargoyle. And unless we get lucky and take him while he's human, the guy will just kill us all."

Eric could practically smell the fear in the car. He glanced around as he considered his options.

Certain people in that limo were expendable. It was a lucky thing he'd already called in some back-up.

"He won't touch us…not if we have her." And that was the trick. Getting close enough to grab Sabrina. According to her signal, she was just past that entrance door. Ten feet inside. So close.

To get her, though, a few people would have to be sacrificed.

"Witch, can you distract him?" Eric barked.

Kevin's mouth dropped open. "Wh-what? Why the hell would I *want* to do that?"

"Because if you don't, I'll put a bullet in your head?" Or rather, one of his guards would. "I'm thinking if you go out there, you throw a little of your magic at him…"

Kevin swayed.

Eric smiled and finished, "Given the guy's history with witches, I'm betting it will piss him off. He'll come at you, and that will give us the chance to get Sabrina. Once I have her, I'll get her to call off her attack dog."

"Interesting plan," Raymond said, inclining his head. "You gonna make her give you the stone?"

Kevin shot his step-brother a surprised glance. Then the witch turned his attention back to Eric.

"If she has it, then absolutely," Eric replied smoothly.

"Um…" Kevin cleared his throat. "What happens if the gargoyle kills me before you get Sabrina?"

Another vehicle slid in behind them. Back-up, perfectly on time.

"I'll have plenty of guards around you. They'll be firing on the gargoyle as soon as we see him. When they start shooting, you duck. Between the bullets and the spells, that should be enough of a distraction to get her." Total bullshit answer. Eric didn't really give a flying fuck what happened to the witch.

But he *was* going to get his hands on Sabrina. She'd turned to another lover. Oh, the hell, *no*. She couldn't go to another. Not happening. So he would break his own rule. He would bring Sabrina close again. *I can't let her weaken me, though. I have to play this very, very carefully.*

He jerked his head. "Let's get this show going." The guards filed out first. Then Kevin, obviously nervous…and next was Raymond.

"Not coming, boss?" Raymond asked quietly.

"I prefer to watch from a distance." And the limo was nearly a tank, thanks to all the upgrades he'd put on the thing. He intended to stay safe.

Raymond grunted. The guards from the second vehicle had already appeared. He'd texted them orders moments before. They were to have minimum contact with Sabrina. *Bring her to me, immediately.* Longer exposure to her would be dangerous to them.

If they didn't bring Sabrina to him, then he didn't really care if any of them lived.

They were replaceable. Everyone was...*but her.*

***

She needed a phone. Only Sabrina didn't think she was going to find one in the closed-down club. Dammit. Her hands slapped against the bar top. Adam might not want help, but she was still going to *give* the guy help. She was going to pull in Cordelia, and her witchy best friend would find a way to break the curse. There *had* to be a way.

If only she had a freaking phone.

Sabrina spun away from the bar and —

Footsteps. Rushing toward the club. She could hear them because there were a *lot* of footsteps. Her body tensed. Adam was on the roof, doing his whole changing into stone routine, but they had company outside, right the hell then.

Gunfire erupted. A fast blast of bullets that had her ducking for cover. The bullets seemed to have been focused on the front doors — she could even see the bullet holes that had pierced through the wood and then —

Those doors burst open. Armed men in black ran inside.

Sabrina jumped behind the bar.

***

Gunshots broke through the night, echoing like thunder. Adam ran to the edge of the roof and glanced down, snarling when he saw the men who were shooting into the front of *his* nightclub. Bastards who were shooting because they were after Sabrina.

A long, black limo idled in front of the building. A black SUV waited just behind it. Men were scrambling everywhere.

Except…one guy just stood there. About ten feet in front of the club. No weapons were in his hands, and his shoulder was bleeding.

Who the hell are you?

But as Adam stared at him, the man lifted his hands…and he began to chant.

Ah, hell. Witch.

Lightning crackled overhead. The wind picked up speed, seeming to howl as it blew against Adam's body.

The men with guns were running into the nightclub. They thought they were going to take Sabrina. The witch thought he'd use his magic to stop Adam.

They all needed to think the hell again.

Stone was spreading over his body. The change wasn't complete, not by any means. He was caught somewhere between a man and a beast, but that wasn't going to slow him down. Adam just stepped right off that roof. He plummeted down, sinking straight to the ground, sinking…just like stone.

Men fired at him. One bullet hit the flesh of his arm, grazing over him and truly pissing him off. Another bullet bounced off the stone that had already spread to cover his chest.

"Oh, shit," the witch cried out, but then, in the next breath, the guy kept right on chanting. A ring of fire circled the man. As if that would keep him safe.

Adam grabbed the fool who'd tried to shoot him in the chest. One squeeze of his now stone-covered hand, and the guy's gun was crunched to dust. Adam threw the human to the side, and the fellow didn't get up after he hit a light pole.

"Adam!" Sabrina screamed.

His head whipped to the right. She was being carried out of the nightclub. Carried—*dragged.* Three men were pulling her and she was fighting with all of her strength.

At her cry, one of those humans actually put his gun to her head.

We aren't playing this game again.

Adam roared his fury and the stone surrounded him completely.

The guards ran with her then, rushing fast and one of the doors to the limo opened.

Eric appeared. "Bring her to me! Now!"

Bullets flew toward Adam. They ricocheted off the stone. The witch sent a wave of fire straight to him. Stupid move. Fire didn't hurt the beast. Adam raced after Sabrina.

But Eric had her. Eric had pulled her close against him and the bastard had put a knife to her throat.

Adam knocked out the other guards — the idiots who were firing at him. He left them all in an unconscious pile at his feet. All but two — the witch...and a guy who seemed to be trying to protect the witch. *Wait, I know him.* Raymond, that had been his name. He was the bastard who'd almost shot Sabrina on that hospital rooftop.

Time to end those two assholes. After he was finished with them, then he'd rip Eric apart. *Mission accomplished.*

"Stop!" Eric shouted. "Stop or I will kill her."

The gargoyle focused on him. "No, you won't." His voice was heavier than the thunder. Eric was obsessed. He needed Sabrina. Adam didn't think for even a moment that the guy would kill her.

But...

Blood trickled down Sabrina's throat.

I will make you bleed, human. I will rip you apart and you will be begging for your own death before I am done with you.

The witch shouted, "Take the beast! Take him far away! Wind blow wide and wind blow hard…take the beast!"

As those words filled the air, the wind seemed to close around Adam, tightening like a noose but blowing with the force of a tornado. He was lifted up and a howling filled his ears. Adam fought to break free, his wings flapping furiously, but the wind was too strong. It was taking him up. Taking him away.

Fuck this shit. "Sabrina!" Adam roared.

He couldn't get out of the wind. The witch was smiling up at him, looking satisfied and damn relieved as he blinked from behind his glasses.

"The wind has you, beast! It won't let you go!"

Was that the way the spell worked? The wind was keeping the beast prisoner? If that was the case…

Then I just have to stop being a beast.

The stone hardened. Inside that stone prison, Adam began to pound with his fists. He'd fight until he became a man again. He'd get out of that witch's trap. And then he would *kill*.

CHAPTER THIRTEEN

The witch cried out, "Holy shit! That worked! It actually worked!"

Sabrina glared at him.

"Get in the car," Eric snapped. "All of you — *now*."

Then he was dragging Sabrina into the back of the limo. Her neck was bleeding, she could feel the blood dripping down onto her shirt. Eric was practically humming with pleasure. Raymond wasn't meeting her gaze and the witch was bleeding more than she was. But he was crowing with pride and pleasure, too.

"I took down a gargoyle!" the witch bragged as he hopped inside. The door slammed behind him and the driver took off moments later. "Did you all see that shit? I am amazing."

"You didn't take him down." They'd left the injured and unconscious men. *And the dead ones.* She knew there were some dead back there. Knowing Eric, he'd have a crew appear immediately and clean up the mess. But he'd better hurry. That particular area of town wasn't deserted…someone would have reported all the gun shots. The cops had to arrive soon.

Provided they aren't on Eric's payroll, too.

"I did so take that gargoyle down." The witch straightened and smirked at her. "Or, I guess, I took him *up* and—"

"You just pissed him off. He'll come after me again. And if you get in his way a second time, he'll kill you."

The witch stopped smirking. His face paled a bit and she saw his fear.

It was her turn to smile.

"You control him." Eric's voice. Quiet. Angry. He did that—when he was at his angriest, he got quiet. When she'd first met him, she'd thought that was a sign of his control. That he could keep himself in check. Too late, she'd realized that the quieter he became, the weaker his control actually was. His whispers came just when he was at his most dangerous. "You have the stone, don't you?"

"The binding stone," the witch added. "Magic, magic, magic!"

"First…who the fuck are you?" She glared at the witch. She wanted a name. She also wanted him to talk to her more. *The better for me to control you.* Because she'd work this guy over in no time…

He licked his lips. "K-Kevin…" His eyes seemed to glaze a bit as he stared at her and—

Raymond punched him in the face. "Don't get caught by her, man! It's a trick."

Poor Raymond. Did he even realize she'd caught him before? *And I will again.* She was actually disappointed her power hadn't made more of an impression on him. She'd been so sure he would turn on Eric. Her mistake.

Again.

Her gaze slid over Kevin's aura. Not much good there. This guy was after power — magic. He was low on the witch totem pole. "Half-human," she murmured. So his spells probably only worked half the time. No wonder he'd been so jazzed about his wind bit. He wanted more magic. He wanted to be as strong as the others in his coven. But if he got power...

You won't use it well. You'll destroy. She saw him very, very clearly.

Her attention shifted back to Raymond. His aura...it had changed a bit since she last saw him. The colors —

Eric's fingers curled around her wrist and he squeezed her so hard she thought he might shatter the bones. "Where is the stone?"

She didn't let even a whimper of pain escape her. "What stone?"

Eric's voice dropped to the whisper she hated. "The stone you use to control the gargoyle. Don't waste my time. I know all about your freak protector."

"So, for the record," she bared her teeth at him, "he's my lover. And he has a name. It's Adam. Don't call him a freak again."

His nostrils flared. "*Where is the stone?*"

"Fuck off."

Eric twisted her wrist, hard, and the bones...snapped. Nausea rolled through her. Pain. Disgust. "Do you think you're the first who went so dark on me?" She laughed—at him and herself. "You aren't. You're just my latest mistake. But I got rid of those mistakes." She leaned toward him. "And I'll get rid of you."

What could have been fear appeared—then vanished—in his gaze. "When did you meet the new lover?"

Her smile grew as she ignored the pain. She just needed to buy herself a bit more time. She was sure that Adam would be appearing any moment. He wasn't going to let her vanish on him. *I trust him.* "I met him when I disappeared from your life. I guess you could say that when I vanished from your world, I dropped into his."

He blinked. "Lie. I know you were held captive. You didn't choose to leave me."

Not that first time, I didn't. But after that, once I saw what you really were? Hells to the yes! "Adam was one of my guards in that prison. How do you think I got away from that place?"

Eric's expression became absolutely blank.

At that same moment, something hard and heavy landed on the top of the car. The limo shuddered, then swerved.

She looked up and saw claws cutting into the top of the limo. "That will be my ride. This has been fun..." *Not even close.*

The top of the limo was being peeled back. Metal groaned and screeched.

"But I've really got to go—" Sabrina's words ended in a gasp because it wasn't Adam who was reaching down to grab her. It was Leo.

Eric jerked a gun out of his jacket and started firing.

Leo snarled. His hand wrapped around her broken wrist and he yanked her up. Even as he lifted her, Leo sent a blast of fire right back into the car.

His wings flapped against the air and he shot into the night. Leo held her tightly against him. Sabrina looked back down and saw the limo swerve off the road as smoke and fire poured from the rear. The vehicle lost control, and it flipped—once, twice, three times...

"Did I just save the day for you, Sabrina?" Leo murmured.

She had a death grip on his shoulders.

"Because if I did..." His voice was grim. "That means you're gonna owe me."

Damn him. Her eyes squeezed shut. "Adam."

"I have no clue where your gargoyle lover is, sweets." His chest vibrated a bit as he laughed. "But don't worry. Something tells me that he'll be coming to find you, very, very soon."

***

Eric shoved open the back door of the limo. Blisters covered his hands and he was choking on smoke.

"*Help me!*"

He glanced back. The witch had gotten trapped in the twisted metal that resulted from the wreck. Raymond was fighting the flames and trying to get his step-brother out. Huh. How about that…maybe Raymond *did* care about the man, after all.

"Witches burn too fast," Raymond yelled. "Eric, help us!"

The driver had escaped the wreckage, too. He ran up to Eric. "Boss, you okay?"

No, he was fucking burned. But…

"I'm far, far better than okay." In fact, everything in his life was about to be perfect. He just had to get back to his estate. Back to the safety that waited for him.

He glanced up at the sky. Sabrina was long gone. Sabrina and whoever the hell that had been who'd taken her away. Eric had barely gotten a glimpse of the man. He'd just seen him long enough to realize...*not Adam Cross.*

I am so sick of these paranormals.

"*Help!*" Kevin screamed.

Eric turned away. He pulled out his phone. A little melted, but still working. He dialed quickly and then said, "I need a car..."

"*Help!*"

Eric kept walking. "Track my phone. Get out here, now." He glanced back. "Raymond, that whole car is about to blow. Get your ass out — or die with your brother."

The driver swore and rushed farther away from the limo.

"*Don't leave me!*" Kevin screamed.

Eric paused. Fear and pain...poor Kevin was absolutely terrified. Death by fire — one hell of a way to go.

"I've got a car close by, sir," a crisp voice said in Eric's ear. "Should be there within five minutes."

Five minutes. Eric hunched his shoulders. Would the gargoyle appear in that time? "I need it faster..." Because he didn't intend to die. He had plans. So many plans.

"*Help me!*" Now Kevin was begging.

And the flames were spreading.

***

Adam hit the ground as a man. He was pretty sure he broke both legs. And some ribs. But he rolled over and ignored that pain. He looked into the sky. The freaking cyclone that had surrounded him before had dissipated as soon as he'd become a man. Would it come back when he transformed again?

No, the witch is long gone. If the witch isn't here, I'm betting it can't manifest again.

Maybe it was a dumb bet but...

Adam called forth the gargoyle. He needed to heal and as soon as the beast took over, he *would* heal. He'd heal and he'd hunt. And he would find Sabrina.

The stone spread. "*Sabrina!*" The roar of her name echoed back to him.

***

"Put me down," Sabrina whispered into Leo's ear. "Right the hell now, or I swear, I will cut your heart out."

He laughed. "With what? You don't even have claws."

She shoved the tip of a knife into his chest. Not deep enough to reach his cold-as-ice heart, but far enough to prove she meant business. "You think I left that limo without a little souvenir?"

Another laugh. "I forgot how much I enjoy you."

But then he opened his hands and he let her fall. Sabrina sucked in a desperate breath as she tumbled down and down and—

She fell into water. A gleaming pool that was lit with dozens of lights. She kicked to the surface and kept a tight grip on her knife. As she swam to the side of that pool, Leo appeared.

"Roof-top pool," he murmured as he knelt near the edge of said pool. "Very convenient, don't you think?"

Sabrina growled at him and then she hauled herself out of the pool. She flopped on the side, sucking in a few deep breaths and choking up some water.

"You *did* say to let you go. I just followed your orders."

She swiped out with the knife.

"Careful! You almost cut me!"

Her eyes were closed. If they'd been open, she was sure that she *would* have cut him. "Leave me the hell alone."

"I will…right after you repay me for saving your ass. I mean, I didn't see the gargoyle swooping in to the rescue. The hero? That was me."

"You are so fucking modest."

"I try."

She cracked open her eyes. "I didn't ask you to save me."

He brushed the wet hair away from her cheek. "I know...that rather pisses me off." His jaw had hardened. His wings were gone. He looked like a man. A normal, handsome man with dark hair and a faint beard covering his jaw. He was even in normal clothes—*dry* clothes. "When you were in trouble, you went to my brother."

"Where is Luke? I could use him right about now." She felt like a drowned rat. *If Luke shows up, I'll find out if he has the stone. If he does have it...*

"You aren't the first person I've let down."

Now she pushed up to get a better view of him. Her broken wrist ached, but she ignored the pain.

"You think I don't know that you hate me?" This time, Leo's laughter was bitter. "Get in line. A very long line."

"Did you know I was being held in Simon Lorne's prison?"

He shook his head.

She wanted to believe him. But he had so many secrets.

"We were friends once, weren't we?" He was still crouched at her side. "Or at least, I thought we were close to being friends."

"We were," she allowed, "until you decided I was one of those pesky bad things that you couldn't have in your world." That had *hurt.*

Leo looked away from her. "I know you made Akin kill himself. I was watching. You thought I arrived after, to help you slip away, but I saw everything. I heard everything."

Her heart jerked in her chest.

"If you could do that, so easily…what else could you do?"

"You think it was easy?" Now she rose. The water slid from her body. Her fingers gripped the knife. She held it in her left hand, not her broken right. "There is nothing easy about taking a life. Not for me. But I saw what Akin was doing—he was going to keep marching, keep attacking. Keep *killing.* I'd created the monster, don't you see that? His lust for power knew no end. He would just keep going. I'd made him. I had to stop him. I had—"

"That was the problem. You did make him. Just as you would make others like him. Like him…like Eric Foster. *You* were the danger. You were the darkness that slipped into their lives. To truly eliminate the evil, I should have eliminated you."

They were alone on that roof, standing on some high-rise in the middle of the city. And she was facing off against a being that was way, way stronger than she was. *Oh, shit. I could seriously use my gargoyle about now.* "Are you…are you going to kill me tonight?"

He looked away from her, turning to stare at the lights of the pool. "I couldn't kill you then, even when you stood with a dead man at your feet. Do you truly think I could kill you now?"

Maybe, yes. Was that a trick question? Sabrina didn't know him any longer. She wasn't sure she ever truly had. But then, Sabrina hadn't been the one who'd been the closest to him. That had been her cousin.

"Where is Fate?"

Her cousin…a being with the title of Fate. The title, the pressure, the never-ending burden…*Fate.* "She goes by Mora now."

A shudder seemed to slip along the length of his body.

"Where is she?"

"Um, yeah." She pushed back her wet hair, then winced when her wrist protested. "She's been hiding from you for centuries. You think I'm just going to give up her location to you? Not happening."

He lunged toward her. His hand flew out— and locked around her broken wrist.

She stilled. Was he going to hurt her? Try to torture Mora's location out of her? He'd have to do more than just break some bones…

But warmth spread from his fingers to her wrist. And the bones snapped back into place. The pain faded.

He'd healed her.

"I'm still not telling you," she muttered.

His eyes narrowed. "What do I have to do…" Leo gritted out, "so that you will tell me where she is?"

That was the thing…Sabrina was actually the only being on the whole face of the earth who knew where Mora was hiding. She smiled at him. "You bring me the binding stone that controls Adam, and I'll give up that location to you."

He growled, then demanded, "Just where in the hell am I supposed to find that stone?"

"I'd start by checking out Luke's place. Because I think he has it." She lifted her chin and tried to act as if she weren't — quite literally — dripping wet at the Lord of the Light's feet. "You get me that stone, and I'll tell you where Mora is."

He gave a jerky nod and stepped back. But then he said, "Why haven't you just made Eric kill himself?"

She felt ice spreading inside of her body.

"Tell me you haven't thought about it." His laugh was cold. "After Akin…how could you not? I know Eric has been hurting humans — "

"He's been hurting them because he can't hurt me," she said, voice breaking a bit.

"So why haven't you stopped him? Why go to my brother? Surely you could have handled this yourself…"

If only. "I tried…I tried to stop Eric as soon as I realized what he was doing. But he knew what I was. He'd learned a lot about paranormals while I was gone. I think…he may have gotten some…enhancements during my absence." It was the only possibility that made sense, the only way he could have resisted her power.

"Enhancements? What the hell?"

"I couldn't get him to obey me." Her lips pressed together. "No one had resisted me before." *And Adam is the only one to resist me since.* "I had to run away, and since then, Eric has been incredibly careful. He doesn't get too physically close to me, and he orders his guards to keep their distance, too."

"So you decided that you'd get a protector who could do your dirty work for you."

Her chin lifted. "What was the alternative? Let him keep killing humans? Taking the deal with Luke was my only choice."

He stared into her eyes. "No, I was a choice, too." Then the guy just shot off into the night.

"Wait! You can't just leave me here!" She didn't even know where *here* was. "Leo? *Leo!*"

But he'd left her.

This is why you weren't a damn choice for me. I can't count on you! Her breath huffed out. "Still a jerk. Guess that part hasn't changed."

***

He saw the flames and smelled smoke. Adam landed on the ground right next to the wreckage. A fast, frantic search showed him — *Sabrina isn't here.* Neither was Eric. The guy's scent still lingered, but he was long gone.

"H-help…"

Adam peered into the crunched remains of the limo. The witch was in there, the flames eating at him and…at the other man, Raymond. Two bastards who were headed for a very swift meeting with death.

Adam stared into the witch's eyes.

"G-get my brother to leave…me," the witch whispered. "Pl-please…"

Raymond was fighting and jerking at a twisted chunk of metal. The metal seemed to be pinning the witch in place.

Adam considered both men a moment. Raymond hadn't even glanced back at him. The witch looked half-dead already. Witches and fire never mixed.

Humans didn't fare so well with fire, either, but Raymond was ignoring his own burns. The guy was choking, probably close to passing out, but still trying to free the witch.

"Give me one reason," Adam growled, his voice that of his beast, "why I should help either of you?"

Neither spoke.

They didn't have a reason.

The scent of gasoline permeated the air. That car—it was going to explode. Adam knew it. The two bastards before him were about to be destroyed. And he was going to watch.

Is this what I have become?

The question slipped through him. And so did an image of Sabrina. Sabrina—staring at him, with tears in her eyes. Telling him that she was the same as Meredith.

Meredith had watched as others burned.

Am I the same as Meredith?

Tears had fallen on Sabrina's cheeks.

He didn't like it when she cried.

Adam's claws grabbed the side of the limo. He ripped the door away. Surged inside and yanked at the metal that pinned the witch. Then he was grabbing both Raymond and the bastard who'd used magic against him before. Adam burst out of the car—with them clenched tightly in his stone grasp—even as the vehicle ignited around him. The witch was screaming. Raymond wasn't making a sound. They were burning...

My stone can't burn.

Adam dropped the two into a nearby lake. He looked down and saw their heads break the surface.

Alive.

Did that count as his good deed for the century? He thought so. It was probably a deed that would come back to bite him hard in the ass but...

At least he didn't have more blood on his hands. Adam flew high into the air. *Where are you, Sabrina? Where did you go?* He flew and he caught her scent...

Her scent and Eric's. They'd gone in two different directions.

He could hunt Eric. Finish the bastard. Or...

Sabrina had been bleeding when she was pulled into the limo by Eric. I saw the blood on her throat.

Or he could find her. *She's my choice.* Adam turned and he followed her scent. He was coming to realize that for him, Sabrina came first.

He wondered if she always would.

CHAPTER FOURTEEN

Something was flying toward her. Something big and strong and…

Don't be Leo. Not again.

Sabrina's body tensed as she stood at the edge of the pool. She'd just been about to search for a way off that building — *off, out, whatever works* – but it looked as if company was coming her way.

The mysterious *something* drew closer and a relieved rasp broke from her. "*Adam.*" In all his gargoyle glory. He was flying fast toward her. She lifted up her hands, reaching for him. He didn't even land on the roof. He just scooped her up, held her against his chest, and flew away with her into the night.

"I knew you'd come for me." She put her cheek against the stone. It was strange, but the stone still felt warm to her. "Just had to make it until you showed up." They were high above the city. The lights gleamed below them. Everyone else seemed to be a million miles away. Sabrina wished they could stay just like this — she was safe here, in his arms. There was only silence around them. Silence and darkness.

"Are you hurt?" His voice was the beast's deep rumble.

Her wrist didn't even ache any longer. Courtesy of Leo's magic. And the cut on her neck? It had healed, too. That would be something else she owed him. Leo liked to collect his debts just as much as Luke did. "I'm fine."

They didn't speak again. Not until they were back at the penthouse. It seemed almost surreal to go back there. To land on the balcony with him and watch as he slowly broke out of his stone prison. When his fingers emerged from the stone, when the rocks fell to his feet, she could only stare at him.

Those rocks vanished after a time. She'd seen them do that before. They just turned to dust and blew away in the breeze.

Magic was a strange thing.

"Your clothes are wet."

Not as wet as they had been, not anymore. Thanks to that windy flight through the sky. "I took a tumble into a pool."

He stalked toward her. "I want to get weapons and grab some new clothes for you, and then we're out of here. I don't want to risk Leo showing up again—"

"Leo is busy with something else right now. You don't need to worry about him." But she turned and left the balcony, leading the way into the penthouse condo. He followed behind her, his steps silent. She went into the bedroom—what she now thought of as *their* bedroom—and stripped.

She didn't fake coyness. She just dropped the clothes onto the floor and then turned toward him.

His eyes raked over her body.

"I need you…to check me."

"Sweetheart, I check you out all the time."

No, not that way. She eased out a slow breath. "Eric is tracking me somehow. He did *something* to me, and I need you to help me figure out what it is." Her hands were by her sides. "He found me at that club. He *always* finds me. No matter where I go, he can locate me. I know he's put something *in* me. I tried to find a cut, a mark, *something* that he left behind when he inserted the tracker, but I can't do it." She took a step toward him. Then another. "You've got better senses than I do. You can catch someone's scent from miles away. Look at me. *Check* me. If something is there…" She reached for his hands. The hands of a man now, but she'd seen how easily claws sprouted from his fingertips. "Then cut the damn thing out."

His eyes widened. "You think I would cut your skin?"

"I'm *asking* you to cut me. Help me! I can't keep doing this. There isn't any escape from him.

He knows every move I take. He's put a tracker in me, and I can't find it." She spun, giving him her back. "Do you see anything? Please, Adam, help me. I am *begging* you."

"How did you get on the roof?"

She looked back at him.

"And how do you know Leo is working on something else right now?"

Her lips trembled. "Because Leo is the one who got me out of the limo…he's also the one who sent a blast of fire at Eric. But that didn't end Eric, I could see the bastard scrambling from the car even as Leo and I flew away."

"Leo saved you." His words were quiet.

"Leo is working his own agenda, believe me. I have something he wants. Or rather, I know the location of *someone* he wants. Apparently, breaking up is not something Leo can understand, not even after a whole lot of centuries." She huffed out a breath. "Get the tracker out of me."

His hands rose and curled around her shoulders. She actually gave a little jump at the contact because an arc of electricity seemed to flow right through her body. His touch did that to her. Gave her a buzz. Turned her on.

Tuned her, to him.

Slowly, his hands slid down, moving over her shoulder blades and then sliding over her spine. Warm and strong, his fingers stroked to the base of her back. He leaned toward her, she could feel him surrounding her, and his breath brushed over her cheek as he said, "I've looked before. I've tried to find out how he was tracking you, but I couldn't."

She turned in his arms. He was naked, she was naked. Flesh to flesh. "Look again."

His hands were on her hips. Slowly, his hands began to slide down her legs. His fingertips were slightly rough against her skin as he dragged his hands over her thighs. Behind her knees. He was stroking every inch of her legs, her calves, her ankles. He even bent before her and lifted her feet.

"There's nothing I can see, Sabrina." He looked up at her.

"Eric keeps finding me."

He was kneeling before her. "The dead can't find anyone."

Then his hands were rising again. His fingers darted between her spread legs. She gave a quick gasp, and then two fingers were sliding into her.

Only he wasn't looking for any tracker. His eyes had changed. Desire had slipped over his face, a heavy mask that told her exactly what he wanted.

"But I'll be thorough," he told her, voice dipping into a guttural growl. "I promise...I'll keep checking."

And he leaned forward and put his mouth on her. She almost fell, but he caught her quickly, and he lifted her up, positioning her so that she was pressed half-against the bed. Her legs were splayed wide, and he was crouched between them. His mouth was on her. Licking her. Stroking her. Her hands flew out blindly and fisted around the bedcovers. "Adam!"

He licked her once more. *Such a wicked, wicked tongue…*

He thrust two fingers into her again even as his mouth worked her clit. She opened her mouth, trying to suck in a desperate gulp of air, and then Sabrina erupted. The pleasure hit her hard and fast and she came against his mouth.

The pleasure was still rolling through her when he drove his cock into her. She was so sensitive — the pressure of his heavy length had her shuddering. He worked in and out of her. She was tight from her release, so tight, and every move of his hips had her heart lurching.

He kissed her. And he came. And she was spinning out of control again because she didn't think the pleasure had ever stopped. Her need for him was growing and growing.

Her lovers had amused her in the past. They'd satisfied her.

Adam was different.

Sex with him…it seemed to pierce her straight to her soul. The pleasure was deeper. The need sharper.

She wanted and she craved and the hunger didn't lessen.

His fingers were trailing over her arms. He pressed a kiss to her breast. "I don't see a tracker on you. I don't feel it."

Her breath was still coming too fast. "It's there."

He withdrew from her. She hated that. She'd wanted him to stay inside of her. When they were together like that, they were part of each other.

She liked being part of him.

"He's running scared." Adam lifted her and placed her carefully in the middle of the bed. "He's fucking terrified because he knows he can't escape from me. However he's tracking you, it won't matter. Like I told you, the dead can't hunt you."

She licked her lips. "We can lock him in Luke's prison. You don't have to kill Eric for me."

He just stared at her.

I'm not Meredith. "Adam…"

He kissed her lips. "I'll be back before you know it."

Oh, great. He was about to do his fly-away routine.

"I have to know you're safe." He pressed another kiss to her lips. "Be here when I come back."

"Adam, just listen—"

But he'd backed away. She could see his skin changing. Darkening. Hardening. He was becoming the beast right before her eyes. And then he was just—gone. Gone into the night. Out flying to hunt while she was left to stay there and wait.

Um, hell, no.

She dressed as quickly as she could, and then Sabrina was running through the penthouse and searching frantically for the phone. She finally found it in Adam's office, in the exact spot she'd thrown it after her disastrous call with Eric. Not even bothering to glance at the clock, she yanked up that phone and called her best friend.

It wasn't as if witches spent their nights sleeping. Not the most powerful ones, anyway. Or at least, Sabrina didn't think—

"Who the hell is this?" A disgruntled—and very sleepy—feminine voice demanded. A hint of the south whispered through her words. "And do you *want* me to hurt you?"

"Cordelia." Relief broke in that name. Sabrina cleared her throat. "I'm in trouble."

"What else is new?" But, suddenly, Cordelia's voice was a lot sharper. Definitely more awake. In the background, Sabrina heard the darker murmur of a man's voice. "No, no, honey, it's fine," Cordelia assured him. "Just girl talk."

Silence.

"It's not girl talk," Sabrina muttered. "I *need* your help."

"Give me a sec…don't like to worry him." Cordelia's voice was soft. "Okay…I'm outside." Her friend exhaled on a sigh. "You know humans, they tend to worry."

Sabrina licked her lips. "I need a spell."

"Where are you?"

"Miami." Her shoulders hunched. "What do you know about gargoyles?"

"Oh, shit. Is one after you? Because if so…run. Run hell fast and hell hard because those monsters don't give up."

"He's not after me. He's…um, protecting me."

"What?"

"It's a really long story—"

"And it's the middle of the freaking night," Cordelia tossed back. "You just ripped me out of bed, so cut to the chase."

"I need a spell to break his curse. You're the most powerful witch I know—"

"Flattery will get you everywhere…Obviously."

"—if anyone can break that spell, it has to be you."

More silence. Sabrina waited. And waited. "Cordelia?"

"I don't know how to break the spell."

Her stomach seemed to drop straight to the floor. "But...you know everything."

Cordelia's laugh was bitter. "I wish."

"Please, please Cordelia. I need your help."

Silence was her answer. Silence and then..."I'm afraid that this time, I don't have any help to give."

No, no, she *wouldn't* give up. "Can you search through all your spell books? Can you scry? Look into the past, the future, look *anywhere!* I know there is a way. There *has* to be a way."

"Why does this matter so much to you?" Cordelia asked quietly.

"Because...because he matters." She held her breath, waiting. "If there is a way, I know you can find it."

"I'll look...but I'm not promising anything."

Sabrina's eyes squeezed closed.

"Do *not* get your hopes up, Sabrina. There may be nothing."

"Bad paranormals don't have hope, you should know that," she whispered.

"You are such a terrible liar." Cordelia gave a faint *hum* as she seemed to consider her options. Then she asked, "Where — exactly — in Miami are you? And why do you need a gargoyle to protect you?"

Sabrina blew out a slow breath. "You really don't want to know why I need him."

"Inspiration gone wrong?" Cordelia's voice was knowing.

"Wrong doesn't even begin to describe things…"

***

Leo landed on the balcony of Luke's home.

His twin brother owned an island in the Florida Keys — an island that included the fucking mansion that Luke had built for himself…and, of course, for Luke's mate, Mina.

He has a home. He has a mate. He has a fucking life.

But according to one screwed up prophesy that had been delivered very, very long ago…one day, Leo was destined to end all of that happiness for his brother. They were supposed to battle. Supposed to fight…until only one remained.

I won't kill him. Leo had held that secret tight for thousands of years. *I can't do it.* Even if it meant plunging the whole world into chaos, he couldn't kill his brother.

"You have got to stop dropping by without an invitation…" Luke's drawling voice came to him from the darkness. "Mina doesn't like surprises." He walked from the shadows of the balcony and snapped his fingers. "Oh, wait. My mistake. My beautiful love just doesn't like *you*."

Leo's lips thinned.

"Lucky for you," Luke added with a flash of his teeth that wasn't *exactly* a smile. "Mina was exhausted from some…rather strenuous activity earlier. She's sleeping."

Like he needed to hear about that strenuous activity shit. "I want the gargoyle's binding stone."

"And I want my brother to not be an asshole. See, we both want interesting things tonight."

The wind blew against them. The waves crashed below.

And behind Luke, the door cracked open.

Leo caught a glimpse of Mina. She was beautiful, Luke was right about that. But she didn't look exhausted. In fact, she looked pissed.

And her fury was directed solidly at Leo. *If looks could kill…*

"What's he doing here?" Mina said.

Luke stiffened. Then he glanced her way. "My love…didn't mean to wake you." He lifted his hand. "Leo just stopped by for a friendly, brotherly visit."

She immediately came toward Luke. Their fingers linked. Their bodies just seemed to…fit. Right next to each other.

Something dark twisted inside of Leo.
Jealousy?

"Bullshit," Mina said flatly. "You two don't do friendly and you don't do brotherly." Her gaze was straight on Leo. "If you've come to try and hurt him…"

Luke laughed. "Sweetness, he can't hurt me. That's just an insulting suggestion."

Mina kept her stare on Leo.

He smiled at her. She didn't smile back.

Right. She might still be a wee bit upset with him because of their past.

Leo glanced back at his brother. "I need the stone that controls Adam Cross."

"Um, good for you." Luke's voice was mild. "And you think I have it because…?"

"Sabrina told me that you sent Adam to her. That he's her protection." Leo kept his hands loose at his sides, not wanting to appear threatening…yet. *But I am getting that fucking stone.* "So since the guy is jumping to follow your orders, I figure that must mean you're the one controlling the binding stone."

"You figure wrong."

Just that. Three words. Then nothing else.

Leo lifted a brow. "Do I look like I buy your lies?"

"No. You look rather desperate. And I have to wonder…why does that stone matter to you? Why do you care about a gargoyle? Surely you have enough of those pesky *good* paranormals who will run to do your bidding, hmmm? You don't need a gargoyle in your arsenal, too. I mean, he's not even one of yours. He's..." Luke's voice dropped to a dramatic whisper, "bad."

"Sabrina wants the stone."

Luke jerked a bit. He rarely showed surprise, so Leo made a mental note of that weakness. But then Luke nodded. "Right, I'd forgotten...once upon a time, you were quite cozy with the muse, weren't you? I mean, before you realized how truly wicked and dark she was. Bad, bad to the core...that's Sabrina."

Leo fought to keep his expression blank.

"Mina, I don't think you know this particular backstory..." Luke announced.

"No, don't think I do," she agreed, her voice drifting magically in the night. She was a siren — her voice was a very big part of her power.

So I can't focus on her voice. I can't let it get to me.

"Let me tell you the story..." Luke said, relish in the words. "Sabrina lost a lover — oh, it was ages ago. A warrior named Akin. A human she just adored. He committed suicide. Stabbed himself in the heart. And a devastated Sabrina had no friends after that. My brother...well, he turned from her. Because *maybe* Sabrina had a hand in what happened to Akin. Maybe she used that wicked, wicked power of hers on him..."

"Shut the hell up," Leo snapped. "You don't know about what happened between us—"

"It's fortunate I was there to help her," Luke continued talking, rolling right over Leo's words. Luke glanced at Mina. "You would have been so proud of me, love. There I was, picking up the pieces that had been left in my brother's wake. The poor muse was shattered."

"Nothing has ever shattered Sabrina," Leo snarled.

Very slowly, Luke turned his head back toward Leo. "Don't be so certain of that."

Leo took a step back, then caught himself. *Fuck. Now I'm showing weakness.* "Give me the binding stone."

"Or…what?" This came from Mina. "If Luke doesn't turn over whatever stone this is…what will you do?" She pulled from Luke and stepped in front of her lover. "Will you fight him? Will you storm through his home, ripping everything apart as you try to find this trinket?"

"It's a stone, love." Luke's hand curled along her shoulder. "Not a trinket. A very, very powerful stone."

Leo's hands had fisted.

"And there's no need for my brother to linger here…no need for him to so much as lift a pillow from my bed. I don't have the stone." Gently, Luke pulled Mina back to his side. "I looked for it, if you want the whole truth. I was hoping to find it after Simon Lorne died. As far as I know, he was the last to wield the binding stone. But I couldn't find a trace of it in the Everglades. I got a bit distracted, you see. Other lives to ruin. Others to save. Blah. Blah. So I didn't get to search the place right away. By the time I arrived back at the scene, the binding stone was long gone."

Hell. "I *need* that stone."

Luke's eyes gleamed, and Leo knew that he'd given too much away. His brother advanced toward him. "And why, again? Could you explain a bit more? I believe you said that Sabrina wanted it?"

Leo clamped his mouth shut.

Luke pursed his lips and then after a tense moment, he said, "I've already made a deal with Adam Cross. He knows he is supposed to do anything necessary to keep her safe. So there is no need for Sabrina to try and control him."

Leo turned away. He knew Luke was telling the truth. *This time*. He could feel it. His brother didn't have the stone.

Luke's hand clamped around his arm. "If there isn't a need for Sabrina to control Adam, then she could only use the binding stone for one reason…"

Leo looked back, making sure to school his expression once more.

He must have done a piss-poor job because Luke's eyes widened. "She wants to set him free."

Leo shrugged out of Luke's hold. "Sabrina has a habit of falling for the wrong kind of guy."

Luke grabbed him again. "She can't break the stone. She can't break the spell. If she does, Adam dies."

Not my problem. He almost said those words. Almost but...

He remembered another time so he didn't speak.

"I was there when the spell was broken for another gargoyle." What could have been sorrow flashed on Luke's face. But the expression was gone too fast for Leo to fully decipher it. "He became human again...and the poor bastard died within the hour. Humans aren't meant to live for centuries. Time caught up with him when the spell was broken. Time will catch up with Adam Cross, too." Luke's lips twisted into a bitter smile.

Shit. This isn't the news I wanted to hear.

But Luke wasn't done. With disgust heavy in his voice, Luke added, "Magic. It can be a real bitch. The same magic that turned Adam into a gargoyle is the same magic that granted him eternal youth. Meredith wanted her warriors at their peak. It was all part of her spell. You break that spell, and Adam will go back to being a human, all right...and then time will catch up to him within the hour. He'll age. He'll wither. He'll die right before your eyes."

And Sabrina would be pissed. *So pissed she won't keep up her deal with me.*

Luke laughed. "Humans…aren't *you* the one who is supposed to watch out for them, dear brother? Because if this spell breaks, you *will* be watching Adam…you *will* be watching him die."

Shit. He breathed slow and easy and tried to ignore his racing heartbeat. "Get your hands off me."

Luke just leaned in closer. "What have you promised Sabrina?"

The binding stone.

"Better question," Luke murmured. "What has she promised you?"

Leo shoved his brother—fucking hard. Luke flew back a good fifteen feet, and Leo launched into the air. His wings sprang from his back as he raced through the darkness.

***

Eric's fingers were shaking as he opened his safe. A quick turn to the right. To the left. To the right again…

And he heard the soft snick that told him he'd just gotten access. His breath heaved out as he shoved his hand into the safe, one that he'd had installed in his study. It was a top of the line safe, the best out there. He'd needed a safe place to store certain prizes that he'd wanted to keep close. Very, very close.

His fingers shoved right past the jewelry — all of those special treasures that he'd taken from his victims. He liked to keep those nearby so that he could look at them any time he wanted. He could touch them. And remember.

But this time, he wasn't going for the jewelry. He wasn't going for the money. No, another item called to him.

He grabbed the small, black bag and pulled it out. He opened the drawstring top and peered inside. So plain. So simple. But...

I knew you were something special the minute I saw you. He'd found this particular token locked away in someone else's safe. Right in the middle of the Everglades. Right in the middle of chaos. He'd been hunting for Sabrina, but she hadn't been there. He'd found this item instead...and something about it had called to him.

So he'd taken the prize for himself.

He'd always been good at making wise decisions.

There was a loud crash from overhead. The walls around him seemed to shake. Swallowing, Eric backed away from his safe and he looked up. He could see a long crack running across the length of his ceiling.

Sabrina's protector had found him.

A roar echoed and then the ceiling was caving in. Eric yelled and rushed toward his desk. He dove underneath it even as chunks of the ceiling rained down on him. Dust, wood, debris and —

"You can't hide." It was the beast's voice.

Eric crawled from beneath the desk. His gaze traveled up the length of that creature. Adam Cross.

The creature didn't look much like a man right then.

"You won't hurt her…or any other woman…again." Such deep, guttural words.

Eric smiled and he rose to his full height.

The gargoyle reached for him.

"Stop." Eric kept his voice quiet. Calm. And he kept his right hand fisted around his treasure.

Like a puppet on a string, the gargoyle instantly froze.

Eric's smile grew. He lifted his hand and slowly uncurled his fingers, wanting to make sure Adam could see the weapon that he possessed. "Does this look familiar?" The reddish stone was warm against Eric's skin. The stone was always warm. *That was how I knew it was special. It carries a constant warmth.* He'd thought he might have discovered some sort of new energy source when he found the stone. He'd been wrong, but…*it is definitely a stone of power.* "I found this item…at a rundown building in the

Everglades. The same building where my Sabrina was being held." He inclined his head. "I think you were a…a guard at that place? Isn't that what Sabrina said?"

The gargoyle's red eyes were on the stone.

"And if that witch I left to burn in that limo was right…this stone is tied to you, isn't it?"

The gargoyle didn't speak.

"*Tell me…*" Eric yelled. "Is this stone tied to you?"

"Yes," the gargoyle gritted out.

He had to answer. Just like he had to stop.

"You have to do what I say…as long as I control the stone, don't you?" It was a fucking stroke of true luck he'd kept the stone.

The gargoyle's burning eyes met his. There was so much hate and fury in that stare. So much rage. But…

"Yes," the gargoyle said again.

Eric laughed. "And here I thought you were a threat…someone I had to eliminate." Perfect. Utterly perfect. "But you're *my* new guard dog, aren't you?"

The gargoyle — Adam — didn't move.

Eric stopped laughing. "*Aren't you?*"

Adam inclined his head.

"Let's test this shit. A real, good test." Eric licked his lips. "Go get Sabrina. Bring her to me. *Now.*" His fingers closed back around the stone and he held it tight. *"Bring Sabrina to me. I want her here within the next fifteen minutes."*

The gargoyle turned away. Then he was flying right back through the gaping hole he'd made in Eric's ceiling. The beast shot into the night just as the thud of footsteps raced into Eric's office. He glared at the guards who'd finally shown up.

Fucking useless.

But he had a new form of protection under his control. Things were about to get even better in his world.

But for Sabrina? Oh, no, things were about to go straight to hell for her.

CHAPTER FIFTEEN

Adam was coming back. Sabrina stood on the balcony, her hands tight around that railing, her eyes glued to the sky. She could see him flying toward her. His powerful wings were stretched wide in the sky.

He's safe. He's alive.

And if Adam was coming back…

Did that mean he'd succeeded? Was Eric no longer a threat?

She stumbled back from the balcony as he landed in front of her. He was so big. His eyes were burning brighter than she'd ever seen them before. His claws were extended, his mouth was open and she could see his wickedly sharp teeth. He truly looked like a monster.

She rushed to him and threw her arms around him. "I'm so glad you're back." Her eyes closed. "I was worried about you. I just…don't leave me alone like that again, okay? We need to be a team. I can help you. I can—"

His hands—tipped with those claws— pushed her back. He stared at her.

She smiled at him. "Adam?"

"I'm...sorry..." His words were so rough. Ragged.

"Sorry?" Her smile dimmed. "For what?"

His arms flew out, locked around her, and he lifted Sabrina up against his chest. "For this." Then he was flying her into the night, holding her in that unbreakable grip, and terror began to stir in her heart.

"Adam?"

He turned his head. The gargoyle's glowing red eyes met her stare.

"Adam, you're scaring me."

"Eric wants you."

Not just scaring me... "Screw Eric."

"He...wants me..." Each word seemed to be a struggle. As if he had to use every bit of his power just to speak. *"Bring you...to him..."*

"What?" Then she shoved against his grip. Even though they were flying past skyscrapers, she fought his hold.

He didn't let her go.

"This isn't funny!"

He kept flying them. Flying so fast.

"What happened? Did you find Eric?" He *must* have found Eric and —

"He sent me...after you."

"And you told him to fuck off, right?" *But, no, you didn't, or this wouldn't be happening.* "Adam, talk to me!"

"No...choice..."

They'd flown so fast. They'd blasted right through the city, but now he was lowering his body and they seemed to be heading toward a big, massive house. One that sat behind a heavy stone fence.

Oh, no. "Why don't you have a choice, Adam?"

He took them through the roof. A hole had been made in that roof, and Adam just flew them right through it.

"Adam?"

"Eric has...stone."

Her heart stopped. *Impossible. No way...*

Adam had reached his destination. He'd landed in the middle of a study—one covered with dust and debris, probably courtesy of the gaping hole in the roof. And in that room, standing beside the desk, with a smug smile on his face...was Eric.

A very much alive, very much *unhurt* Eric.

"That was awesome," Eric announced. He looked at his watch. "You were back in ten minutes. I am definitely impressed."

Adam still held Sabrina in his arms.

"Let her go. Just drop her right on the floor. Now," Eric barked.

Adam let her go. Sabrina fell right on her ass.

Eric tossed the stone in his right hand. Tossed it up into the air and them immediately caught it.

Sabrina couldn't breathe.

Eric sauntered toward her. "When I was looking for you…you won't believe what little item I found in the Everglades…"

Adam's stone.

And Adam's grating voice whispered through her mind once more. *No…choice.*

Tears pricked her eyes. Adam was a prisoner again. Because he'd been trying to help her, he'd wound up in another monster's hands.

Eric stared down at her. "We are going to have so much fun."

She jumped to her feet. Her fists flew toward him.

"Stop her!" Eric bellowed. "Stop her from attacking!"

Immediately, Adam's arms—those arms made of stone—locked around her body and he pulled her back against him. He held her tightly, so that she could barely move.

"Isn't that amazing?" Eric asked her. He opened his hand and stared at the stone. "He has to do every single thing that I say. I mean, when the witch started telling me how a gargoyle was controlled by a stone…and then I remembered this interesting little piece that I'd picked up while I was looking for you in the Everglades…I thought, no way, right? I mean, what are the odds that would happen? Fate can't really be that kind to me."

"Fate isn't kind," she whispered. *Not even to the ones she loves. She can't be.*

"No." Eric rolled back his shoulders. "I don't guess Fate is kind. At least, not to you, is she?"

She had to get that stone from him. She'd get it, and then she'd smash the damn thing into a million pieces.

"Can I control him when he's in human form, too?" Eric asked her.

Sabrina had no clue, but she feared the answer would be yes. She just glared at Eric.

Eric sighed. "Let's try this again…*Adam!* Do I control you in human form, too?"

"Yes," the gargoyle snapped.

Eric smiled. "Perfect. Because you don't really bleed when you're a gargoyle, do you? And I think it would only be fitting…that you bleed and you suffer."

"No," Sabrina cried out. "Eric, don't do this!"

He came toward her. His left hand lifted and smoothed over her face. "When you're gone from my life, I feel empty. I thought it would work…just always knowing where you were. Just always being able to find you, instantly. I thought I could live that way. But then you went…and you started fucking this freak."

She flinched. "I didn't—"

"*Adam!*"

Her eyes closed.

"Adam, did you fuck my Sabrina?"

"Yes…"

The stone arms were so hard around her. She could almost picture Adam in her mind. A man, trapped inside that stone. Fighting so fiercely against the magic that compelled him.

Her eyes opened.

"You just lied to me, Sabrina." Eric shook his head. "I'll have to hurt you for that. See, if this is going to work, if I'm going to let you come back to me, we must have honesty between us."

If I'm going to let you come back to me.

Her eyes narrowed. "Eric, it's not me you want to hurt." She pulled up her power. Channeled it as much as she could. He'd been careful not to get close to her…to hurt her from a distance. To hurt others.

He'd made a mistake.

He'd resisted her the time she found the jewelry in his safe—those horrible trophies he'd taken from his victims. But if she pushed hard enough, maybe she'd be able to get to him. Maybe.

I have to try.

"It's not me you want to hurt," she said again, "it's—"

"Don't let her talk, Adam."

Her mouth was immediately covered by stone.

"You're going to hurt her for me, Adam."

No. *No!*

"And then you're going to hurt yourself."
Eric's gaze slowly slid from Adam...back to
Sabrina. "You'll see everything that happens, my
love. And you will *never, ever* want to betray me
again."

***

He'd tied Sabrina up.

Adam stared at the ropes that bound Sabrina.
She was sitting in a chair, the thick ropes around
her body, a gag in her mouth, and her eyes were
on him.

Such beautiful eyes.

Eric had forced Adam to tie her up. He'd
gotten Adam to transform back into the body of a
man, and then the sonofabitch had ordered him
to bind Sabrina.

She'd been crying.

And he'd been fucking *helpless*.

He was a prisoner again. So was she. Now he
was just fucking standing in front of her while
those tears slid down her cheeks. Her eyes were
on his, but Sabrina didn't stare at Adam as if he
were a monster.

He wished that she would. He wished that
she would stare at him with hate or fury or
something other than that stark sorrow.

"Adam..." Eric was to the left of him.
Fucking bastard. The binding stone was cradled

in his hand. "Adam, I want you to pick up the knife that's on the table near the wall. Then I want you to come back to this exact spot. Stand in front of Sabrina with the knife."

Fuck. No! But Adam's legs started moving. He lurched toward that table. He couldn't stop the movement. He couldn't control himself no matter how hard he tried.

Sabrina couldn't talk. She couldn't try to influence Eric. She could only sit there and watch as Adam grabbed the knife. The blade was long and sharp, and Adam wondered if Eric had used that weapon on some of his victims.

His fingers fisted around the handle and then he was dragging his feet back toward Sabrina. Adam kept going, kept staring at her until he was standing right in front of her again.

"Wonderful." Eric's breath was heaving out. "Put the blade to her cheek."

Adam's heart was about to burst right out of his chest. He didn't want to hurt Sabrina. Not her. Never *her*.

She was special. So special to him. He'd wanted to free her from this bastard who got off on hurting women. He'd wanted to...

I wanted to be with her.

The knife lifted. And Adam put the blade to her cheek.

Another tear slid from Sabrina's eyes. She still didn't look at him as if he were a monster.

Why the hell not? Why wasn't she staring at him in horror?

She…

Nodded.

Her gaze had softened. He gazed into her eyes and saw the sorrow, but he saw trust, too. Fucking trust? Was the woman insane? She couldn't trust him — he had no control. He was a puppet on a string. He was —

"If I told you to slice her face, you'd do it, wouldn't you?" Eric asked.

Adam just stared at Sabrina. In her eyes, dammit, he saw everything that could have been. Everything he *could* have possessed.

I'm so sorry.

Meredith had made him stare into the eyes of his best friend, too. And then she'd given the order that they had to battle until death. They'd both been in human form. There had been so much blood.

"Answer the freaking question!" Eric yelled. Adam's head turned toward him. Spittle flew from Eric's mouth as he shouted, "Tell me…if I told you to slice her face, would you do it?"

Adam's jaws had clamped together. His body was shaking. Sweat covered him. "Y-yes…" That voice wasn't his. It wasn't *his.*

I can't hurt her. I need to turn the knife on myself. On Eric. Not her. Never her.

She's…

Everything.
My everything.
I can't hurt her.

Eric laughed. "Did you hear that, Sabrina? Your new lover wouldn't even hesitate if I told him to carve up your perfect face. He'd do it in a heartbeat."

Can't. Hurt. Her.

"Get the hell away from her," Eric ordered.

Adam stumbled back.

Eric bent and pressed a kiss to Sabrina's cheek. "I wouldn't let that happen. Not to your face. You're too perfect. See…that's why I never go after you with my knife, Sabrina. I can't kill *you.* Sure, I might bruise you a bit. I might scare you sometimes, but deep down, we both know the truth, don't we? I'd never kill you. I'd never scar you." He pointed to Adam. "*He* would. You can't trust him. He'll hurt you. He'll destroy you if given the chance."

Sabrina shook her head.

But Eric wasn't looking at her any longer. He'd turned to stare at Adam. "I think you need to learn a lesson."

Adam had learned plenty of lessons during the very long course of his life. Lessons about loss and pain. Lessons about hell and torture.

But…he hadn't learned about love.

Not until Sabrina.

Fuck.

"I want you to stab yourself, Adam." Eric's gaze swept over his chest. "Take that knife and stab yourself in the chest."

Sabrina was frantically shaking her head. Her eyes were wide—and now, finally, horrified.

Adam lifted the knife. The blade sank into his chest.

Sabrina strained against the bonds that held her. She was jerking and heaving in the chair.

"Do it again," Eric murmured.

Adam sank the knife into his chest.

Sabrina was making a desperate, keening sound behind the gag.

Eric bent next to her once more. "He matters to you."

Adam could feel the blood soaking his shirt. Eric had given him the shirt—the shirt and the jeans had been thrown at Adam after he'd transformed.

There's a lot of blood, but it's not as bad as it looks. He'd been careful with the stabs. He'd made sure not to hit anything vital. *Eric, if you wanted me incapacitated, you should have chosen your words more carefully.*

"He matters," Eric snapped again. "I can see it on your face, Sabrina."

Adam could see it, too. And…

She matters to me. More than anyone else.

The knife clattered to the floor.

Adam blinked, shocked that he'd managed to let go of that weapon.

Eric immediately spun around. "Pick it up!" he bellowed.

Adam picked up the knife. His blood dripped onto the floor. He wanted to shove that knife into Eric's throat, but Eric still held the fucking stone.

"Do you heal?" Eric demanded as he closed in on Adam. They stood toe to toe. "Or will you die as a human?"

"I only heal...if I transform." That was why his best friend had died in that bloody fight. Meredith hadn't allowed him to transform. *Because she was trying to show me that I was helpless.*

Eric's eyes narrowed. Then he looked back at Sabrina. She was still struggling against her bonds. "We're alike."

Sabrina ignored him.

"Did you hear me, love?" Eric pushed. "You and I...we're alike. I can get a man to kill himself just with one whispered order. That's the same thing you did, isn't it, Sabrina?"

She stilled. Her gaze lifted to Eric's face.

He inclined his head toward her. "You talk in your sleep."

She blinked.

"I know about the lover you had to kill. Some general or something, right? I think the name you called out in your sleep was Akin. '*Akin, I'm sorry!*' He was mad with power and you—you still feel guilty because you had to tell him to take his own life. You gave an order and he complied." His hand rubbed over his heart. "I keep trying to figure out how your magic works." Now he was muttering. "Is it in your voice? Your eyes? Or is it just something *in* you?"

She slowly shook her head.

"Doesn't matter." Eric stood right next to Sabrina's chair. "I'm going to give an order now. And another lover will take his life before your eyes. I'd thought I might keep Adam around but...I don't like the way you look at him. You weren't supposed to ever love another, Sabrina."

She doesn't love me.

Does she?

A loud bang sounded on the door. Adam had known someone was approaching the room, he'd heard the quick thud of approaching footsteps, but Eric gave a quick jump. "Not now!"

But the bang came again. "Boss! It's Raymond! He's here and says that he has to talk to you. He's got information you need about Sabrina."

Eric glanced down at Sabrina. "I have her." His fingers fluttered over her cheek. "I thought the tracker I injected into your body would keep me feeling secure enough. I'd always know where you were, but I've discovered...I really can't stand the thought of you being out there, fucking someone else. *Loving* someone else. So I'll have to keep you close from now on. Just have to make sure you don't get the chance to give *me* any orders…not like you did to that unfortunate Akin."

A fist pounded on the door again and then a voice called out, "He says he knows how her power works!"

Eric smiled. "Then I guess Raymond is still useful." He pressed a kiss to Sabrina's cheek. "I'll be right back." He turned for the door.

Adam still held the knife.

Eric paused. He smiled at Sabrina. "One more thing…while I'm gone…" Now he looked at Adam. "You fucking keep stabbing yourself. Bleed out and die right in front of her. I think that will help to teach Sabrina a lesson, too, right?"

And then he was gone.

Adam lifted the knife and the blade cut into him again.

His eyes were on Sabrina. She was frantically shaking her head. Jerking and twisting in the chair.

He lifted the knife.

I'm so sorry, love. I didn't want this –

The blade sank into him again.

CHAPTER SIXTEEN

No. *No!* Adam was bleeding. He was *dying* right in front of her eyes.

Sabrina twisted against the ropes. They were cutting deeply into her skin. She was bleeding and hurting and she didn't care. All that mattered was getting to Adam. All that mattered was helping him.

Saving him.

She rocked forward and backward in the chair.

The knife went into him again. She'd lost count of the number of times that blade had pierced his skin.

No, Adam! No!

The chair crashed to the floor. Her face hit the floor. The wooden chair legs smashed at the impact and the chair's back snapped. The ropes were suddenly loose around her. She shoved them out of her way and ripped the gag out of her mouth.

"Adam, stop!"

He was still staring at her. He'd been staring at her the whole time he'd been stabbing himself.

She ran to him and tried to yank the knife out his grip, but he wouldn't let go.

"I...can't..." Each word from him was a rasp. "Have...no...choice..."

"Yes, you do. We have a choice. Together, me and you. And I am *not* going to watch you kill yourself, do you hear me?"

"S-sorry..."

"No!" She pressed her mouth to his. She kissed him—frantic, desperate, deep. She had to break through to him. "You listen to me!" she whispered—*begged*—against his lips. "You hear me...you are more than this. You are strong and you are brave and you are the best thing that has ever happened to me. I love you, and I am not going to let you die. Do you hear me? You aren't going to die! You're going to fight!"

But he wouldn't let go of the knife.

She kissed him again. His blood soaked her clothes. "Fight!" she cried against his mouth.

His body was hard. Not as warm as it usually was. She could have sworn he was already colder, as if death were reaching out to him.

And then...

They fell.

Adam tumbled down on top of her and when they hit the floor, the knife fell from his hand, clattering away. His weight pinned Sabrina and she pushed him over, heaving him off her body. The front of his shirt was completely covered in blood. He was too pale.

Because he was dying.

She put her hands on either side of his face. "Transform."

His eyelids were closing.

"Transform, right the hell now. You become the beast, and you'll live. You transform *right now*."

His eyelids flickered. His gaze...so dark...met hers.

"Transform." She was still begging. "I need you, Adam. I need you to stay here with me."

His hand lifted. He touched her cheek. "Did you...mean it?"

"Mean what?" Dammit, he had to transform! "Love...me?"

Sabrina nodded, then she realized, no, that wasn't good enough. She wanted him to have the words. "I meant it. I love you, Adam." She leaned in closer to him. "And I am *not* letting you die."

Eric had the stone. Adam had to do whatever the possessor of that stone ordered.

Then I'll get the fucking stone. I'll make Adam transform. I'll make him live.

"Fight," she ordered him flatly. "Fight and live, do you hear me? I'm getting that stone. Then we're getting out of here." *After* she took care of Eric.

She kissed Adam once more. He was dying. She could watch him die or she could fight to save him.

Sabrina flew to her feet. She ran for the door. Eric had been arrogantly certain of his power over Adam. And he'd been so sure she couldn't get out of the ropes. So he'd made a terrible mistake.

He hadn't locked her in.

Sabrina yanked open the door and ran into the hallway.

***

He was dying. Adam watched as Sabrina raced away. She was going after the binding stone. Would she get it in time?

He felt so cold. A cold that sank into his very bones.

Chained to a fucking binding stone. Brought down by something so small — a rock. A damn rock. He hated being trapped…

Sabrina wants me to fight.

She'd kissed him. She'd said she loved him. And she'd asked him to fight.

Sabrina wants me to fight.

Sabrina…loves me.

Inside, the beast began to stir. The beast should have been silent, controlled so completely by the stone but…

Sabrina loves me.

The beast began to claw at his insides.

Adam lifted his hand, and he saw his skin begin to harden.

Transform, right the hell now. You become the beast, and you'll live. He wanted to live. For her. For them both. He wanted to live because he wanted to see what could happen next for them. He wanted to live…

Because I love her.

Eric had ordered him to bleed out and to die…right in front of Sabrina. But Sabrina wasn't there any longer. She'd left the room. If he died then…he wouldn't be bleeding out in front of her.

Adam's lips curled into the faintest of smiles. *The sonofabitch should have been more careful with his command.*

Stone began to spread over Adam's body and Sabrina's words whispered through his mind once more, giving him power, giving him strength. Giving him hope.

You are strong and you are brave and you are the best thing that has ever happened to me. I love you, and I am not going to let you die.

He wouldn't let her die, either.

CHAPTER SEVENTEEN

"Sorry I couldn't get you out of the limo, Raymond." Eric's voice carried easily as Sabrina crept toward his study. "But the fire was raging. I had to look after myself. Surely you understand that."

Soft, rough laughter came in response to Eric's words. "Self-interest...yeah, I understand that."

She had the knife gripped in her hand. The same knife that Eric had ordered Adam to turn on himself. She hadn't been about to leave that knife in the room with Adam. The guy might have started cutting himself again.

Not happening.

She inched toward the door. She'd been lucky. None of Eric's goons had appeared during her frantic rush down the hallway. Maybe Eric had sent them all away so that he could better enjoy Adam's bloodbath.

"You have news about Sabrina." Eric sounded curt now. *He wants to get back to the blood.* "That's why I agreed to see you. Tell me...and then you can walk away."

"I want money. Cash. Fifty thousand. I *think* that was the price we discussed before. Payment for intel."

Eric gave a grating laugh. "Not like I have that money here..."

"It's in your safe, asshole. I know it is. Open the safe and give me the money. Before he...he died, my brother told me how Sabrina's power works. I know how you can control her magic. Pay me, and I'll give you that information. I'll let you know how to control Sabrina."

No one controls me. Sabrina inched a bit closer. His words about controlling her were a lie, but what about the witch? Was he dead? Had he died in that limo fire? Or was Raymond lying about that, too?

"Don't mean to tell you about your business..." Eric drawled. "But you look like you may need to be in a hospital. Those burns are pretty bad."

"The fifty thousand. Give it to me...or I won't talk. You'll never know her secrets."

She was right outside of the study. Sabrina drew in a deep breath. This was it. She'd have to attack as fast as she could. Attack and get the damn stone.

She risked a quick glance around the edge of the doorway. Eric's back was turned to her. He was opening his safe. Raymond stood a few feet away from him. Her gaze swept quickly over him, noting the changes in his aura. Red — as red as the burns on his body. Anger. Fury. And...

Raymond looked up. He met her stare. He didn't say a word.

"I plan to keep Sabrina very close from now on," Eric announced. "I think that's for the best."

Sabrina slipped into the room. Raymond's aura had definitely changed. *He* had changed. She could see that now.

"She's a muse," Raymond said. He inclined his head toward Eric's back. "She inspires people...to be their very best...or even their very worst."

Eric's fingers stilled on the lock. "Are you saying she inspired me to be my worst?"

He started to look back at Raymond, but the other man was already attacking. Raymond lunged forward and slammed Eric's head into the open door of that safe. "No, you bastard, you were already fucked up."

Eric screamed and stumbled away from Raymond, and when he did, she saw that he was gripping a gun in his right hand. He looked as if he'd just pulled it from the safe.

He's holding the gun...so where is the stone?

Eric fired, shooting wildly at Raymond. The bullet hit Raymond in the stomach and he fell, groaning and twisting.

Sabrina attacked. She drove her knife into Eric's side. He yelled and then he was aiming that gun at her. Right at her heart.

Where is the stone?

"Sabrina?" Eric blinked. Blood trickled from his temple. "How did you get loose?" His gaze shot to the door behind her. "Where is the stone freak? Is he dead?"

"*You're* dead." She stood before him the same way she'd stood before another lover...one who'd taken the wrong path. "You went too far. And now the only way to stop the madness...it's to use that gun." She was pushing forth all of her power, trying desperately to get into his mind once again. She'd done it before, so long ago...*I must do it again.*

Eric's gaze seemed to turn bleary. "You...stop talking..."

"You don't want to point it at me. I'm not the one you want to shoot." She smiled and moved closer to him. The gun pressed to her chest. She had nothing to lose, so Sabrina was going all in. She was using every bit of her power, every single drop of her magic. If she didn't reach him, if he proved himself immune again, then she'd be dead. *But I have to try...for Adam. I have to fight.* "You want to end the pain, don't you? The pain is inside you. To end the pain, you have to fire the bullet. Fire the bullet at the one person you know is responsible for all of this..."

He was sweating. The knife was still stuck in his side. She didn't think her magic was working on him. Again. He'd gotten too strong, somehow, and —

Where is the damn stone?

"What are you…doing to me?" The gun was sliding away from Sabrina's chest.

It's working! Her whole body was shaking from the strain, but her power seemed to be getting to him. "I'm taking away your control," she whispered back. "How does it feel, you sonofabitch?"

He stared at her in dawning horror, and then the gun was pointing at his own chest. She thought he'd fire. That he'd squeeze that trigger, that —

"No!" Eric bellowed. He lunged away from her and hit some button on the side of his desk. "Guards…coming now…stop you." He was holding the gun, it was trembling in his grasp.

He'd resisted her power, again. This was what she'd feared. Somehow, he'd grown immune to her. He could fight her when she tried to influence him.

I won't give up. "You *will* end the pain," Sabrina said, moving closer to him. "You will…"

But he shook his head.

A roar echoed through the cavernous house. Sabrina's horrified gaze turned to the door. She could hear the rush of footsteps pounding toward them. Eric's guards. He'd sounded the alarm and they were racing to the study but…

Someone else was coming, too.

She recognized that roar.

Gargoyle.

Her gaze flew back to Eric. His eyes had widened. His left hand started pawing at his pockets…

He's keeping the stone on him. Sabrina threw her body against his. They fell back, rolling against the edge of the desk.

And the gun went off.

***

Men with guns were running toward Adam.

They lifted their weapons. They fired. Fools. Their bullets couldn't hurt stone. The men should have known better. Gunshots seemed to thunder all around him.

He grabbed the two closest men. Ripped away their weapons. Used his claws to slash against the weak human bodies.

Some of the guards gave up right then. They dropped their weapons and fled.

Others didn't. So Adam attacked them. He threw one against the nearest wall — the man went *through* that wall. Adam knocked out two more and then…

"Stop, gargoyle!" Eric's voice.

Adam looked at the men around him. Eric's attack force. Only they weren't attacking any longer. They were on the ground, limp. They were finished. So he followed the sound of Eric's voice. He entered that study. And he was sure that his world stopped.

Eric stood beside the desk, a gun in one hand and the fucking binding stone in the other. And at his feet...Sabrina lay bleeding. Her face was pale, her eyes huge, and for once — that brilliant blue color seemed muted.

"Kill the human." Eric pointed to another man in the room. A man Adam hadn't even noticed at first glance because he'd been so focused on Sabrina.

Sabrina is hurt. Sabrina is...dying?

Could a muse die from a bullet wound? It sure looked as if she could.

"Kill Raymond!" Eric shouted. He dropped his gun and reached for Sabrina. His hand went to the wound on her chest. He pressed down.

Adam glanced at Raymond. The guy was dragging himself to his feet. Swaying.

Adam looked back at Eric. The bastard was still holding the stone, but he was obviously freaking out over Sabrina. Whispering to her, telling her how sorry he was, that she was going to be all right, that—

"Nothing will be all right." Sabrina's weak voice. But her hand suddenly flew out and she wrenched the stone out of Eric's grip. She threw that stone, sending it crashing against the wall. A chunk of it broke loose on impact. "Never again…it's not going to be all right…not…for you…"

Adam charged forward. He grabbed Eric, locking one hand around the human's neck and lifting him high into the air.

"R-Raymond!" Eric croaked. "Get…stone!"

He was trying to bark orders to the same man he'd just wanted to kill? No way would Raymond be dumb enough to do what the jerk wanted. No—

Adam glanced to the left. Raymond had grabbed the stone. He held it tight.

"S-smash it…" Sabrina cried, her voice breaking. "Be strong…be more than…than Eric…Smash—"

Raymond slammed that rock against the wall. This time, one piece didn't just break off. The entire thing shattered into a dozen pieces and as it broke, the stone that had been covering Adam's body shattered, too. The stone fell away from his skin. For the first time, he didn't have to fight his way to freedom. He just…became a man again.

Eric was staring at him with shock in his eyes. "No, hell, no!"

Grimly, Adam smiled back at him. "Yes, hell, yes." Then he drove his fist into Eric's face. Again and again. Bones smashed beneath his blows. Blood covered Eric's face. The guy tried to fight back, but he was useless.

Eric fell.

Adam grabbed the gun from the floor, ready to finish the guy…

"Adam?" Sabrina's voice. Too weak. Too soft.

With the gun in his hand, he whirled toward her.

She was smiling at him. "You…you're a man now…not a monster."

She'd become even paler. He bent next to her, and he saw just why Eric had been frantic over her. Her wound—it was bad.

"Your heart?" Eric whispered.

She pulled the gun from his hand. He wasn't even sure where she'd gotten that energy. "Don't…start your life…being on the wrong side…" She licked her lips. Was that blood trickling from her mouth? "It can be…good. You can be."

Behind him, Eric groaned. The bastard was still alive.

Adam put his hand to Sabrina's chest, trying to stop the blood flow. "Tell me how to fix you."

"I don't…think you can…"

No, no, she wasn't dying. He scooped her into his arms and leapt to his feet. He'd fly her to Luke. He'd—

I can't fly. I don't have wings anymore.

"Luke!" Adam bellowed as he tilted back his head and stared up at the gaping hole in the ceiling. "Luke, dammit, I need you!" Sabrina was one of the dark paranormals...that meant the Lord of the Dark could help her. He held dominion over her, so he could surely find a way to heal her, right? Or, shit, maybe she just could be sewn up at a hospital. That was all she needed. A hospital and—

"I do...love you." Sabrina's lashes were closing.

"And I love you and you're going to be fine. Do you hear me? *Fine.* Luke will appear. He'll heal you, and everything will be fine. You are—"

A gunshot blasted. The blast was so close—it had come from the gun that Sabrina still held. Even so weak, she'd fired.

Adam looked over his shoulder.

A bullet had blasted into Eric's chest. The man was on his feet, as if he'd been caught mid-attack. Eric blinked in shock. Then he looked down at his chest. "S-Sabrina?"

She was smiling as he died.

Raymond was staggering around—Adam figured that guy was going to make it. Sabrina was his priority. She was what mattered. She was—

The room seemed to shake. Wind whipped around him—wind, in a closed room. *Closed except for the roof.* He looked up once more, and sure the hell enough, they had new company.

Powerful wings beat against the air — and then Leo was slamming his feet down onto the floor as he landed near Adam.

"You're not the one I need," Adam snarled at him. "Luke has to get his ass here right now. Sabrina is hurt!"

Leo blinked. "How can you always tell us apart so easily? We're twins, after all."

Adam growled. "*Get Luke.*"

Leo's gaze swept over him, then over Sabrina, and finally…over Eric's still form.

Raymond ran from the room. Or…staggered out.

Then Leo's gaze returned to Adam. "Something's different."

He wanted to rip that bastard apart. "*Sabrina is dying! She needs help! Get Luke here!*"

More wind. Only this time, the whole house seemed to shake — and a new hole was made in the roof as Luke came crashing down to join them.

Luke stood there for a moment, his wings spread behind him and his head bowed. "I get so tired…" he muttered, "of everyone needing me for something. A vacation would be nice. A little alone time with Mina."

"Fuck your vacation!" Fear and anger cracked in Adam's voice. "Sabrina is dying!"

Luke's head snapped up. "She can't die."

"No, no, she fucking *can't*! I need her! I love her and I can't let her go! I can't—"

Luke crossed to them. He put his hand on Sabrina's cheek. "No, you aren't listening to me. I mean…Sabrina literally *can't* die. I don't know what she told you, but according to Fate…"

Behind him, Leo swore.

"Sabrina will always walk this earth. A muse has to be here. Good or bad, she's here. It's the way for certain paranormals. Nature won't let the most powerful die out completely. She's the last muse standing…so that means she *always* stands."

Hope stirred but when Adam looked at Sabrina's face, she was still far too pale. *And still.* She also damn well wasn't standing. Instead…"She's bleeding out."

Luke's hand lingered on her cheek. "It takes a while for her to heal. But she *will* heal. You think this is the worst wound she's had?" He gave a rough laugh. "I've seen her nearly decapitated, seen her with a dozen broken bones, I've seen—"

"Who the fuck hurt her?" Adam demanded. He'd find the bastards. He'd rip them apart.

Luke's gaze slowly rose to meet his. "Something is different here." And he was…worried? His gaze flew around the room, as if he was looking for something. Then he moved back and seriously started to search.

"Who hurt her?" Adam bellowed.

"Humans, mostly." It was Leo who answered. Luke was ripping apart the room — searching for who the hell knew what — but Leo was just standing there, watching Adam. "Some paranormals. When you live as long as she has, you do make enemies. A lot of them. Sometimes, those enemies were even once your friends." He pointed to Eric's still body. "Or your lovers." His lips thinned. "Sabrina had vowed to me that she'd never kill another human, not after Akin. Guess that proves you just can't trust — "

"Don't say another fucking word." Adam's voice was low and lethal, but the hands that held Sabrina were gentle.

At his tone, both Luke and Leo seemed to focus completely on him.

"I don't care what you *think*, Leo," Adam continued as the rage and fear grew in him. "Sabrina is good. She only killed that bastard because he was a monster. Have you seen what he did to his victims?"

"Sabrina inspired — "

"Evil lives in some people," Adam rasped, cutting through Leo's words. "No matter how hard they try to fight it…it's there. She didn't make that jerk evil. He already was." His gaze fell to her. "And now she's hurt and you two aren't doing a damn thing for her. She's *bleeding* and it won't stop. I need it to stop. I need *her*." He whirled from them, heading for the door. They weren't going to help him. He'd get Sabrina to a hospital. A real doctor who could stitch her up and—

Luke was in his path. As fast as a blink, the guy was there. "If you lift up her shirt you'll see that the wound has already closed."

Adam's heart stopped. Was it true?

"Put her on the desk. See for yourself." Luke's voice was surprisingly calm, but his hands were fisted at his sides.

Adam hesitated.

"See for yourself," Luke said again. Only his words sounded more like an order this time.

Adam whirled and rushed for the desk. Leo shoved everything off the surface, and then Adam carefully, tenderly, put Sabrina on top of the wood. He squared his shoulders and reached for the hem of her blood-soaked shirt. Her skin was stained red from blood but…"The wound is closed."

"Like I said…" Luke murmured. "Sabrina can't die, but you're a whole other fucking matter."

What? Adam's head whipped up as he glared at the guy. Luke was supposed to be on *his* side. Luke had been the one who sent him to Sabrina in the first place.

"This shit did not go down the way I planned." Luke opened his hand. Nestled in his palm, Adam could see broken shards from the binding stone that had made Adam a prisoner for so long. "I'm sorry about that."

Sorry that Adam was free? Screw that shit. Screw—

"Adam?" Sabrina's soft voice. Calling to him. Making him actually able to *breathe* again as the heavy fear finally left his chest. He looked at her face and saw the faint color returning to her cheeks.

His heart thudded in his chest. She was all right. "Sabrina." His head bent over hers and he pressed a soft kiss to her lips.

She kissed him back.

I am never letting her go.

Her hand rose and stroked against his cheek. "Sorry," she whispered against his mouth. "I think I passed out for a minute there."

More than a minute. And Adam would never forget the terror he'd felt.

Leo cleared his throat. "This is tender and touching and all...but I really must insist on some private time to discuss a very important matter with Sabrina. Right now."

What?

Adam's head whipped up and he glared at the Lord of the Light. "Screw. Off."

Leo winced. "I did expect that response but...sorry, human, you don't hold any power here."

Human.

"Human?" Sabrina's voice. She pushed up to a sitting position on the desk and a broad smile spread across her face. "The stone shattered, didn't it? I remember…" Then she was throwing her arms around Adam's neck and holding him tightly. "You're free!"

He hadn't even wrapped his mind around that part, not yet. He'd been so consumed by her. *But she's safe. She's alive. And she's acting as if she weren't as still as the dead moments before.*

"I am *insisting* on that private talk, Sabrina." Leo's voice was flat. "And it has to happen *now.*"

She kept hugging Adam. "Leo, you heard Adam…Screw off."

But in the next instant, Adam was ripped away from Sabrina. Leo's hold was hard, unbreakable, and in a flash, he'd tossed Adam out of that study. Then the bastard barred the doors.

Adam found himself standing in the hallway, still nude because of his change. A nudity he'd only just noticed. His hands pounded against the wooden door. "Open the door!" Fear was back, clawing at him because he knew something bad was happening inside that room. "Don't even think of touching Sabrina!"

He didn't have supernatural strength. Not any longer. His hands began to bruise, then to bleed, as he pounded on the door. *"Don't touch her!"* Then he started ramming his shoulder into the wood.

CHAPTER EIGHTEEN

"Someone sure is fierce, even as a human." Luke's voice was low, barely carrying to Sabrina's ears.

She jumped off the desk and would have fallen, but Leo grabbed her arms. He steadied her. "Easy."

She shoved his hands away. "Never liked easy. Never wanted it." *Not my style.* "Say your piece then get out of my way. I *am* going to Adam. I am going to be with him and—"

What could have been sympathy—if it were any other person—flashed on Leo's face. "He's dead, Sabrina."

Her heart stopped. "What?" No, no, Adam wasn't dead. She could hear him. He was pounding on the door. He was about to break the door down. He was—

Luke lifted his palm. The shattered pieces of stone were in his hand. "There was a…a rather unfortunate part of the spell that I don't think you knew about. When the stone shattered, your knight became human again."

Right. That wasn't unfortunate. That was wonderful. That was —

"A human can't live as long as he has." Leo's voice was a soft murmur. His lips curled down. "Time is about to catch up with him."

The words weren't quite registering. Maybe it was because a dull ringing was filling her ears. Or because her cheeks suddenly felt ice cold. Or because her knees were giving way. Or —

Leo held her up. "I'm sorry." He truly sounded it. *Leo.* Sorry for something. The world must truly be ending.

Maybe not the whole word. *Just my world.* "He's...dying?" She stared at Leo, then at Luke, hoping one of them would offer a denial.

"Adam has got less than an hour," Luke said. Those words weren't a denial. They were hell.

Her lips were trembling. "No."

Luke swallowed. "I can't do anything. I'd thought...maybe the spell could be broken another way...that you could reach the man inside the stone..."

She shook her head. "He can't die."

Leo's fingers wiped over her cheek. Was he brushing away her tears? "He's already dead. He just doesn't know it."

Her heart was being ripped out. Clawed out. "Help him. Please. If he's human now, then he's under your command, right? *Help him.*"

But Leo shook his head. "I can't stop time. That's not a power even I have."

Her hands flew out so that she was the one holding so desperately to him. "You can make him into something else. You can change him. Make him a vampire—"

"That's not my realm." Leo's voice was still soft. His head jerked toward Luke. "You know the dark ones are his." A pause. "And is that really what you think your Adam would want? After centuries of being one monster...would he just want to become another?"

"I don't care!" Those words burst from her. Selfish. Cold. *True.* "I need him to stay with me. Don't you see that? I want him in this world. I *need* him here! He has to stay with me. He has to—"

"What do you think would happen if he did stay?" Leo's face was now devoid of expression. "A human...with someone like you. Your last human lover is dead in the corner. You think your power wouldn't sink into Adam, too? Even if he became a vampire...he'd be susceptible to you. Vampires *are* better than other paranormals at resisting you, but, in the end, he wouldn't be able to hold out forever. A vampire inspired by a muse. Think of the people he'd kill. He'd probably go on a bloodlust filled rampage."

"Y-you don't know that."

"Didn't it happen before?"

Her eyes squeezed shut.

"The 1300s, I believe. Another lover who fell beneath your power. If I remember right, Luke had to cover that scene by saying a plague had killed everyone. A plague, and not the vampire who became maddened by you."

Luke didn't speak. Neither did Sabrina.

"Adam has an hour left," Leo added. "Maybe...maybe you should just spend that time with him. And then let him go."

Her eyes flew open. "You don't know what it means to love someone."

He didn't deny her words.

"You don't know what it feels like when they are *in* your heart. When you think something bad is happening to them and the fear is so thick that you can't breathe."

"Sabrina..." Leo sighed her name. "You *are* the something bad that happened to Adam."

Her heart was as shattered as the binding stone.

The door shook. And cracked. She saw the long spider-web like line that appeared in the wood. Adam had almost broken through to reach her.

Her nails dug into Leo's chest. "I'll give you Fate's location."

His jaw hardened. "We've already made a deal—"

"I will take you to her, I swear I will. But you have to help me. You let him die, and I don't care about any deal we've made...I will never tell you where she is."

"Sabrina..."

She leaned up on her tip toes. Her mouth brushed against his ear as she said, "You've never been in love, so you don't know how much I'm hurting right now. But you came close, didn't you? You came close with Fate. You've been looking for her all these years. I'll take you to her, but you have to find a way for him to live. Just— let him live. That's all I'm asking."

All. Everything.

The door broke open. *"Sabrina!"* Adam roared.

She rushed away from Leo and grabbed Adam's hand. Warm and strong. And alive. She threw her body against his chest and held him, as tightly as she could. "Let's get out of here." She wanted to be far away. She wanted them to be alone. To be safe.

"Sabrina..." Leo's voice.

She glanced at him.

He waved his hand vaguely at Adam and she saw clothes appear on Adam's body. Jeans. T-shirt. Shoes. But Leo's face remained grave. "The clock is ticking. An hour..."

Her chin notched up. "That's right. You have an hour...or you'll never see Fate. She can hide forever, and you know that."

Then she and Adam were running out of that blood-soaked room. Out of that house. They found an SUV in the driveway. Adam hot-wired it and he got them the hell out of there.

The clock is ticking...

***

Leo glanced at the dead man in the corner. The scent of blood and death were strong in the room.

"Well, that didn't go according to plan." Luke rolled back his shoulders in a weary shrug. "Guess somethings just don't work out." His wings spread behind him.

The guy was going to fly away. To just let things end...

Leo's hand flew out and locked around Luke's wrist. "Just what *was* the plan? How did you think this was going to work?" Each word was bitten off.

Luke glanced down at Leo's hand. "I thought a muse was going to wind up owing me. A muse's inspiration can be a powerful thing. So powerful that it can even tame a beast."

Leo frowned at him.

"Destroying the binding stone wasn't the only way to break the spell. That's the sad part of all this. Sabrina's power could have done it. I told her I wanted inspiration in return for the protection I was giving her…but I never said who would be getting that inspiration."

Leo's brows furrowed. "Stop with the damn riddles. You know I hate them."

"Her power is incredibly strong. I thought…*she* could do it. She could break through the stone and reach the man inside. I'd hoped her power would push him over the edge so that he could resist control from anyone who held his fucking stone." Luke still held the pieces of the binding stone. But his hand fisted and when he opened his fingers again, dust drifted to the floor.

"Why didn't you tell me this before?"

Luke's mouth twisted into a mirthless smile. "Because you would have told her. And things would have gotten screwed to hell."

"Like they *aren't* screwed to hell now?"

Luke's eyes were narrowed. "You couldn't tell her. *I* couldn't tell her, not if she was going to fall for the guy. If I'd told her I was just using her to free a gargoyle, she never would have fallen in love with him. And a muse's power…it's always stronger when her heart is involved."

He couldn't believe this. "You were using her, all along?"

Luke stared into his eyes. "I use everyone. I'm the bad one, remember?"

No one ever let them forget.

"What are we supposed to do now?" Leo demanded.

Luke frowned. Then he extracted his wrist from Leo's grip. "You speak as if we're partners in this mess."

"Do we always have to be enemies?"

"Since according to…Fate…one of us will kill the other eventually, yes, I think we do."

"Fate could be wrong."

Luke smiled at him. "Is that why you want to find her so badly? Because you want her to be wrong?" His head cocked to the side. "Or do you actually think you can make her change things for you? That's what you tried before, isn't it? You seduced Fate, and then you betrayed her." He laughed. "After all of that, do you seriously think she'd ever want to do anything to help you?"

"I need to help Adam Cross."

"I *was* going to help him. But then you got your ass involved and you messed it all up."

What? "I didn't—"

"You want to save him? You want to stop Sabrina from going on what I am sure will be the worst vengeance seeking episode of her life? Then I'd suggest you get yourself some witches.

Maybe they can turn him back before it's too late." Luke's wings spread once more.

"Turn him back…" Leo smiled. "That's brilliant!"

"No, it's not. It's condemning a human to hell all over again." Luke stared at him. "And here I thought you were the one who was supposed to protect the humans."

Leo didn't speak.

"Good and bad. So fucking relative." Luke flew away.

Leo stood there a moment longer, then he walked from the study. In the hallway, guards were on the floor, some slowly waking, some still out cold. He strode right past them. He went outside and—

"*Help!*"

His head turned to the left. The cry had come from just beyond the bushes near the sidewalk. Frowning, he moved closer. Then he saw a human he recognized. He'd been keeping tabs on those close to Eric. "You're Raymond Bannon."

The man had his hand over his bloody wound.

Leo smiled at him. "And your step-brother is a witch." He grabbed the human, hefting him up high. "Tell me…did the witch die in that limo fire?"

Raymond shook his head. "No."

"That's absolutely fantastic…"

CHAPTER NINETEEN

"Stop the car." Sabrina's voice was shaking. She couldn't help that because she was absolutely terrified. At her words, Adam slammed on the brakes. They were near the beach. She could hear the waves crashing.

How much time has passed? She shoved open her door and jumped outside.

"Sabrina!" Adam exited the vehicle, rushing after her. But she hadn't been running away. She wouldn't run away from him. Not ever.

They stood on the edge of the road. The beach was deserted. She swallowed and took his hand. "Come with me."

Because she needed to be with him. If he was leaving her...if time was catching up to them...

Their fingers twined together. They walked onto the beach, heading down to the edge of the shore where the waves washed against the sand. They stood there a moment, and then she turned toward him. The wind caught her hair, blowing it around her face.

She stared up at him. "I love you."

The faint lines on his face…they were just the slightest bit deeper. A touch of gray had appeared in his hair.

She smiled at him. "Do you know…I've lived a really, really long time, and I've never felt about anyone the way I feel about you?"

His head bent. His lips feathered over hers. "I can be just a man with you now."

Just a man. "You'll always be more than that." She looked at him then, truly looked at him. "The shadow is gone." The heavy shadow that had hung over him, and now she could see his true aura. So bright and clear. A dozen shades of gold. A protector, straight to his soul. With just the right inspiration, he would have done great things…

He is something great.

"I love you, Sabrina." He stared at her with eyes that didn't seem as dark. "I want to spend the rest of my life with you."

Those words hurt so much. Because if Leo didn't pull through for her…*you will.* "What if your life could be longer?" Sabrina asked. A lock of her hair blew over her cheek. "What if you could live forever, with me? Would you want that?"

A furrow appeared between his brows. "Humans don't live forever."

No, they didn't. "What if you could be more?" And Leo's damn voice was echoing in her head. Telling her that Adam didn't want to be a monster. But she had to know. She needed to hear his choice. "What if you could spend an eternity with me? Only...only maybe there's a price. Maybe you have to—have to do some things that you don't want to do..."

He kissed her again.

"Adam..." She pulled away. "I need your answer. What if you could spend eternity with me and maybe...maybe you just had to—to pay a price for that life?"

"I would pay any price for you."

Relief had her heart stuttering. He'd do it. He'd...

Become a monster again, for me.

The smile on her lips froze.

Adam frowned. His hand rose and pressed to his chest. "Something is...wrong."

"Adam?"

"Hurts." His eyes squeezed shut. "Beating...too fast..." He fell.

"Adam!" She sank to her knees beside him, desperately reaching out to him.

The wind blew harder against her.

His eyes opened. "Squeezing...so tight...I can't..."

"*Leo!*" Sabrina screamed. "*Leo, help me!*"

And Leo appeared. He seemed to shoot out of the very sky itself. Only he wasn't alone. He had a half-burned man with him—a bandaged up man. A guy who was staring in shock at Sabrina. *I know him — the witch!*

"Here's the thing..." Leo drawled as he dropped the man onto the sand. "Kevin is the only witch I could find on such short notice."

Her lips parted in surprise.

"I had to drag him out of a hospital. Turns out, he's only living because your Adam saved his ass. So I figure...that means you owe the guy, right, Kevin?"

Kevin gave a weak nod. "But I don't...know how to do the spell. I...I told you..."

Adam's breath rasped out. "What's...happening...?"

She made herself smile at him. "It's...okay."

"No, it's...not." A pause. "I'm...dying?"

She licked her lips. "We can fix you. We have a witch." She made her smile flash again.

"The witch will turn him back into a gargoyle," Leo announced, sounding pleased with himself. "Adam will become immortal again. Time won't be able to catch up with him and —"

"No," Adam gasped.

No? Sabrina shook her head. "Adam?"

"Won't...be prisoner..."

"No, no, you won't be. I'll make sure of it." She kissed his lips. They were already cold. "You'll be with me. We'll be together. We'll never let anyone control you again. We'll —"

"I don't know how to work the binding spell!" Kevin cried. "Listen, man, I keep trying to tell you. This is over my head. I can...I can maybe make him into a zombie or um, I can—"

"You can get the hell out of our way." Another voice joined the mix. Luke's booming voice. She wasn't particularly surprised that he'd joined their group on the beach. "This isn't amateur hour," Luke snapped. "Let a professional work."

A professional? Sabrina pulled her gaze from Adam's face...and she saw that Luke had come to the beach with his own witch. A tall, beautiful, African American woman stood at his side. And the woman's gaze was on Sabrina.

"Cordelia?" Sabrina barely breathed the witch's name. The witch...her best friend. The most powerful witch that Sabrina had ever known. Relief had her shaking. If anyone could help...if any witch could cast that spell..."*Cordelia, I need you to give Adam more time.*"

Cordelia approached Sabrina slowly, and magic seemed to crackle in the very air around the witch.

"Oh, sweet hell," Kevin muttered. He immediately backed away. "Out of my league...out of my..."

Cordelia put her hand on Sabrina's shoulder. "I can't make him into a stone beast again. Even I'm not on Meredith's level."

"H-he can be a vampire. Or a—"

"Or he can be a man."

Sabrina's breath caught.

"I can let him just be a man, Sabrina." Cordelia's voice was soft as the waves crashed. "He can be human, with the right magic. He can be a man who walks away from this beach and he leads a normal life."

"Yes!" She could feel hope exploding within her. "Let him—"

"A human life, Sabrina. One that will eventually end."

I can solve that problem. Give me enough time. I'll find a way. He just has to keep living now.

"You're a very strong being, Sabrina." Cordelia stared at her with eyes that gleamed with power. "Others have tried to steal your magic, but they weren't successful. Because that isn't the way the transfer works, is it? No one can *take* your magic. You have to give it to them."

"Y-yes…" Just as she gave inspiration. She had to choose. It could never be taken from her.

"You have nothing but time," Cordelia continued. "After your two sisters died, Fate was kind to you. She granted you endless time on this earth."

No, she's not kind. People always get that wrong. Not kind or cruel. She just…is.

Cordelia squeezed her shoulder. "You can give some of your time to Adam. You can give him your power. I'll help you channel it...and it will buy him life."

Adam was gasping beside her. *Dying* beside her. "He can have it all," Sabrina said without any hesitation. "Give him everything he needs." If he would survive, if he would live...

Cordelia opened her left hand, offering her palm to Sabrina.

Sabrina's fingers curled around hers.

"Now lock your other hand around his," Cordelia ordered her.

Sabrina wrapped her hand around Adam's. "Please hurry," she begged her friend. "Hurry."

Luke came forward then. He took Cordelia's free hand in his. She nodded and began to chant.

The waves crashed. The wind blew.

"There's a price," Luke said.

Sabrina was staring at Adam. "I don't care." If he would just live...she'd pay any price...

"That's what they always say," Luke told her quietly. "But then it's time to collect and all you hear is bitching and moaning..."

"Any price," Sabrina vowed. Adam was dying right before her eyes. Just...withering away. "Please..."

Leo put his hand on her back. Sabrina felt raw power rip through her. Leo's power? Luke's? Cordelia's magic?

It hit her all at once, like an electric shock and she screamed. She screamed and screamed because the terrible power was burning right through her…no, no, it was being *drained* from her.

It's not their power. It's mine.

Her power was being drained…and when she looked at her and Adam's joined hands, she could see the sparks — the power — dancing in the air as it pumped into him.

She tried to smile. He was going to be all right.

But then the whole world around her went black.

***

Sabrina's eyes flashed open. "Adam!" Sabrina screamed his name even as she lurched into a sitting position. She was on the beach. The waves were soaking her legs and Adam…

"Sorry, Sabrina." Luke stood a short distance away. "But Leo took him away."

Sabrina shook her head. "What?" Then she scrambled to her feet. "No, no, that wasn't part of the deal—"

"Bitching and moaning," Luke muttered as he cast a quick gaze toward Cordelia. "Didn't I tell you that would happen?"

Sabrina lifted her hand and shoved her palm against her chest. Her heart *hurt*. "Is Adam alive?"

Cordelia crept toward her with slumped shoulders. Her friend appeared tired. *Way beyond tired – more like exhausted.* "Very much alive. And…very much human. A normal human. Not one who is about to be ripped apart by time."

Relief burst inside of Sabrina and she grabbed Cordelia, holding her friend tight. "Thank you!" She squeezed the witch even tighter. "You are the best friend ever!"

Cordelia was tense in her embrace. Not a good sign.

Sabrina slowly let her go. "Cordelia?"

Cordelia glanced away, turning her stare to the waves. "He's human now. Totally human. And to be totally human…he had to lose the life he'd had."

"Okay. I hate riddles. Mostly because I suck at them." She whirled away and started to scamper up the beach. "I'll go find Adam and I'll make this all—"

"He doesn't know you." Cordelia's soft voice seemed incredibly, terribly loud.

Sabrina froze.

"He doesn't remember being a gargoyle. He doesn't remember being a knight. Because none of that could exist in a *normal* human's life. That was what your magic gave him, you see. Life…years."

Sabrina turned back slowly. "I don't understand." But now her gaze slid to a watchful Luke. "Tell me what's happening."

He crossed his arms over his chest. "It's for the best. You have a very bad track record with humans. You wouldn't want to…inspire him…but you would. He'd become obsessed. It wouldn't be love, not anymore. He'd be lost to the madness that is…you."

Her spine straightened. "I'm not madness."

Luke just lifted a brow.

"I'm not madness!"

"No, you're inspiration. Only madness and that genius inspiration often get twisted, don't they?"

"I—"

Luke dropped his hands and walked toward her. "Do you want that for him? Do you want him to get lost in you? Or do you want Adam—a man who has suffered and been a prisoner for centuries—do you want him to finally have a normal life?"

A life that doesn't include me. "He…he doesn't remember anything about me?"

Luke shook his head. "And now you get to decide…will it stay that way? Will you let him go? Let him live…or will you go after him? Go find the man you loved and make him remember you? Because I'm sure it would be so easy for you. You'd walk up to him, touch him…and bam, just like every other human, he'd fall under your spell. Be it for good or bad."

The wind was cold against her. "This is the price, isn't it?"

Luke just looked at her.

She wanted to punch him. She wanted to scream. She wanted *Adam.* "He gets to live, but he has to live without me. That's the price. Only you didn't tell me before I agreed—"

"You said you'd pay any price," Luke cut in. "You promised. Or were you lying?"

She looked at the water. She could feel Cordelia's gaze on her. The waves were rough. A storm was coming.

The storm is already here.

"I wasn't lying," she whispered.

"No, I didn't think so." His voice was quiet. Luke cleared his throat. "And, by the way, I think this concludes the original deal that we made, too."

She couldn't look away from the waves.

"You wanted protection. I provided it. Eric has been taken care of…"

"*I'm* the one who shot him. I don't see how you get to take credit for that."

The sky darkened. "I set a chain of events into motion." His voice had deepened. "Without me, you wouldn't be where you are now."

"Stuck on a beach, with my lover long gone? Right, I wouldn't be. Thanks so much."

He growled.

Her hands fisted. "Don't worry, Luke. I keep my deals. You want inspiration. You got it. Just tell me where and when."

He moved to stand in front of her, forcing Sabrina to meet his stare. She was so cold on the inside. Icy. Her heart seemed to be freezing in her chest.

Not freezing. I think it's turning to stone.

"I will…" Luke smiled. She didn't like his smile. "When the time comes."

Then he turned away and began to walk down the beach. She didn't speak, not until he was long gone. "I think I may hate him."

Cordelia's hand curled around her shoulder. "Are you okay?"

"Adam's alive."

"Yes."

The pain in her chest was growing worse. Spreading…"If he's alive, then I'm okay." *Lie.* Her heart was changing. She could feel it.

I have to think. I have to figure this out.

"I'm sorry…" Cordelia's voice was halting. "I wish I could have done more for you."

She looked at her friend. "You saved Adam. You did *everything*."

***

Leo found her that night. Maybe finding her wasn't exactly hard since Sabrina had just gone back to the penthouse she'd shared with Adam. She'd memorized the security codes so getting inside wasn't hard. And she'd even found a keycard for the elevator waiting for her in the lobby.

Luke's doing? Probably. Bastard.

Being in that penthouse...it made her feel close to Adam.

And it was a safe place, right? A paranormal haven...

She wasn't particularly surprised when Leo appeared on the balcony. No, not surprised. She'd been waiting for him.

"Fate is in Nevada," she said curtly. "The last time I spoke to her, she was working in a bar on the outskirts of Vegas."

There. She'd done it. Kept her deal with him...and betrayed the last family member that she had.

If anything, his face turned harder as he ordered, "Tell me the name of the bar."

She stepped toward him. The moon was overhead, shining down on them. "Tell me where Adam is."

"Why? So you can go and work your magic on him? He's human...he'd be putty in your hands." He paused. "Is that what you want? A mindless lover? Or...with Adam's past...maybe you'll get another guy like Eric. Someone who steps into the darkness because you get beneath his skin and you don't—"

"Maybe Eric was just bad to begin with. Maybe I reached out to him too late. Maybe you need to stop blaming shit on me. *Maybe* you need to own the fact that you screw up, too." She lifted one hand and put it on his chest. She stared into his eyes and she called up every bit of power that she had. "Maybe you need to finally see yourself for who you really are."

He blinked. His gaze…shuttered.

That's right, Leo. You're not made of stone. I can get to you. I can and I will.

"Your aura has always been so interesting to me. You and Luke. To be twins, your auras are so completely different." She paused. "Want to know what I see?"

His fingers curled around her wrist. "What game are you playing?"

"Where. Is. Adam?"

"Right here in Miami," he gritted out. "I gave him back his nightclub. I gave him a whole life…he thinks he's Adam Cross, a twenty-nine year old entrepreneur. He doesn't have a care in the freaking world. He's normal, and he will be *happy*."

She sucked in a breath. "You'll find Fate in a bar called Resurrection. She's living as a waitress, as a human. She thinks you won't ever find her.

She's living a normal life, and I think she is as happy as it is possible for her to be."

They glared at each other.

"Do we leave them to those lives?" Sabrina asked him. "Or do we fucking fight for what we want?"

His face was as hard...as stone.

"We used to be more alike than we were different," Sabrina whispered. "Remember?"

"Sabrina..."

"Why don't you reach your full potential again?" she pressed softly.

"You...aren't going to get beneath my skin."

Oh, Leo, I'm already there.

"Is there another way I can get Adam back?" Sabrina asked him carefully. "Something you didn't share with me before...because I do know how you like your secrets." She knew better than most.

He licked his lips. "Luke said...he said you could have broken the spell without smashing the stone. That he was hoping you'd be able to reach Adam. He'd thought that you would *make* Adam break free on his own. But...that didn't happen." Now his eyes had gone hard. Cold. "If he'd done that, things would have been different."

Very different.

"But I guess you can't change Fate," he murmured.

Her eyes turned to slits. "Don't bet on it. I'm not giving up on Adam. I will *fight* for him."

"You mean you'll destroy him. Another miscalculation on my brother's part. Luke didn't realize…you weren't ready to pay any price after all. At your core, you are as bad as the other dark paranormals."

Her teeth clenched.

"You won't sacrifice your own happiness. See…Adam? He's not grieving. He's not hurting. He's happy. You're the one in hell, and you're going to drag a human down with you." Leo backed away from her. "And for the record, your magic does *not* work on me." He leapt off the balcony.

She didn't move. "Don't be too sure of that…"

CHAPTER TWENTY

Three weeks, two days…and way too many hours later…

"Holy hell. She should *not* be here," the bartender muttered. "This is bad. Very, very bad."

From where Adam Cross was standing…things looked very, very good. "Who is she?" Adam asked as he stared across the crowded club. *His* club. His place. He'd busted ass to make this grand opening happen, and from the size of that packed crowd…he'd succeeded.

But his gaze was drawn helplessly to the beautiful blonde. The woman who wore a tight, black dress like a second skin. The woman who slipped through the crowd without touching another person but who still seemed to draw every gaze in the room.

She'd certainly drawn his attention He'd been standing near the bar when she'd walked into the club. As crazy as it seemed, her scent had hit him first.

Sweet. Light.

Seductive.

From all the way across the room, he'd smelled her. *Impossible.*

She hadn't looked up at him. She hadn't even glanced his way. The woman moved around the club as if she'd been there hundreds of times before.

This is the first time I've ever opened it to the public.

She paused near the big mirror that he'd hung at the bottom of his stairs. For just a moment, her back pressed to that mirror as she turned to look at the crowd. And her eyes—the most gorgeous shade of blue that he'd ever seen—swept toward him.

Adam was pretty sure he stopped breathing. "Who is she?" he rasped again. Because from the way his bartender was talking, the guy knew her.

"How the hell am I supposed to know that?" Raymond asked.

Adam dragged his gaze off the woman and glared at Raymond. Raymond Bannon had shown up on the club's doorstep a week ago, asking for work. He'd been moving a bit slowly, as if the guy was recovering from some kind of injury, but he'd sworn he could handle *any* kind of work. Adam had felt a connection with the other man—there had just been too much grim determination in Raymond's gaze for Adam to turn him away.

So he'd hired himself a new bartender.

"Raymond…" Adam sighed out the other man's name as his fingers tapped on the bar top. "You just told me that *she* shouldn't be here. That her being here was, and I quote, 'bad, very bad.' Now you're going to act as if you've never seen her before in your life?"

"Have…*you* seen her before?" Raymond asked carefully. He was sweating.

Adam laughed. "No, and I doubt I'd forget a woman like her."

Raymond gulped down a drink. "Don't be too sure," he mumbled.

Adam frowned at him. "You know her. And you're going to hold out on me? Man, that's not what friends do." He gave the guy a little salute. "Don't worry, though, I'll just go over and introduce myself."

Before he could swing away from the bar, Raymond's hand flew out and locked around his arm. "Is that what we are?" he asked quietly. "Friends?"

Adam nodded. "Yeah, we are." His head tilted. "You okay?" Because the guy was acting weird. Even weirder than normal.

Raymond let him go. He offered Adam a weak smile. "Busy night, you know. Guess I'm a little stressed." He raked his hand over his face. "Her name's Sabrina. She's…not the kind of woman you want to fall for, got me? She…she was involved with, uh, my former boss." His gaze had turned somber. "It didn't end well."

"Broke the bastard's heart, huh?" Sure, he could buy that.

"She put him straight in the grave."

That was a new slang expression for him. But, obviously, Raymond meant the guy had been so devastated that the break-up had been like death for him. "That's too bad."

Raymond grunted.

Fresh from a break-up. She probably wasn't looking for a new guy. He should walk away. Steer clear. But…

His gaze slid back toward the mirror.

She was gone.

Immediately, his heart squeezed in his chest and he took a fast step forward.

I can't lose her! The thought raced through his mind. Totally irrational. Totally insane. He didn't know her. There was no *losing her* involved. There was no need for this choking panic that was consuming him. There was—

He saw her on the stairs. She was just strolling right up them. Still acting as if she owned the place. Acting as if she'd been there so many times before.

"Keep an eye on things down here," Adam directed without glancing at Raymond. "I'll be right back."

Then he started pushing his way through the crowd, and his gaze never left the stairs.

I can't lose her.

***

This is bad.

Raymond drowned a quick scotch and then his shaking fingers pulled out his phone. He dialed fast, knowing there wasn't any time to lose. And his call was answered on the second ring. Raymond didn't bother to identify himself. He just said, "She just walked into the club…and he's already trailing after her. *It's started.*" A pause. "Dammit, I *like* the guy. So help him. Help—"

The line went dead.

Raymond glanced toward the staircase. He didn't see Adam. And he didn't see Sabrina.

Shit.

***

Adam shoved open the door that led to the roof. "Hello?" he called out. "Miss, you're not supposed to be up here!" He wasn't even sure how she'd gotten up there. The door should have been locked.

Obviously, it wasn't.

"Miss?" He stepped away from the doorway, searching for her.

And there she was. Standing near the edge of the building, glancing down. The wind caught her hair, tossing it back just a bit, and as he stared at her…

I swear, we've been here before.

"My name is Sabrina," she said, not looking up at him.

"I know."

Her head immediately whipped up and turned toward him. "You do?" Hope was there, dancing in her voice as she took a few quick steps toward him. The moon was shining down on them. A full moon, big and bright, and it showed the utter beauty of her face.

He swallowed. "Yeah. Turns out my bartender, Raymond, he knows you."

"Raymond." She seemed to be tasting the name. She'd also stopped advancing toward him. She gave a little laugh that danced along his nerve endings. "I can't believe he's working for you. Didn't expect that." She tilted her head as she seemed to consider things. "Only maybe…maybe it's not *you* he's really working for."

She was gorgeous. She was sexy as all hell. She also seemed…maybe a little crazy. "Uh, yeah, he's working for me. It's my club. He's my bartender." He flashed her a broad grin.

She didn't smile back.

Okay. He took a step toward her and held out his hand. "My name is Adam. Adam Cross."

She looked at his hand. Didn't take it. Just looked. "I don't think I should touch you."

What?

"It's probably a bad idea. Coming here was a bad idea, but I just needed to see you. I wanted to…I don't know, make sure you were happy?"

Then she smiled, but it was mocking.

That's not her real smile.

How did he know what her real smile looked like?

"Your opening seems to be a big success," she told him, nodding. "Congratulations. I know this place means a lot to you."

He slowly lowered his hand. "Am I missing something? Because I swear…you talk as if you know me."

"Impossible, right?"

He inched closer to her. He *loved* the way she smelled.

But she stepped back. "I told you, touching is probably a mistake."

I want to touch her. She feels like silk beneath my hands. I want to kiss her because I love the way her lips open so sweetly beneath mine.

He shook his head.

"Is…something wrong?"

I have more pleasure with her than I've ever had – or will ever have – with any other woman.
"I…I'm having weird thoughts."

"That's because of me." Now she seemed sad.

I don't want Sabrina to be sad.

"I tend to have that effect on people. Especially humans. And that's what you are now."

He laughed. "Right. I'm human." Wasn't *everyone* human?

"I wanted to fight for you. I wanted to find a way to be with you…but even the strongest witch I know can't figure out a way to make it work."

It was a shame that someone so beautiful seemed to be riding on the crazy train.

And yet…he was still not moving away from her. He was still standing right there, drinking her in and thinking…*I've missed you.*

Maybe he was riding on the crazy train with her. If so, Adam wasn't so sure he wanted the ride to stop.

"So I came here tonight, because I wanted a memory of you being happy. The last memory I had of you…it wasn't so good." She turned away and walked to the edge of the roof. "I'm sure Luke or Leo will appear after I'm gone. They'll make this little visit vanish from your mind, just like everything else vanished."

I can't lose her.

He bounded forward and his hands curled around her shoulders. He spun her to face him.

Hunger, need…desire…blasted right through him.

"Touching me was a bad idea," she whispered. "I warned—"

He kissed her. His lips took hers in a frantic kiss and a dozen visions seemed to explode in his mind.

Sabrina…wearing a dress the same shade as her eyes, standing in a ballroom, surrounded by fawning men.

Sabrina…trapped in a wrecked car, hurt, scared.

Sabrina…kissing him. Staring at him as she wore absolutely nothing.

Sabrina…crying as she bent over him and begged for his life.

Sabrina…My Sabrina…

Inside of him, something woke up. Something dark. Something strong. Something that seemed to be clawing at his insides…

She is mine.

Sabrina shoved against him. "Bad, very bad." Her breath choked out. "Coming here was a bad mistake, but I'm selfish and I've never exactly had the best nature. So I wanted to see you once more. I didn't want to—oh, dammit, I can see streaks in your aura already. You need to get away from me!"

"No." That hardly even sounded like his voice. Deep. Growling. But…he couldn't let her go.

"Adam?" Sabrina blinked and stared at him uncertainly.

"I won't leave you."

Her lips were trembling…

And then the whole building seemed to tremble. Was that some kind of earthquake? What the fuck? Adam grabbed Sabrina and held on tight. He—

"*Sabrina…Sabrina…Sabrina…*" That was a male voice, rumbling from the darkness. A man had just appeared on the roof. Tall, broad-shouldered, with dark hair and the faint stubble of a beard covering his jaw. "What part of *stay away from the human* did you misunderstand?"

"Luke," she breathed the name. "Figured you'd show up."

The stranger—Luke—inclined his head toward her. "But…what? You thought you'd be out of here long before I actually arrived?"

"Raymond is working for you, isn't he?" Sabrina said, her voice louder and stronger. "What did he do? Call you as soon as I walked into the club?"

"Pretty much, yes." Luke flashed a broad smile. "Now, it's time to say good-bye to the human, Sabrina. A seriously, *forever* good-bye this time. Think you can manage that? Or should

I just throw your sweet ass off the roof so that you can let the guy go?"

Adam surged toward the stranger, immediately going toe-to-toe with him. "Don't you even think it." *Throw her off the roof? Was the asshole insane?*

Luke sighed. "You were with her — what? Five minutes? Four? Three? And already you're in protective mode." He slapped his hand on Adam's shoulder. "You're choosing the wrong side, my friend."

"Luke, don't hurt him!" Sabrina cried out.

"Let him try," Adam invited. His head was pounding and he could have sworn that something was still clawing at him from the inside. The world around him didn't make sense but Sabrina...

She's mine.

That certainty went soul deep.

Luke leaned closer. "I wouldn't just try. I'd succeed. And then all the work I've done...well, it would have been for nothing." He quirked one brow. "She's not worth it, Adam. You're finally on the good side. Stay near her, and she'll drag you back into the darkness. Most people don't get the chance you have. I thought Sabrina could sacrifice for you. She offered to pay any price, but I guess that was a lie."

"It wasn't!" Sabrina yelled. "I was saying good-bye..."

"It looked to me like you were saying hello..." Luke drawled. "You know, with your tongue in his mouth—"

Adam grabbed the guy and lifted him a foot into the air, holding tight to the bastard's shoulders.

"My, my..." Now surprise could be heard in Luke's voice. "Aren't you strong...for a human?" His gaze cut toward Sabrina. "What did you do?" Suspicion had entered his voice. "Did you get your witch to work her magic? Knew I should've watched Cordelia more carefully..."

"You *won't* hurt Sabrina," Adam shouted at him.

That clawing in his chest was worse. Something was in him—and it wanted to break free.

He dropped Luke, and Adam's hands flew over his own chest. "What is happening to me?"

Luke straightened. "I have no idea."

"Adam?" Sabrina's hands reached for him. "Adam, are you okay?"

He looked up at her. "It...hurts, sweetheart."

"Did you just call her sweetheart?" Luke snarled.

"What hurts?" Sabrina ran her hands over his shoulders. "Tell me...I'll help you. I'll—"

He stared into her eyes. "*I remember you.*"

"Fuck," Luke said. "Now I have to be the bad guy." He grabbed Sabrina, hoisting her into the air.

"Luke, stop it!" Sabrina yelled. "What are you doing?"

"Testing a theory…let's see what happens when a muse decides to fly…" He held her over the side of the building. His eyes glittered. "If I were you, I'd try really, really hard to…inspire."

"*Sabrina!*" Adam bellowed.

Luke let her go.

Sabrina plummeted.

CHAPTER TWENTY-ONE

"Sabrina!" Rage and terror exploded inside of Adam. He didn't stop to think. Didn't hesitate.

He jumped off that roof, racing after her. She was falling and—

He caught her. Right before her body would have slammed into the ground. He caught her and he held her tight. "It's okay," Adam whispered into her hair. His heart was pounding like a damn drum. "You're okay."

Her head lifted. She stared up at him with stunned eyes. "Adam?"

He flew them right back up to the top of the club. Four stories. That sonofabitch Luke had just dropped Sabrina four stories. *I will kill him.*

He landed on the roof. Carefully put Sabrina on her feet. Then he whirled, ready to rip apart his prey. "*Luke!*"

The bastard was still there. Standing with his arms crossed over his chest. Looking as if he didn't have a care in the world.

"Yes?" Luke lifted his brows. "You need something else?"

Growling, Adam charged for him. His hands flew out to attack—

What's wrong with my hands?

Adam stumbled. His gaze flew over his hands…hands that weren't human, not any longer. They were covered with stone, not flesh. Stone…and tipped with razor-sharp claws.

"I think we…misinterpreted a few things…" Luke announced.

And then Sabrina was in front of Adam, standing between him and…*He's the Lord of the Dark. I remember him. I remember her.*

Sweet fuck, I remember everything.

He stared at the stone on his hands.

"You flew," Sabrina breathed the words. "I…I can see your wings. They're back. I thought you were supposed to be human again."

His gaze rose to hers. Desperate hope was in her eyes. Hope and fear.

She whirled to face Luke. "What happened to him? He *can't* be a prisoner of the stone again. That can't happen. Throw my ass off the roof once more—do it a dozen times—but *don't* make him a prisoner again—"

"He's only half-stone, love. This is different. Not like before." Luke's voice was musing. "Because I don't think…he's quite like he was before."

Sabrina and Luke both studied him.

Adam closed his eyes. He breathed, nice and slow...

"Look at that." Luke had turned admiring now. "He's even managing to control it now. No breaking to freedom needed. No bursting out of the stone shell to become a man again. It's almost like a normal shifter's transformation."

Sabrina grabbed Adam's hand. His eyes flew open. He stared at her fingers — so soft against the stone. Until that stone turned straight to dust and vanished.

"I thought this might be the case." Luke sauntered closer. "Before I left her on the beach with you — you know, during that unfortunate time when you passed straight out from agony, Sabrina — I did get Cordelia to scry for me. I wanted to see that big battle scene with Eric for myself. I was a bit curious about things...I mean, I'm not wrong very often. And I was so sure that a muse with your power could help Adam to break free of his curse."

"I didn't help him," Sabrina denied. "I wish that I had." Her fingers were linked with Adam's. "Raymond shattered the binding stone, that's how Adam got free of the curse —"

"No." A flat denial from Luke. "Your gargoyle came rushing into the room in order to save you...though I am pretty sure he had orders to the contrary. He went against those orders. He fought for you…and that was even before the stone was shattered."

Her lips parted. "Eric told him…to kill himself. He wanted Adam to bleed out in front of me."

"Right…but when Adam got in front of you in that study, I didn't see him suddenly start attacking himself. That's not what went down. He was there, fighting *for* you." Luke seemed incredibly pleased with himself. "I swear, it's like the world wants to bend to my will."

Her eyes were so wide. "Adam?"

He was almost afraid to hope.

"What we had…" Luke continued as he seemed to consider things even more. "What we had at play were two events that occurred at the same time. We all just *assumed* Adam was free because the binding stone was broken…but what if…*what if…*Adam had freed himself before that stone so much as shattered? That would certainly change things."

"When the binding stone shattered, the gargoyle vanished," Sabrina said, voice tight. "I saw—"

"You saw a curse ending, but not for the reason you thought," Luke explained.

Sabrina pulled her hand from Adam's. "No." She stepped back and her shoulder bumped into Luke's. "No," she said again. "Time was catching up to him. I *saw* it. He was dying right before my eyes on that damn beach."

"Was he?" Luke murmured. He scratched his chin. "Sometimes, what you see…it isn't always what you get."

"What?" Sabrina screamed.

Adam shook his head. Memories were bursting inside his mind, and the force of the past was about to drive him to his knees.

"I may have…played a bit with reality on that beach," Luke confessed. "Perhaps I made things seem a bit more desperate than they were."

Sabrina drew back her fist and punched him in the jaw.

"Deserved," he muttered.

"Luke…" Sabrina drew back her fist again.

"I needed to see what you'd do for him…it's not easy to get a muse's power. I mean, look at all those who have tried! I knew the power wasn't in your eyes. Or your voice. You're no siren." His hand rose and pressed over her heart. "It's in here."

"Get your hands off her," Adam snarled.

Once more, Luke sighed. "Always the jealous lover, even after the amazing solid I did for you." But his hand dropped. "You sacrificed for him, Sabrina. You *gave* him half your power. That's the only way to take a muse's power. A willing sacrifice. And that's why Adam has got all of these lovely supernatural bonuses now. You did that for him. *You* gave him the ability to transform. To be super strong. To be super fast. You *inspired* him to be so much more than just a human. Did you make yourself weaker in the process? Sure. I mean, damn, it was too easy to toss you from the roof a few minutes ago…thought you could pack more fight than that…" But his words trailed off and he started to grin. He snapped his fingers as if he'd just realized another fact. "Sonofabitch…you *wanted* to provoke an emotional response from him, didn't you, Sabrina? You didn't need me to tell you to inspire the guy. You came here with your own plan. You thought something was up with him…that I'd tricked you…"

She wasn't aiming her fist at Luke any longer. "You do have a habit of twisting the truth into a lie." She turned her head and gave Adam a weak smile. "And I wasn't going to let the man I love go without a fight."

Luke clapped his hands together. "You pulled one over on me…that is impressive."

"I try to be impressive," Sabrina murmured.

The roller coaster of images had finally halted in Adam's head. The last image had frozen…

Sabrina. Leaning over him on a beach. Tears glittered in her eyes as Luke asked if she'd give her power to Adam…

He can have it all…Give him everything he needs.

"What…am I?" Adam asked. His voice sounded rusty.

Luke waved toward him. "You're an immortal…half man, half gargoyle…with a little bit of inspiration thrown in for fun. No one controls you. You control your own self *and*…" Luke added with a meaningful glance at Sabrina. "You're immune to a certain muse's powers."

Adam's gaze slid to Sabrina. "I missed you," he rasped.

A sob slipped from her. But she didn't rush to Adam. Instead, she spun — and hugged Luke. "Thank you."

The Lord of the Dark seemed stunned. "You're not supposed to thank me." He patted her awkwardly on the back. "I…I turned your lover into one of my dark paranormal soldiers. All of the strengths he had before, but none of the weaknesses. I did this for me, not for you."

She slowly pulled back from him. "Thank you," Sabrina said again as she stared up at Luke. "You are such a liar."

"True." Luke inclined his head.

Adam was still trying to wrap his head around his new life. "I'm…I'm going to spend forever with Sabrina?"

She let out a cry of delight.

"Yes, you are." Luke's voice held a hint of amusement. "You'll have to decide if that's heaven or hell."

Heaven.

But Luke was eyeing Sabrina again. "I was wondering when you were going to drag your ass over here to him. Expected it a lot sooner…"

"I thought I was being *good*," Sabrina threw at him.

"How'd that work for you?" Luke wanted to know.

Adam couldn't stand it any longer. He grabbed Sabrina. *My Sabrina. I missed her…my heart was fucking gone without her…* And he kissed her. Deep and hot.

And she kissed him back the same way. When he finally lifted his head, Luke was still watching.

Seriously, the guy needed to *leave*.

"Being good didn't work so well," Sabrina said softly, her words directed at their watcher. "I think I like being bad better."

Luke laughed. And, finally, he turned away.

Adam focused on Sabrina. His memories were there. Bright and strong. It was as if he'd been sleeping. And he'd finally woken up to the real world.

Made sense, she *was* his world.

But…

Sabrina pulled from him. "I kept my end of the bargain!" Sabrina yelled.

Luke was just about to step off the roof. He looked back at her shout.

"So don't return and try to screw with our lives. Adam is safe now, got it?"

Luke rubbed his chin. "Just how do you think you *kept* your bargain? I haven't asked you for payment yet."

"I understood part of your game. I'm not like the others that you play with..." Her fingers were twined with Adam's. "I inspired...I gave your brother Leo just the right amount of inspiration. That's why he's not dodging our steps right now. He's taking his turn with Fate, and what happens next...that's going to be the end game that you've been waiting for. So I hope you're ready."

Luke's wings spread behind him. "I've always been ready." And then Luke flew into the night.

Sabrina started to step away from Adam.

Hell, no. He yanked her right back. "You think I'm letting you go?"

He wanted to chain her to his side.

"Better question," Sabrina whispered. "You think I'm letting *you* go?" Then she rose onto her toes. Her lips brushed his, but, unlike the kiss before, this one was soft. Gentle.

Tender.

"I'd fight anyone and anything for you, Adam Cross. You might have started as my protector..."

And I'll be that for the rest of our lives.

"But I can battle for you, too. I can and I will because nothing matters more to me than you do. *Nothing.*"

The Lord of the Dark was gone. And Adam didn't give a shit about where Leo might be. *Go tangle with Fate, asshole.*

I'm not human. I'm not a prisoner. He was strong and he was free and the woman he loved was right in front of him. "I would have found you."

A furrow appeared between her eyes.

"You think I wouldn't search this earth until I found the other half of my soul?" His words were rough. "Sweetheart, I would have *found you.*"

She smiled for him. The real smile that he remembered. The one that hinted at hope and joy, the one that showed her love. The one that made him finally feel whole again. Because that was what Sabrina did for him.

More than a mate, more than a lover.

She was the woman who possessed his heart. He was certain she held it in the palm of her hand.

And that she always would.

He kissed her again.

***

Luke wasn't really into voyeurism. Not one of his kinks. So he left the lovers on the rooftop, and he counted the night as another win for him.

Most nights were wins.

The fact that Sabrina had figured out his game...that she'd been going to push her lover into revealing his more...primal side? *And* she'd already used her power on Leo?

Well, that just meant he'd need to keep a closer eye on Sabrina. The woman was a little too smart. And dangerous.

That was why he'd worked to give her Adam. Sabrina was happy with the fellow. And a happy muse...that was a muse who wouldn't get in Luke's way. That was a muse who would owe him.

When the battle came...and it *was* coming...Sabrina wouldn't let her old friendship with Leo sway her. She'd choose Luke's side.

He'd covered all the bases.

Now...now he just had to wait and see exactly what Fate had in store for him...

And for Leo.

###

Ready for Leo's story? TEMPTED BY FATE will be available in April 25, 2017!

Tempted By Fate - Available April 25, 2017

You can't cheat Fate...and for the record, she *really* doesn't like it when you betray her, either.

Leo is used to having power. After all, he carries the title *Lord of the Light* for a reason—he's a supernatural powerhouse and his job is protect all of the "light" paranormals in the world. He's used to snapping his fingers and getting anything—or anyone—he wants. But when he fell for Fate, Leo learned that power didn't get a man everything. In fact, it didn't even get him the one woman he wanted most...

Fate...AKA *Mora* (that's the name she prefers to use—a lot less weighty on her shoulders) has spent centuries hiding from her supernatural ex-lover Leo. Most people fear Leo and rightly so. He's got immense power and a definite date with an unfortunate end-of-the-world calamity. When Leo seduced Mora and promised to put the world at her feet, she actually thought the guy had fallen for her. Too late, she discovered he was just using her in an attempt to change his destiny.

And Leo's destiny? It's not pretty. Some very, very bad things are coming for him. Mora shouldn't care about the danger he faces. She should turn her back on her ex. His heart is ice cold, she knows that, but her own heart...it's still a little weak where Leo is concerned.

Leo has tried to walk on the side of good for a long time…but his sins are coming back to haunt him. A darkness is trying to consume him, and if Mora can't help him…then it's not just Leo who will pay the price for his past. The whole world will change.

You think you know the Lord of the Light? Think again.

A NOTE FROM THE AUTHOR

Thank you so much for taking the time to read HEART OF STONE. I hope that you enjoyed the story.

If you'd like to stay updated on my releases and sales, please join my newsletter list www.cynthiaeden.com/newsletter/. You can also check out my Facebook page www.facebook.com/cynthiaedenfanpage. I love to post giveaways over at Facebook!

Again, thank you for reading HEART OF STONE.

Best,
Cynthia Eden
www.cynthiaeden.com

ABOUT THE AUTHOR

Award-winning author Cynthia Eden writes dark tales of paranormal romance and romantic suspense. She is a *New York Times, USA Today, Digital Book World,* and *IndieReader* best-seller. Cynthia is also a three-time finalist for the RITA® award. Since she began writing full-time in 2005, Cynthia has written over fifty novels and novellas.

Cynthia is a southern girl who loves horror movies, chocolate, and happy endings. More information about Cynthia and her books may be found at: http://www.cynthiaeden.com or on her Facebook page at: http://www.facebook.com/cynthiaedenfanpage. Cynthia is also on Twitter at http://www.twitter.com/cynthiaeden.

HER WORKS

Free Reads
Purgatory Series
- The Wolf Within (Purgatory, Book 1)
Mine Series
- Mine To Take (Mine, Book 1)
Bound Series
- Bound By Blood (Bound Book 1)
Other Paranormal
- A Bit of Bite

Boxed Sets

Blood and Moonlight Series
- Blood and Moonlight (The Complete Series)

Dark Obsession Series
- Only For Me (Dark Obsession, Books 1 to 4)

Purgatory Series
- The Beasts Inside (Purgatory, Books 1 to 4)
Mine Series

- Mine Series Box Set Volume 1 (Mine, Books 1-3)
- Mine Series Box Set Volume 2 (Mine, Books 4-6)

Bound Series
- Forever Bound (Bound, Books 1 to 4)

Romantic Suspense

Killer Instinct
- The Gathering Dusk (Killer Instinct, Prequel)
- After The Dark (Killer Instinct, Book 1) - Available 03/28/2017
- Before The Dawn (Killer Instinct, Book 2) - Available 07/25/2017

- Abduction
- Hunted - Available 06/20/2017

LOST Series
- Broken (LOST, Book 1)
- Twisted (LOST, Book 2)
- Shattered (LOST, Book 3)
- Torn (LOST, Book 4)
- Taken (LOST, Book 5)
- Wrecked (LOST, Book 6) - Available 05/30/2017

Dark Obsession Series

- Watch Me (Dark Obsession, Book 1)
- Want Me (Dark Obsession, Book 2)
- Need Me (Dark Obsession, Book 3)
- Beware Of Me (Dark Obsession, Book 4)
- Only For Me (Dark Obsession, Books 1 to 4)

Mine Series
- Mine To Take (Mine, Book 1)
- Mine To Keep (Mine, Book 2)
- Mine To Hold (Mine, Book 3)
- Mine To Crave (Mine, Book 4)
- Mine To Have (Mine, Book 5)
- Mine To Protect (Mine, Book 6)
- Mine Series Box Set Volume 1 (Mine, Books 1-3)
- Mine Series Box Set Volume 2 (Mine, Books 4-6)

Montlake - For Me Series
- Die For Me (For Me, Book 1)
- Fear For Me (For Me, Book 2)
- Scream For Me (For Me, Book 3)

Harlequin Intrigue - The Battling McGuire Boys
- Confessions (Battling McGuire Boys...Book 1)
- Secrets (Battling McGuire Boys...Book 2)
- Suspicions (Battling McGuire Boys...Book 3)

- Reckonings (Battling McGuire Boys…Book 4)
- Deceptions (Battling McGuire Boys…Book 5)
- Allegiances (Battling McGuire Boys…Book 6)

Harlequin Intrigue - Shadow Agents Series
- Alpha One (Shadow Agents, Book 1)
- Guardian Ranger (Shadow Agents, Book 2)
- Sharpshooter (Shadow Agents, Book 3)
- Glitter And Gunfire (Shadow Agents, Book 4)
- Undercover Captor (Shadow Agents, Book 5)
- The Girl Next Door (Shadow Agents, Book 6)
- Evidence of Passion (Shadow Agents, Book 7)
- Way of the Shadows (Shadow Agents, Book 8)

Deadly Series
- Deadly Fear (Book One of the Deadly Series)
- Deadly Heat (Book Two of the Deadly Series)
- Deadly Lies (Book Three of the Deadly Series)

Contemporary Anthologies
- First Taste of Darkness
- Sinful Secrets

Other Romantic Suspense
- Until Death
- Femme Fatale
- Christmas With A Spy

Paranormal Romance

Bad Things
- The Devil In Disguise (Bad Things, Book 1)
- On The Prowl (Bad Things, Book 2)
- Undead Or Alive (Bad Things, Book 3)
- Broken Angel (Bad Things, Book 4)
- Heart Of Stone (Bad Things, Book 5) - Available 03/14/2017
- Tempted By Fate (Bad Things, Book 6) - Available 04/25/2017

Blood and Moonlight Series
- Bite The Dust (Blood and Moonlight, Book 1)
- Better Off Undead (Blood and Moonlight, Book 2)
- Bitter Blood (Blood and Moonlight, Book 3)
- Blood and Moonlight (The Complete Series)
  Purgatory Series

- The Wolf Within (Purgatory, Book 1)
- Marked By The Vampire (Purgatory, Book 2)
- Charming The Beast (Purgatory, Book 3)
- Deal with the Devil (Purgatory, Book 4)
- The Beasts Inside (Purgatory, Books 1 to 4)

Bound Series
- Bound By Blood (Bound Book 1)
- Bound In Darkness (Bound Book 2)
- Bound In Sin (Bound Book 3)
- Bound By The Night (Bound Book 4)
- Forever Bound (Bound, Books 1 to 4)
- Bound in Death (Bound Book 5)

Night Watch Series
- Eternal Hunter (Night Watch Book 1)
- I'll Be Slaying You (Night Watch Book 2)
- Eternal Flame (Night Watch Book 3)

Phoenix Fire Series
- Burn For Me (Phoenix Fire, Book 1)
- Once Bitten, Twice Burned (Phoenix Fire, Book 2)
- Playing With Fire (Phoenix Fire, Book 3)

The Fallen Series
- Angel of Darkness (The Fallen Book 1)
- Angel Betrayed (The Fallen Book 2)
- Angel In Chains (The Fallen Book 3)
- Avenging Angel (The Fallen Book 4)

Midnight Trilogy
- Hotter After Midnight (Book One in the Midnight Trilogy)
- Midnight Sins (Book Two in the Midnight Trilogy)
- Midnight's Master (Book Three in the Midnight Trilogy)

Paranormal Anthologies
- A Vampire's Christmas Carol
Loved By Gods Series
- Bleed For Me

ImaJinn
- The Vampire's Kiss
- The Wizard's Spell

Other Paranormal
- Immortal Danger
- Never Cry Wolf
- A Bit of Bite

Young Adult Paranormal

Other Young Adult Paranormal
- The Better To Bite (A Young Adult Paranormal Romance)

Anthologies

Contemporary Anthologies

- "All I Want for Christmas" in The Naughty List

Paranormal Anthologies
- "New Year's Bites" in A Red Hot New Year
- "Wicked Ways" in When He Was Bad
- "Spellbound" in Everlasting Bad Boys
- "In the Dark" in Belong to the Night
- Howl For It

Holidays

Contemporary Anthologies
- "All I Want for Christmas" in The Naughty List

Paranormal Anthologies
- A Vampire's Christmas Carol

Other Romantic Suspense
- Christmas With A Spy

Made in the USA
Middletown, DE
07 May 2017